Of
Secrets
and
Slippers

Of Secrets and Slippers

CHANDA HAHN

Of Secrets and Slippers
Copyright © 2022 by Chanda Hahn
www.chandahahn.com
Neverwood Press
Editor: A.L.D Editing
Proof Readers: Corrine Doxey, Brandy Michelle Barber
Cover Design Covers by Christian
Map Illustration by Hanna Sandvig
www.chandahahn.com
(Hardcover) 978-1950440375
(Ingram) 978-1950440337
(Paperback) 978-1950440382

Also By Chanda Hahn

Daughters of Eville
Of Beast and Beauty
Of Glass and Glamour
Of Sea and Song
Of Thorn and Thread
Of Mist and Murder
Of Secrets and Slippers

The Unfortunate Fairy Tales
UnEnchanted
Fairest
Fable
Reign
Forever

The Neverwood Chronicles
Lost Girl
Lost Boy
Lost Shadow

The Underland Duology
Underland
Underlord

The Iron Butterfly Series
The Iron Butterfly
The Steele Wolf
The Silver Siren

For Bob
The best Father-in-law I could ever ask for.
Miss you lots.

CHAPTER ONE

The Dread Knot Tavern was busier than usual. A clamor of raucous sounds filled the air; the thuds of heavy mugs crashing onto the table, drunk and rowdy patrons calling out to the passing servant girls for refills. From the kitchen, the scent of roasting meat filtered out into the hall and mixed with the acrid scent of body sweat and ale. The floor, once a light oak, was now stained a dark brown from years of use and spillage.

The serving girl's hair was matted, her eyes filled with despair as she brought me a complimentary roll with my penny ale.

She dropped the wooden platter on the table and left, her boots making a sucking sound as they stuck to the viscous floor.

I swirled the contents of my mug and looked at the questionable brown contents before I scrunched up my nose in disgust. It looked like slop and smelled the same. The roll seemed dry, and I couldn't help but pick it up and knock it against the table. I sighed, then dropped the roll and set the mug back onto the table as I leaned back to study the elf sitting across the table from me.

Lorn pulled his hood further over his head, keeping his

pointed ears covered, but there was no hiding his silver-colored eyes. Even though he sat in a tavern surrounded by people, his aura was almost completely invisible. Using his elven gifts, he faded into the background noise of the tavern, where even the serving girl ignored him.

"You shouldn't have come," I said softly, running my fingers down the side of the mug, feeling the hairline crack in the ceramic. "I'm doing fine."

"You haven't been back to visit the Northern Woods since you went to Kiln. I was worried about you," Lorn answered.

Northern Woods. The place where the elves lived, and where I'd spent most of my life passing through before heading back out on the road. My life was a careful balance of always moving, never staying in one place too long for fear of harming those I loved. Visiting my six sisters in Nihill and adoptive mother and then traveling along the ley lines for added protection.

"I don't want to be a burden on you anymore," I said. "I've seen almost twenty years. I can take care of myself. You've seen to that." I crooked an eyebrow at him, daring him to deny that he was faulty in my training.

"Twenty," he scoffed. "A baby in elven years, as it were." Lorn smiled wanly.

"To your two hundred, I would expect as much." I leaned back and dropped my hands to my lap. My mouth was dry, and my hands clasped tightly together under the table as I tried to tell my mentor I was ready to move on. "You've kept your promise to my mother. You've protected me; trained me how to live off the land. Figuratively and magically," I added, referring to my curse that caused me to either block others' magic or drain them. It was the reason I had to stay close to the magical ley lines. They were my support when I couldn't control myself.

"Honor," he began.

"Now that my training is complete," I said, rushing to speak before him, "there's nothing keeping you from being free to love . . . who you love."

Lorn's shoulders stiffened. We'd never spoken about his affection for my adoptive mother, Lorelai Eville, but I knew. I had always known. The hidden glances, the lingering touches.

"Where are you going to go?" he asked gruffly, changing the subject.

"I'll travel the ley lines and head south. Sion's always nice this time of the year."

"And dangerous," he warned.

"Everywhere is dangerous." I shrugged. "Remember that time in Candor when we stepped into a pit of drake-fowls during mating season?"

Lorn chuckled. "I never told your mother about that one."

"Good. She'd skin you alive if she found out. I still have a nasty scar from that encounter." I held up the underside of my wrist, showing off the jagged mark that looked like a pine tree.

"It was only slightly poisonous," Loran added.

"Slightly . . . I was heavily medicated and out of my mind. I think I proposed marriage to every person that week."

"You did leave a trail of disappointed suitors," he teased. Lorn froze, his eyes going to the door. After a few moments of tense silence, he released a strained breath. There was something bothering him, but he didn't want to talk about it. The furtive looks and the quiet stillness were both signs that he needed to be going, but he was delaying because of me.

I reached across the table and touched the top of his hand. Lorn stiffened. Elves did not like to be touched unnecessarily, but I did it to prove a point. His eyes drew to me. "You are the closest thing I've ever had to a father. I promise I won't let you down. Besides—" I tapped my back and the slight bulge hidden under my cloak. "I won't be alone. I have backup."

Lorn's lips twisted into a rare smile. "Backup. That's more of a liability. I'm not sure why you were saddled with it."

"I promised Rhea."

"Are you sure that she doesn't hate you?"

I laughed. "I'm sure."

I could see when Lorn's mood changed, and he knew he couldn't convince me to come with him. He stood up, scanning the tavern one more time. "Be mindful. There have been random attacks throughout the kingdoms. There are rumors that it's the son of Allemar who has been orchestrating them."

"The son of Allemar?" I said in disbelief. "He didn't have any children?"

"We believe it is one of the dark sorcerer's apprentices using that name to wreak havoc and fear. But we're uncertain because after each attack, they disappear with little to no trace." His knuckles clenched in frustration. "Promise me you won't get involved."

"I promise I'll stay out of trouble."

Lorn sighed. He drew close, placed his open palm on

the top of my head. "I doubt that very much. Trouble always has a way of finding you."

"I know, but I promise. If I see trouble, I'll run the other way." I drew my finger across my heart in the shape of an X.

The silence in the air was awkward as it hung between us. "Okay."

He reached out and touched the top of my hand. "Be careful," he whispered.

Without another word, Lorn slipped away without making a sound. I watched his retreating back as he headed out the exit. The door let in a whiff of bitter cold air before slamming closed.

Even now, I could see the trouble brewing. The man at the table next to me was eyeing my coin purse and licking his lips, probably hoping to relieve me of it as soon as I stepped through the doors. I smirked. I was itching for a fight and was kind of hoping he would try.

"You no good lying cheat. I'm going to kill you," a loud voice said from the balcony above.

The upper floors of the tavern held a gambling den filled with card tables, where players frequently lost their gold and dignity. The thud of a meaty fist hitting flesh sounded. A crash followed as a table was overturned and cards flew over the banister and scattered like leaves upon the patrons below. A king of diamonds landed face up on the table in front of me, next to a black jack and a red two. I picked up the king and studied it.

My keen eyes took in the slight variation of thickness on the king, and the bright ink print compared to the faded print of the other two. I knew it wasn't from the Dread

Knot's deck. Someone was cheating by sneaking in other cards.

I snorted at the lack of finesse. No wonder he was caught.

A loud crack resonated, and I looked up as the banister above me splintered outward and a body flew backward over the broken railing.

Fast as a whip, I stood, grabbing the mug and sliding my chair back as the man hit the middle of the table and groaned. His hooded cowl covered his hair, his eyes were closed in pain as he rolled off the table and landed gracefully on his feet. His fingers moved to his belt as he palmed his stolen winnings into a hidden slit in his dark cloak.

He looked up, and we made eye contact. My heart raced in panic. He stared, his mouth dropping open in recognition. "Honor?"

I spun and headed out of the tavern as fast as my legs could carry me.

I promised Lorn I would stay away from trouble, but this time it landed in my lap.

"Honor, wait." The man called out and took a step after me, but before he could take another, he was surrounded. Two burly bouncers grabbed his arms and lifted him off his feet, dragging him backward, farther into the tavern.

"We'll teach you to cheat at our card tables. The owner wants to have a word with you."

I cast a look over my shoulder at the man, the back of his boots sliding across the muck covered floor. His eyes pleading as he struggled against the bouncers and their much larger build.

"Honor!" he called my name one last time. This time it wasn't a plea for help, but one of remorse.

I ignored his cry, pulled the hood further over my head and stepped out into the freezing cold night.

I shuddered, but not from the chill air. It was the guilt that assailed me for not helping him. But I refused to help a notorious thief and gambler.

Even if he was once my best friend.

The snow crunched softly beneath my fox fur wrapped leather boots. The air was bitterly cold and burned my lungs with every breath.

I'd been tracking the creature for three days straight through the mountain pass and I could feel my own body begin to betray me. I blinked, clearing my vision as I shook off the cobwebs of delusion. I was exhausted. I wanted to sleep, but this wolf I was tracking wouldn't let me. He was a loner, without a pack, and that made him dangerous. He wasn't protecting a territory and didn't have anywhere he would hole up for the night. He was moving quickly, and I was always one step behind.

I'd first seen the poster about the rogue wolf nailed on the magical notice board at the waystation in Creed. Then I saw a second one farther south, and this time the bounty was even higher. It appeared the beast had moved on from poaching sheep and cattle and had attacked and killed a person.

The townspeople had sent out hunters and trackers, but they'd always lose him. It was as if his tracks kept changing, or he knew he was being followed.

Which only left one option.

I wasn't hunting a wolf.

My guess? A werewolf or a true blood shapeshifter that had gone mad from the change.

This was my sister Maeve's specialty. She was the one who was born a shapeshifter. It should be her out hunting this thing, not me—but she was in Florin, too far away.

"*It will always be you.*" The memory of Lorn's frequent chastising cut through my thoughts. "*You have to work six times harder than your sisters because they have what you do not.*"

"*Magic,*" I said bitterly.

"*Control. They can control their power. Yours is unstable. A threat. Which is why you will always be on the run. You can never stay in one place. It is safer for you to keep near the ley lines. They will be your safety. They will keep you alive.*"

Closing my eyes, I raised my head and felt the direction of the wind. I concentrated; listening for the twitter of the mourning doves and the rustling cries of the scavenging ravens.

The wind was silent; her song mute.

My eyes flew open, and I ducked behind the trunk of a tree, pressing my back to the rough bark. I pulled the bow from my back and strung the cord, testing the tautness, then reached for an arrow.

"Marry me!" a cocky voice whispered from behind me.

"Shh," I hissed. "Rumple, I swear if you don't quiet down, I will throw you down to the bottom of the nearest well."

"You know I can't swim. I don't have hands," the disembodied voice spoke behind my back.

8

An evil smile crept up to my lips. "Exactly."

"You're a cruel, cruel mistress," the talking axe pouted.

I shook my head and scanned the white hills below me. Thankfully, even though it was spring, the snow hadn't melted yet farther up in the mountains. It made hunting easier, if you could survive the harsh temperatures.

But could I survive babysitting Rumple? Rhea and Kash wanted some time alone after tying the knot in a small wedding ceremony in Kiln. They didn't want Rumple Stiltskin, a dwarf whose soul was trapped in an enchanted axe, to come with them on their tour of the king-dom. I didn't blame them. I'd returned to my adoptive mother's childhood home in Kiln and promised to take him on some crazy adventure. Since then, he had gotten me kicked out of two taverns with his bawdy caterwauling, made me lose at a game of cards for telling my hand out loud, and scared off two deer. I couldn't afford to lose the bounty on my prey today.

I sighed, sighting along the arrow.

Nothing moved among the tree line.

The hair on the back of my neck rose.

A twig snapped behind me and I spun, releasing my fingers from the arrow as the dark form lurched toward me. Impossibly fast, it ducked and rolled into the underbrush.

That wasn't a wolf.

"Let me at him!" Rumple begged from his harness on my back.

"Shut it," I hissed. I drew another arrow and sighted along the shaft, searching for any movement from the brush.

There!

I released, and then heard a cry of disdain.

"That was my best cloak, Honor!"

"Percy! Leave before I send you back to the clan in pieces," I growled, calling him out into the open.

"I would gladly oblige and do the chopping," Rumple added.

The bushes moved and the man from the Dread Knot Tavern appeared. Although I wouldn't necessarily call the elf standing before me a man. There was an allure about elves, and Percy was the epitome of elven heritage and looks. His long blond hair shimmered as if it was coated with magic, and he stood tall, his frame muscular and lean. For all I knew, he was part siren for how his presence always made my heart skip a beat. He brushed a leaf out of his hair and his impish green eyes laughed at me.

Percy cocked his head and took notice of the large axe on my back. "Seems you've picked up a stray?" He sauntered over to me and ran a finger over the wood handle of the axe. I swatted his hand away.

"What are you doing here?" I snapped.

"Following you, of course."

"Why?"

"No reason, except that I think you owe me an explanation for abandoning me in my time of need at the Dread Knot. I was truly in dire straits, and you left me," he accused.

"You didn't need my help." I turned and walked down the mountain, still following the wolf trail. "You could escape them with your eyes closed. In fact, I'm sure that was part of your grand plan all along."

"What was?" he asked innocently, easily keeping up with me with his much longer stride.

"To get caught cheating on cards and dragged into the

back office. I bet that's where the safe was. Judging by the bulge in your cloak that wasn't there a few nights ago, you came out ahead."

"Indeed. I could never get one over on you, Honor."

"It's because I was the one who usually planned your escapades for you. But not anymore. You're a scout."

I slowed and turned to take in his very normal attire of brown pants, black leather boots, green wrap jacket, and a cloak.

"Why aren't you in uniform?" I asked. "You should be patrolling the Doring route with Einan and Rulah."

"Honor, I'm done." Percy's face was like stone.

"What do you mean, you're done? That's all you ever talked about. It was your dream to be part of the scouts," I said.

I could feel my own disappointment building. It was all I'd ever wanted as well. Ever since I was little and Lorn had first taken me to the Northern Woods. The scouts appeared out of thin air, hidden by glamour, their arrows and swords aimed at me.

Lorn explained his mission. Who I was. The adoptive daughter of Lorelai Eville. The scout leader, Einan, leaned down to take a look at me. His white hair reflected the moon. In his vest were throwing knives that looked like stars. I'd immediately thought Einan was the most beautiful person I'd ever seen. The other scouts let us pass before disappearing into the shadows . . . like magic.

I'd since learned that the scouts were "the elite." They were the finest fighters, the most swift-footed, and the best at hiding in all the elven armies. When they returned home, they were greeted like royalty and given a banquet.

If I could have, I would have joined the scouts. But I could never, not because of *who* I was, but *what* I was.

"I've revoked my vow," Percy said, breaking my daydream.

"I'm sorry, what?" I choked out the words that didn't make sense. "Why?"

He made a sour face. Most of the elves of the Northern Woods were like Lorn. They were majestic, calm, and hid their feelings behind stony expressions. Except for Percy. His face was broken, and he didn't seem to care.

"Does it matter?" he retorted. "I *was* a scout, and now I'm not."

It did matter. It mattered to me, but I couldn't tell him that. I didn't want him to know the jealousy that was bubbling up inside of me. How I wanted to change places with him. That all the training I did every single night was because I wanted to be where he was. I wanted what he so easily gave up. It made me all the more frustrated.

I pinched my lips together and held back my bitter words. Instead, I spun on my heel, and yelled at myself for missing the wolf tracks that were quickly filling back in with the light snow.

I cursed under my breath and took off running, following the trail down the mountain and toward the small village. My heart plummeted when the tracks changed. Four evenly spread paw prints slowly became two as they shifted from wolf to human.

I hated being right.

CHAPTER TWO

"Werewolf," Percy said in surprise.

"I feared as much," I said. "It's getting bolder. We have to stop it before it kills again."

He leaned forward, sniffed the tracks, and glanced down the mountain toward a small village. His keen elven eyes saw far more than my mere human vision could. The layout of the village, the main roads in and out, the most sheltered route into town. His training kicked in.

Percy stood, his body rigid as he took in the seriousness of the situation. As much as he'd become a lazy thief or joker, he was still one of the best scouts in the kingdoms.

"Let's not waste time." Percy took off running, and I sprinted after him. He could always outrun me, but it didn't mean that I wouldn't try to beat him every single time. This was my hunt. My kill. I would not let him outdo me.

My lungs burned, but I continued to run. When we came to the outskirts of the village, Percy went left. He beckoned for me to follow, but I intuitively knew to go right. Lorn had always told me to trust my instincts. They wouldn't fail me.

It was still daylight. The town was buzzing with

activity as people went about their daily business. The fresh snow brought a brightness to the town. Children threw snowballs at the wooden placards outside of the shops. An old woman had a stall where she was selling roasted nuts. This nameless village, accustomed to the harsh winters, even had a covered outdoor market where one could walk the rows freely under a manmade canopy tent, safe and warm. Every twenty feet were manned coal burners.

I walked down the aisle of the covered market, my eyes and ears searching for any clues; a hint of the beast. I paused by a burner to get warm while I waited, observing and gauging the people coming and going. *Did anyone look out of place? Were they lingering too long? Paying too much attention to a person or item? What were their tells?*

My heart thudded in my chest, and I calmed my breathing, focusing my attention outward. When I walked to the end of the row, I was frustrated that I didn't get anything. Not a sign of him.

"Relax, it's daylight," Rumple spoke up. "It won't strike until night falls."

"I should've got him before he made it to the town. I could've stopped him, but Percy distracted me."

"Don't blame yourself. You'll get him this time. I'm sure. Best thing to do is rest up and wait until dark. You haven't slept in three days."

Rumple was right. It was too visible.

I bought a bag of roasted pecans from a vendor and made my way to the center of town. Scanning each of the rooftops for a good perch, I took my time before choosing the loft above the blacksmith's barn. It had a central location with an open second-story window where I could relax and watch the streets below.

It was the perfect spot to spy. I easily scaled the building's siding and swung into the loft. Inside there was a long wooden crate that I turned over and used as a bench as I settled in to wait.

One of the hardest jobs of reconnaissance was the boredom that would come with it. You had to learn to occupy your mind for long periods without losing focus on your target and also not let a nature call rob you of your prey.

As I chewed on a warm pecan, I settled Rumple on the floor next to me.

"What's the story with the elf?" Rumple asked.

"There's no story," I said, popping a nut in my mouth.

"There may not be a story now, but there's *history*. I can tell."

"We used to be friends. And now we're not."

"Why not?" he pressed.

"Because it's none of your business," I said.

"You might as well tell him," Percy said as he swung onto the window ledge gracefully and landed on the loft floor without a sound. "Because I'm interested to know the reasons for us not being friends as well."

I refused to answer, chewing on my snack with a vengeance. My eyes narrowed as I focused even harder on the street below, ignoring the handsome elf as he sat on the other half of the already small crate, his thigh pressing close to mine. Immediately, the freezing chill that permeated my body lessened.

Percy gave me a questioning look as he waited for my

answer, but I didn't move or give a hint of a reply. I couldn't. He wouldn't understand. It was better this way.

"Are you going to tell me why you left the scouts?" I countered.

"No," he said firmly.

"Then there's no need to talk about me."

"You? Don't you mean us?"

I shook my head. "Don't go there. Don't *ever* go there."

The muscle in Percy's jaw clenched ever so slightly. He was angry.

Good. Because so was I.

He was the only person I knew that could get beneath my skin. Called me out whenever I lied. He knew all of my flaws and weaknesses, except for one—and that one I'd take to the grave. I decided to try to clear the tension between us by changing subjects.

"How's Einan?" I asked, referring to his old captain.

"Still as heroic as ever. He never changes, the old fart."

I smirked as he used a very human nickname; one he had picked up from me. "You don't either. Still as annoying as ever."

Percy didn't move. Humans were always moving, twitching, blinking. Even when we tried, we could never hold ourselves still. But elves could go for minutes without blinking, and by them not reacting *was* reacting. I had hit another nerve.

"Do you really think that of me?" he asked. His voice was serious.

"I meant it as a joke," I said flatly.

Percy gazed out the window, his sea-green eyes making him look almost unearthly beautiful. I studied him out of the corner of my eye; the sculpted jaw, his narrow nose, lips that were thin and perfect. But I could see the tension in the corner of his mouth. He looked forlorn, and I had a feeling I was the one causing his unhappiness. "Honor, there's something I need to tell you."

"Please, not now," I begged, fearing that he was going to give me horrible news that would make my world come crumbling down. "It can wait. Let's just stay in this moment a bit longer."

He nodded, seeming to understand my pain.

We weren't always this close. At one point, we hated each other, but not anymore. The same, and yet completely different. The only problem was he was an elf with a duty to fulfill . . . and I was cursed to hurt those closest to me.

I was four when my powers first came into fruition, and I'd almost killed my parents. The neighbor found them both passed out on the wood floor of our home in Denford. I'd been playing on the floor next to their prone bodies as if nothing had happened. Later that week, I'd fallen sick and spent days running a fever so hot it was apparently painful to the touch. Then my breathing had slowed. My temperature dropped so low my parents feared I was dead. Then it would start all over again.

A local hedge witch came to examine me and she recoiled so fast after her first brush with my skin. "Cursed is this child."

My parents became afraid of me. For it seemed *I* was the cause of their own maladies. They became gaunt, and all who heard of me became terrified. It wasn't until a tinker made mention of a woman more powerful than any hedge witch and he suggested she may have a cure. They brought me to Lorelai Eville.

17

I remembered riding in the back of a flatbed wagon, my parents sitting as far away from me as possible as we rode up to the tower. It was the most magnificent thing I had ever seen. A mini castle out of a storybook. One old guard tower with an addition of a main house and work room. A plume of purple smoke rose out of the chimney, and it shifted into pink then white. A garden full of fresh herbs carefully planted in rows in front of the house were tended by three different breeds of butterflies and even a few hobs. There was a stable with a horse and a donkey grazing peacefully in the field beyond, and clean laundry hung on a line, drying in the summer sun. A shutter opened in the tower, and I saw a redhead and blonde-haired girl peer out at me from the upper floor. They looked to be close to my age.

Lady Eville stepped out of the main house and addressed my parents. Her hair was pulled back in a bun, and she wore a deep blue work dress with a black apron.

"What is the problem?" she had said by way of greeting, her eyes picking me out in the back of the wagon.

"Our daughter is a plague. Anyone that goes near her ends up sick. She almost killed our local healer, and look at what she's done to us."

"Let me see." The tall woman drew closer to me. She'd raised a hand, and I saw a touch of gold light gather around the tip of her finger.

"Pretty," I remembered saying, and I reached for the ball of light.

She'd pulled it away, just out of reach.

"You can see magic?" she had asked.

I nodded and focused on the golden light. It was so

beautiful, I wanted it. Then the magic around her flickered out and vanished.

"Interesting. You've nullified my magic. I wonder what else you can do."

I remembered being frustrated that the golden light disappeared, and I wanted it back. So I'd concentrated on making it appear again. Lady Eville had gasped in pain as a string of gold began to pull from within her chest, and it floated out of her and into mine. My chest had glowed as I took the golden string.

"Not so fast, little one." She'd clenched her hand into a fist and the magic string snapped back into her. "It's not nice to take things that aren't yours. Especially magic."

I'd jutted my chin at her, and she'd laughed. "You *are* very much an enigma. I don't know what to do with you." She'd bit her lip, her dark brows furrowed in thought.

But then I'd felt dizzy, and the world went dark as I'd passed out, falling forward out of the wagon bed and into her arms.

A few days later, I'd woken up on a cot by the fireplace inside her home. A strange creature, called a brownie, was stoking the fire, and a tall man with long black hair, pointed ears, and gray eyes had been speaking to Lady Eville. His uniform was green and trimmed in silver.

"You can't be serious. Do you know what you are asking of me?"

"I know it's asking a lot, Lorn. Those horrible people abandoned her, and I can't keep her here. Her gift will interfere with the others' training. It's just too powerful."

"What is it exactly?" he'd asked, looking over at me.

I'd closed my eyes and pretended to sleep, watching the handsome elf through heavy lids.

"I don't know. I've never seen anything like her. She nullifies magic, but not only that. Over the last few days, when she is at her weakest, her body pulls magic from those closest to her. I've been able to protect the girls by supplementing her hunger with my own magic. But I find it best when I take her to the ley line near the fairy circle. It seems to stabilize her. Gives her strength. But what happens when she's older and stronger? If she isn't trained right, she could kill those closest to her."

"But I'm expendable?" Lorn had asked.

"No, never. You're the only one I can trust with her. I need you to do this for me, Lorn. You're the only one who can train her to live off the land, away from people. Where she can't harm anyone."

"She's going to have questions," he'd answered. "What do you want me to say?"

"Speak the truth, but hide her ability from others. They won't understand. They will fear her and may even hate her. You know what that's like."

Lorn had nodded. "I do. I will do as you ask, Lorelai, because it is you who is asking."

The next time I saw Lorn, he was no longer wearing his green scout uniform, and he never donned it again.

I assumed that loss was the reason I wanted Percy to be a scout so badly. To try to earn the uniform Lorn had given up because of me.

I'd learned years later that the couple that abandoned me weren't my real parents. They admitted to Lorelai Eville after she'd pressured them under the threat of a curse. They'd found me crying in a basket in the arms of a dead young woman, a black and gold arrow buried in her heart—arrows only used by the southern elves. They had to assume the woman had trespassed and was killed for doing so.

The couple took me in as their daughter and never admitted what they had done—until confronted by Lady Eville.

"Have you ever seen the southern elves of Sion?" I asked Percy.

He was always reluctant to talk about the southern elves. Everyone was, for they were like a bad omen. One didn't speak of their kind or name. "I have."

"And?" I pressed for more.

"Only humans have this unnecessary need for information," he rebuked.

"We're curious, that's all. Our lives are shorter. What do you expect?"

"True." I thought he was going to ignore me, but he opened up. "They're currently led by Allrick, and they keep to themselves. "

"I know all of this." I sighed. "But what *about* them? Their magic, a weakness. Tell me something I don't know."

"Honor, you need to let it go, this obsession you have with them."

"I don't know if I can," I said. "Not until I know if they really killed my mother."

"A black arrow doesn't prove guilt."

"It doesn't prove innocence, either."

"Why don't you tell me what you know already?" he said.

"Centuries ago, the elven king of the Thornhaven Court wasn't happy with the gifts the earth bestowed upon the elves. He wanted more powerful magic than the normal elemental affinities and he did something that caused a split," I said, reciting the answer I'd learned from Lorn.

Percy nodded. "The elder king made a deal with a dark sorcerer and allowed him access to the sacred hollow of Thornhaven. There was a great backlash of magic that spiraled out of the southern realm of Sion. It destroyed the temple of the sacred hollow, and it almost killed everyone in the realm. Dark magic leaked into the nearest ley lines which caused many of the creatures in the realm to become unnatural. Creatures like the brackenbeasts and the omnis began to appear. The elves of Thornhaven, their magic became . . . twisted," Percy said, his eyes looking sad. "And they would forever become blamed for one man's greed. Feared and hated by all, and the direct descendants of that leader are charged with guarding the tainted hollow for all eternity."

I shivered somewhat and felt the slightest pressure as my old friend leaned a hair closer to me, pressing more of his leg and arm into mine. Most would not have noticed the elf's movements. But I did, and soon heat seeped into my bones, enveloping me in warmth and safety. I struggled to keep my eyes open. I could feel them close. Each blink became longer than the previous. Until they didn't open again.

CHAPTER THREE

I snapped awake, my head dropping forward as I started to fall off the crate. I caught myself, instantly alert, and I knew something was wrong.

It was night.

I was alone . . . and Rumple was gone.

I flung off the canvas tarp that had mysteriously appeared around my shoulders and ran to the window ledge, scanning the road below me. The streets were empty.

That thief!

He'd done it again. He'd stolen from me. I screamed internally. He'd probably spotted the axe at the tavern and followed me just so he could steal it.

When I get my hands on him, I'm going to kill him.

I jumped from the second-floor window and landed on my feet, my hand hitting the snow to steady me. I spun in a circle, searching the road, looking for the prints. It was a mass of hundreds of footsteps, and the falling snow made it quite difficult to find the right set.

There! A print that didn't sink into the snow as deep as the others. It was barely discernible as it was quickly being covered by the fresh snow.

Percy's footprint. One of the first lessons I'd learned from Lorn was that elves were light of foot. They could walk on top of snow, barely leaving a print behind. I followed the lighter footprints down a side road, into an alley that came out by the stables on the outskirts of town.

Was he running away? Stealing my sister's axe? I actually wondered if it would be the end of the world if I let Percy take Rumple off my hands. That axe was quite the talker.

No. I owed it to Rheanon and Kash to take care of him. I said that I would bring him back.

The prints suddenly disappeared near a wall, and I looked up. The roof was low, perfect for scaling and getting onto the rooftops. Grabbing the overhang, I pulled myself up and took the easiest route, avoiding the snow-covered thatched roofs. I would hate to fall through one of those onto an unsuspecting family. About the eighth one over, I found a handprint on the gable. Percy was definitely here. But he didn't seem to be running away, instead he was circling back toward the market.

A scream filled the night air, and I turned, trying to gauge where it had come from. It was definitely female. I stood, sliding down the roof, and jumped over to the next lowered roof. From there, I leapt into a wagon and hopped onto the road, running into the covered market. It had closed up hours ago, the tables and stalls still stood, but the merchandise had long been packed away. Most of the coal in the burners had been left to die out. An ebbing orange glow flickered within the tent, creating haunting shadows on the canvas walls.

A whimper came from below a nearby table. Stooping low, I found a woman with brown hair, her white blouse was spotted with blood, cradling a fair-haired girl protectively. The girl's eyes glistened with tears. The woman's hand was covering the child's mouth as she tried to keep her from crying out.

I placed a finger to my lips, and she nodded. I mouthed the word "where" and she pointed farther down the aisle across the market. Standing, I reached for my short blades. Both were only the length of my arm, which made them easier to hide than a short sword.

My eyes searched the shadows for movement. Where was it? Then I paused and turned toward the table where the woman and child were cowering. My intuition said something was wrong. There had been something more than just fear on the child's face. A pleading look. I replayed the encounter in my mind. The woman: brown hair, white blouse . . . she wasn't wearing shoes. I leaned down and the space beneath the table was empty. The woman and child were gone.

I swore under my breath and jumped up onto the table and took off running in the opposite direction. A female werewolf. Of course, she would send me downwind.

Now I was angry. Leaping from table to table, I saw a shadow running on the other side of the canvas. I crossed, leapt in the air, and ripped my blade through cloth and crashed into the person, tackling them to the ground.

Hands wrestled for my blade. I grunted, and then was easily flipped over their head where I landed on my back. The air was forced out of my lungs and I gasped as a shadow loomed over me.

I expected a killing blow, but a hand reached out and pulled me to my feet.

"You're getting slow," Percy said.

"Shut it," I snapped. "Come on, she's getting away."

"She?" He looked confused.

"Women are capable of being killers too."

Percy didn't miss a beat. "I don't doubt it."

"That way," Rumple called from Percy's back. "In the woods."

We took off running toward the path, through the bushes and up a hill. We approached a clearing and slowed when we came to the girl, left abandoned in the middle of the snow. I raced to the child and checked her to make sure she wasn't injured.

Percy stood over us protectively. "The werewolf wouldn't just abandon her prey so easily."

"No, she wouldn't," I agreed, pulling the girl's arm out to see the bite mark on her wrist. "But I don't think this is about food."

"What?" He turned his head down to look at me as I met his gaze

"Watch out!" I pulled the child back as the werewolf dropped from the trees above, landing on Percy and knocking him to the ground. Percy raised the axe as the wolf snapped at his face. He shoved the handle into the wolf's mouth, pushing her jaw up and away from his head and neck. Her claws dug into his shoulders, ripping through his skin.

I grabbed my knives and slashed at the werewolf's arms. She howled and leapt backward off of Percy. Now she was injured and crazed. Percy got to his feet, his arm dripping blood.

"She bit me!" Rumple called out indignantly. "It's only fair that I bite her back. Let me at her."

The werewolf in front of us stood at almost seven feet

tall, her chest gaunt and her body misshapen. Her mouth was now a maw of jagged yellow teeth, with fingers elongated into claws, and her eyes yellow with madness.

She attacked me, her claws swinging for my head. I ducked, spun, and kicked out my leg to sweep her feet out from under her. The werewolf leapt straight up, avoiding my attack, and clawed again. I wasn't so fast dodging it a second time and her claw raked my shoulder.

"Honor!" Percy rushed forth, swinging the axe toward the werewolf, aiming to cleave her in half.

"No, don't harm her!" I jumped between them, and he arched the axe upward, barely missing my face.

"Are you crazy?" Percy cried out. "I could have killed you!"

I ignored Percy. "I'm sorry," I whispered, walking toward the werewolf. "For the pain you're in, and your loneliness. But you have no right to steal what doesn't belong to you," I said, repeating the same words Lady Eville had spoken to me years ago.

The werewolf's jaw snapped and froth fell from her lips, then her head turned back to the cowering child. She took a step forward, and I cut her off, my swords at my side. "I know you must have lost a great deal. But nothing will bring them back."

The wolf shook her head and her shoulders lowered as if in remorse. I took another step closer. "This is not who you are. What happened was an accident. But you've become a killer, and I can't let you continue this course. Think about what you are doing. Your family wouldn't want you to become this."

"Honor, what are you doing?" Percy tried to take a step closer, but I held my hand out, keeping him at bay and motioning to the child. He sidestepped and picked her up in his arms, preparing to run to safety.

"Don't do this to them. You can be stronger than this. You don't have to continue on this path." I took another step, and the werewolf snarled. She snapped at my outstretched hand, but I didn't back down. "I can help you."

The werewolf looked over my shoulder at the child and then back to me. She shook—head to toe—and I watched the horror of her shift. The bones in her arms and legs cracked and broke as they reshaped themselves. The snout began to mold back into her skull, and I couldn't take my eyes away as the fur peeled back to reveal a quivering naked human woman, cowering in the snow. I took off my cloak and wrapped it around her shoulders.

She clutched it closed in front of her and looked up at me, tears running down her face. "It hurts so much. The pain. It never stops."

"It's the werewolf curse. You weren't born a shifter. Your body's not handling the change well."

She trembled, her eyes looking through me, like she was remembering. "They attacked our village. There were so many. Monstrous wolf-like creatures ravaging through our homes. My husband died protecting me as I tried to escape with my daughter, but they caught us. Those monsters caught us," she repeated and raised her trembling hand to her throat, where I saw faint scars that had healed. "I thought I'd died that day."

"What else can you tell me about the attack?" I said softly.

She shook her head. "I don't know. It was dark. Middle of the night. Wait. I remember . . . I remember hearing music. A haunting melody right before a beast burst through our front door. After the attack, when I came to, everyone was dead, and all that was left was dust."

Was this one of the attacks Lorn was worried about? The son of Allemar?

When I thought of the evil sorcerer, I shuddered. He was killed by my sister, Maeve, or at least his soul was. He had come back before, but we knew he had apprentices spread throughout the land. In Florin, he was trying to create a shifter army. It seems that was still the case, but now it was led by someone else.

"What's your name?" I asked. Reaching out, I pressed my hand against her back and could feel the heat radiating from under the clothing. Her face was dripping with perspiration, and her breathing was becoming quick and ragged.

"Arisole," she whimpered, and clutched her stomach. Her face contorted, and the pressure caused the veins on her face to surface.

"Think of the child, Arisole. You don't want to harm the innocent." I thought the change was coming on her again, but she pushed it down.

"But I'm so lonely," she whimpered. "I just want my family back." Her body trembled again, and I looked up at Percy and shook my head. This wasn't good. This was a very sick werewolf. She wasn't taking to the shifting well, and her body was slowly killing her. It was known to drive some mad; it killed others. Not everyone could survive the werewolf change.

"Arisole, I know someone that can help you."

"No." She pushed my hands away and got to her feet. She looked at the child in Percy's arms, seeing the bloody bite mark on her hand. She recoiled in disgust. "Did I do that?"

I nodded.

She clutched her head. "I don't remember. I don't remember hurting her. I just wanted my family back."

"There were more," I said. "In another town. A man."

Her hands flew to her mouth. "I killed him. I didn't want to. I remember. He looked so much like Henry. I just wanted him to be with me." Fresh tears spilled anew from her eyes, and she looked behind her over the mountainside. "I can't live like this anymore. I don't want to hurt people."

"You don't have to. I know someone that is a werewolf, cursed like you. He can help you. Teach you to live a normal life."

As I pleaded with the cursed woman, torches flickered through the trees. Drawing closer like dancing fireflies, the clearing became a halo of light as townspeople came out of the woods carrying weapons.

"There she is!" A stocky man in a red wool jacket and fur hat pointed toward the trembling Arisole. "That's the woman that kidnapped my Polina!"

The child's mother raced toward Percy, and he kneeled to give the child back to her. While the mob of angry villagers pressed on toward Arisole, she turned and ran.

They gave chase, screaming obscenities and threats. I tried to follow. To call out and calm the angry crowd, but I was shuffled to the back, cut off.

The mob stopped and the angry cries died as a heavy silence followed. I pushed through the throng of villagers, elbowing and shoving people out of the way until I came to a cliff. It had come out of nowhere, hidden by the blinding white snow in the darkness. I saw the single set of footprints race off the precipice. I leaned forward and glanced over the edge of the cliff. On the rocks below, I could make out my cloak surrounding a still form.

Was it an accident? Was it her choice to jump over and end it, or was she forced by the crowd? My stomach turned sour with bitterness. It wasn't her fault she was going mad. For weeks she had fought the curse alone, eating to survive, and she had attempted to create a new family the only way she could. The man in the village didn't survive her attempts. But the child would. She was bitten and would become a werewolf if not treated with a counteragent. I would need to find the parents and get them wolfsbane as soon as possible.

"Arisole," I whispered, bowing my head and praying for her. "Your pain is gone."

I slipped back through the crowd and headed to the clearing. I picked up Rumple who had remained blessedly quiet, and slung him in his leather holster over my shoulder.

CHAPTER FOUR

"Apply this to the cut." I handed Polina's parents the wolfsbane I had ground into a powder and added to a salve. "Use it in small amounts and watch her closely on the first full moon. Only then will we know if we caught it before it spread."

I had wasted no time. While the rest of the mob had been in a confused frenzy, I'd gone into town and found the only hedge witch and pounded on her door, pulling her from a dazed sleep. After I'd explained what I needed, the hedge witch gave it to me freely.

"It wasn't a deep cut, so if this salve doesn't work, she shouldn't turn anytime soon. It could take a while." I continued my lecture on werewolves. "But just to be safe, you should travel to the kingdom of Baist and speak with King Xander. If you leave now, you can get there in plenty of time. There are wards in place at the palace, places where she can be protected if she does shift."

"How do you know she will shift at all?" Polina's mother asked, worried, as she dabbed the salve onto Polina's wound.

"I don't . . . Not really. Some people that are bitten never become werewolves. But if she does, the first shift can be deadly, and she might not survive it. The wolfsbane should lessen the effects of the curse. I don't know if it will cure it."

The father, still wearing his fur hat, paced the small living room the whole time I was there. He shook his head in denial. "I think you're mistaken. It's just a dog bite."

Polina was asleep on a cot by the fire. Her face was pale, and a shimmer of sweat appeared on her brow. I briefly touched her forehead. It was burning hot. It could be an infection, or the curse already taking hold.

"I'm sorry." I turned to the parents. "I want to be wrong, but in this case, I know I'm not. I witnessed the woman's transformation. I will send a missive and arrange for transportation to Baist if you can't afford it yourself. If anything, think of your family."

The mother turned to her husband. "We must, James. We have to think of our daughter."

"Very well." He took off his hat, wiped his bald head, and nodded to me. "Make the arrangements. We will do as you say."

"As you wish." I gave them a bow and then headed outside. The sun was just starting to rise over the mountain. My feet crunched on the soft snow, and I headed back toward the market to find a mirror vendor. They had become all the rage since King Xander placed them throughout his kingdom. Other kingdoms had followed suit shortly after. For a small coin, you could use them to contact a loved one.

Of course, my six sorceress sisters never needed to use the public mirrors. They could enchant almost any reflective surface to speak to each other. Except for me. I had to pay like everyone else. I shouldered my jealousy as I dug into my pouch and produced a coin, handing it to the same hedge witch I had woken up the night before. The woman stood outside a wooden box with the image of a moon and sun on it.

"Sorry, Auntie, for the rude awakening last night." I used the familiar greeting bestowed on an elder hedge witch. Even though I wasn't of the same bloodline or family of magic as my sisters, I was still taken with using the names and terminology. "The sun and the moon are rising."

The hedge witch's hair was silver, with a single streak of brown down the side. Her face was kind, and her eyes ringed with laugh wrinkles. "Yes, I see. Never you mind. You were on a mission to save a child. Was it successful?"

"Only time will tell," I answered.

Her green eyes met mine, and her hands trembled as she clasped and unclasped them. I could see her reluctance to speak, but she found the words, not mincing them. "It was probably too late for the wolfsbane."

"I know. But I had to try."

"That you did, dearie." She stood up from the stool in front of the booth and handed the coin back to me. "The call's on me. Just press the edge of the mirror and speak clearly the name of the person you want to appear in the mirror. If they hear the hum, they can respond. But you know that already, don't you?" she said with a smile on her face.

"I do."

"Strange. I feel an odd aura about you." The hedge witch reached out her hand to touch me, but I pulled away before she made contact. Stepping quickly into the booth, I closed the door behind me.

The booth was cozy. A circular mirror hung on the wall; a padded bench on the floor in front of it. On the sides of the booth were small windows to let in sunlight and fresh air. Candles lined a table in front of the mirror, giving even more light to the calling booth. A sweet smell hit my nose, and I saw the incense burner hanging from a hook on the wall.

Before I began, I ran my fingers through my hair, tucking away stray strands that had come out of the braid. My eyes had dark circles under them from lack of sleep, and there may have been a smudge of blood on my cheek. Using my sleeve, I wiped it away as best I could and wished that I had another cloak.

"Do you think you could ask Rhea to make another enchanted weapon?" Rumple pleaded.

"No. I'm not bothering Rhea."

"Why not? I bet they miss me. They probably want to hear my voice. Especially sissy hands."

"They are on their honeymoon and a tour of the kingdom. I would be daft to interrupt them. And I'm still mad at you for going off with Percy and not alerting me."

"You hadn't slept in days. We were only trying to take care of the werewolf problem for you."

"I thought dwarves didn't get along with elves."

"He's an elf? He sure doesn't act like one," Rumple muttered.

"You don't necessarily act like a dwarf, either."

Incessant grumbling followed, and I had to remind myself to be nicer to Rumple. It wasn't his fault that he had been displaced or brought back as an enchanted weapon.

I took my knife and nicked the tip of my finger, then placed a single drop of blood on the mirror. It wasn't needed, but I knew the extra precaution would make the call more stable—and keep people from eavesdropping.

"Rosalie," I commanded, picturing my raven-haired sister.

The mirror shimmered, and I felt a hum. I waited, imagining where my eldest sister could be at this time of the morning. Last I'd heard, she was back in Baist after having established Maeve and her brother as the rightful heirs and rulers of Florin.

A few moments later, a room came into focus, and I could see Rosalie sitting in front of a small desk.

"Why hello, Honor." Her eyes lit with joy before her perfect mouth turned down into a frown. "You look horrible."

I chuckled. "Why hello to you, sister dear. You look unspeakably well. Is that rosy glow to your cheeks called motherhood?" Rosalie was wearing all white, her glossy dark hair flowing over one side of her face, hiding the silver scars she'd received in the battle with Allemar years ago. Behind her, I could make out a giant four-poster bed. Violet, her daughter, slept in the middle of it on a mass of covers, and beside the bed, a bassinet.

She had only weeks ago borne her second child. A boy named after his father, Alexander.

"You will know it soon enough," she teased.

I frowned. "I highly doubt that."

"You're like an angel," Rumple blurted out.

Rosalie laughed. "Is this the magnificent Rumple I've heard so much about?"

"You've heard of me?" He preened. "I can guarantee you, whatever you've heard, it's all true."

Rosalie shook her head and laughed. Before she could

say more, I interrupted. "We have a problem. I just came across a woman who was the sole survivor of an attack by werewolf-like creatures."

"Not werewolves, surely? For we have been tracking all the rogue werewolf packs with a tracking spell, and they are all in the southern part of Baist. None have been sighted in Kiln for years."

"She said they were *werewolf-like*, but their bite was the same. She turned at the next full moon. Do you know of anything like that? A creature that is a werewolf, but not?"

"She's sure it wasn't a shifter?" Rosalie asked.

"I don't know. But a shifter's bite doesn't create werewolves."

"That is unfortunate. We've had our hands full with similar cases," Rosalie said. "Always striking in the middle of the night. In Baist, it was ogre attacks; in Florin, a nasty group of Omnis. There have been about one a week. All spread out, never attacking the same place twice, leaving little trace. Eden, Meri, and I are in communication trying to track them. It definitely smells of dark magic . . . and him."

"Do you think—?" I asked, trailing off.

Rosalie gently touched the scar on the side of her face.

"I don't want to think about anything yet. Allemar's reach and influence are far and wide. But if this is someone posing as his protégé, they must be stopped."

I agreed and quickly explained my fear for little Polina and how I was sending her family there.

"Of course. We will send someone to fetch the family right away, and we'll prepare for her arrival. If anyone can teach a werewolf how to control her curse, it's another werewolf."

I sighed in relief, grateful that King Xander, a werewolf in secret, was willing to help others of his kind. He had been bitten when he was younger and had to overcome the werewolf curse for years. My mother helped him by creating wards in his palace. Polina's family would be safe on the castle grounds. Over the last few years, the stray werewolves had made it to the hidden sanctuary, and it was moved out into the woods. The wards and lands had grown in acreage as well. It was the perfect safe place . . . especially for Polina.

"Allemar was tough enough on his own, and if there are more . . . A true son of Allemar? I'm terrified of what it could mean for the seven kingdoms," I said.

"I will do what I can to find out more about these creatures. But Honor, there is another thing to consider. This is the year of the high council."

"Already?" I leaned forward. The high council was when all the royal families of the seven kingdoms got together to speak of peace treaties and marriages between the kingdoms. "Where is it held this year?"

"The summer palace of Sion," she said. "And all the daughters of Eville have been banned from attending."

"What?" I asked in surprise.

"It seems that King Leonel still has a grudge against Mother. He's accused her of using magic to unnecessarily influence the outcomes of the last six royal weddings, and he fears that our presence will only muddle the murky waters since he has a brood of his own that he's trying to marry off." She smirked. I knew she was thinking of the arranged marriage that Mother had forced Rosalie into with the Prince of Baist. Luckily, it had turned out to be a love match in the end.

"I don't like that. All the kings gathered together in one place while these rogue magical attacks are happening? It seems suspicious."

"My thoughts exactly," Rosalie said. "I will speak with Xander, and we will keep you and the others up-to-date. And Honor?"

I could feel a yawn coming on, but I was unable to hold it back.

"Get some rest. You look peaky."

I knew the warning was more than just tiredness. I needed to get to the ley line soon.

"I will," I promised.

"Take care."

The mirror went dark, and I leaned back in the chair. Rosalie was right. I needed to get some sleep. I pulled out the worn leather map and laid it across the bench, tracing my finger along the dotted lines. I had strayed too far from the nearest ley line, and I could feel exhaustion settle into my body. And I was dangerous when exhausted. I had traveled farther west than I'd thought. The closest ley line was the Northern Woods. It was time to return home.

CHAPTER FIVE

The cold earth penetrated through my clothes as I lay prone on the ground, staring up at the black cave wall above me. Smoke from the fire burned my eyes as the pine needle kindling caught and a good size blaze erupted. I'd traveled through the day, avoiding all the main roads, heading deep into the mountains. I'd found a small cave that ran over an outlying ley line that originated from the Northern Woods. By the time I'd arrived, I was sweating, trembling, and struggling to stand upright. I'd collapsed onto my knees and pressed my forehead onto the earth, and then waited for my curse to take over.

Little by little, I could feel my soul reach deep into the ground and take strength from the earth. My sisters had learned to tap into the magic of the earth through these ley lines of power and they would use them to amplify their magic. Not me. I needed it to survive.

Trembling, I waited for my soul to fully connect. For the warmth to spread through my body as I fed on magic. I wasn't sure what else to call the exchange my body went through. I knew it could look odd to a passerby as my body slipped into a hypothermic sleep. For at this moment, I was in my cold stage. I had to leave Rumple outside. I was scared that I'd siphon all the magic from him if I lost control. I'd hung him in a tree a good thirty paces away to keep watch.

I closed my eyes and finally let myself rest.

Rest didn't come, for not more than a candle mark later, I was awoken by bawdy name-calling as Rumple laid into an intruder. "Back off before I cut you down into kindling." He was better than any guard dog.

I pulled my bow out and pressed my back against the cave wall, scanning the woods. Rumple was still where I'd left him hanging from a tree, but I couldn't see who he was talking to. But he had sensed them—which meant elves.

Two short whistles resembling a native bird pierced the air. I grinned and placed my fingers to my mouth and responded with the return call of three trills. Lowering my bow, I stepped out of the cave and waited for the scouts to materialize out of the woods. It was always a treat to watch their magic at work. An elf stepped out from behind a thin ash tree. Impossible as it may seem, they were able to cloak their bodies behind something so small. He wore the green formfitting uniform of the scouts, with feather patterns running along his arms, giving them the semblance of wings. His brown hair was braided along the sides and left long down his back. To his right, a beautiful elven woman with hair like fire appeared from the underbrush. She didn't lower her bow and still had it trained on me. Silver tree roots ran up her legs and folded into the trunk that connected with her torso. Her affinity. Earth.

I turned back to the first scout with the feathers on his uniform. "Greetings, Captain Einan." I nodded my head toward the beautiful red-haired elf at his side. "Rulah."

Rulah's eyes narrowed, and in that micro expression I could tell how much she hated me.

I took a deep breath. Glancing around the woods, I began to pick out the faint shimmer by the rocks, the second one by an evergreen, a third by the small stream, and I turned to look behind me and above the cave. I called out to each of the scouts. "Greetings to you as well; Aflin, Ardax, Corill, and Taris."

"Greetings, Honor Eville." Einan let out the rarest of smiles. "It seems your skills are as keen as ever. To detect an elf in hiding, but to also identify them by name . . . is quite a rare talent."

"I was trained well," I said, leaning my bow against the side of the cave wall. "Your brother, Lorn, spared no expense."

"Pity he couldn't train our other younglings as well as he trained you." Einan waved his hand, and the four other scouts appeared, dropping their magic and revealing themselves. Ardax was the elf who had scaled the rocky outcropping, and he nimbly leapt down in close proximity in an attempt to startle me.

"We don't need Lorn, or the girl," Ardax snapped. He brushed past me roughly, his shoulder purposely nailing me in the back. His uniform didn't have any markings to identify his gifts. He was one of three elves that chose not to showcase their affinity.

My anger started to rise to the surface as I bit back my irritated retort. I got along with almost all the elves in the Northern Woods except for two, and they both happened to be here. Ardax and Rulah.

Einan barked out an order in elvish and Ardax moved to stand by Rulah, his head cocked and chin raised. I had a feeling that if Ardax had the chance, he would kill me in my sleep and not get a spot of blood on his uniform.

"I'm surprised you would come this close to our home and not visit us," Einan said.

"I wasn't sure of my welcome since I'm not with Lorn," I said warily, keeping an eye on Ardax.

"You, Honor, will always be welcome. Come. Rest. It is almost time for the Affinity Celebration. You can be our guest."

I had completely forgotten about the elven ceremony. "I would enjoy that," I said.

Einan raised his hand, and the scouts fell back, slowly disappearing into the woods behind him. He paused and studied the double-headed axe hanging from the tree. He could sense the magic emanating from it.

"What are you looking at, long-face?" Rumple spoke up.

Einan gave me a questioning look.

"It's a long story," I said.

"All I have is time, and I do love a good story," he replied.

After I put out my fire, gathered my pack, and slung Rumple over my shoulder, we were off, running at a brisk pace. For most, this would be an impossible speed to keep up with, and even I was barely able to.

"So he was a dwarf?" Einan asked after I filled him in.

"Still a dwarf, you no good maggot-eater," Rumple challenged.

"My apologies," Einan corrected, his voice filled with regret. "It must be the lack of beard that had me confused."

"I'll have you know, I had one of the most glorious

beards. It was long and could hold many surprises," Rumple said.

Einan gave me a questioning look, asking me to expound.

"Apparently, their beards have pockets," I explained.

Einan threw his head back and laughed. It was so unexpected that it caused scouts to suddenly halt. Einan leaned forward and grabbed his chest. "I like him," Einan added as his laughter died down.

"Well, the feeling is *not* mutual," Rumple grumbled. "Stupid elves. Should be out doing something useful like making shoes, not running through the woods like fairies."

"Well, I could make a comment about dwarves running their mouths off and spending all of their days hiding in the ground like grubby moles . . . but that would be beneath me," Einan said slyly.

I pinched my lips together to hold back my mirth.

Within a few candle marks, we had made it to the outer wards of the Northern Woods. Snow no longer covered the ground. Winter had faded away, and the air was warm with the scent of spring. There was a long line of ash trees, and I knew we were about to cross over into the hidden realm.

My heart raced as I got excited at the prospect. I loved the hidden elven realm of the Northern Woods. Few humans ever got to enter because you could only find the realm and pass through the magic veil unless an elf accompanied you.

We drew closer, and the scouts before me all walked through the tree line. They shimmered and then disappeared. Einan held out his arm to me, and I politely placed my hand on top of his as he escorted me through the veil of magic.

My body tingled as magic kissed my skin, the feeling akin to butterfly wings racing over my face. The scent of plumeria flowers tickled my nose and my tongue tasted of sweet honey.

Everyone's experience as they passed through the veil was different. Some could feel the warmth, others only got a hint of a faint scent. When I passed through the veil, my body drank deep of the magic and reacted differently. No other had responded to so many of their senses being triggered. Which made me another enigma.

As I stepped over to the other side, tears fell from my eyes.

Einan looked at my glistening face. His finger reached out and touched my wet cheeks. "I've never crossed with you before. Is this a common occurrence?" He held up his wet fingertips.

I didn't hide the smile. "Always . . . every time." I wasn't ashamed of how I reacted to their magic. I loved it. I wished it were mine.

He seemed perplexed by my tears. The first time I'd passed over as a child, Lorn had thought I was sick because I'd immediately begun to wail and cry because I'd wanted to go back inside the veil.

I still cried with each passing through the veils, but not as dramatically as I had back then. I had gained control.

I took a deep breath and turned to face Northenial Woodfaelon Court, or, as the humans called it, Northern Woods.

We stood upon a cliff and overlooked a beautiful city made of glowing white stone, surrounded by rivers and streams that ran through it like watery tree roots. Elaborate natural-looking bridges made crossing the streams easy, and the air was always filled with the sound of a gently babbling brook. Across the city, a waterfall cascaded down from a mountain, and on either side, two great towers like half-moons arced toward each other, with the waterfall as the barrier between. There, the great council of elves met.

Einan and I crossed behind the scouts as we headed into the city. A trumpet blared, followed by a second and third, as they led a trail of waving blue flags up to the citadel where the council lived. It was always a thrill when the scouts returned. Many times they were gone for weeks on end, visiting the other three elven courts. Each of the elven courts settled where a ley line of magic erupted above the earth, creating what was known as a sacred hollow. The elves dedicated themselves to guarding the sacred hollow and hiding it behind a veil of magic. That was how the elven realms were created, and the families and clans protected them.

Northern Woods was run by a high council made up of ambassadors from each of the clan's oldest families. Most neutral in their beliefs and training, they were considered the peacemakers.

Farther south in Sion were the southern elves of the Thornhaven Court.

Then across the seas, further than the kingdom of Isla, was the Lightwood Court. I'd heard Rulah brag many times about being the daughter of one of the council members.

Then there was the Wynterbrook Court; a gentle drove of elves high in the mountain's eastern edge of the kingdom of Rya.

I was almost lost among the hustle and bustle of the crowds as we passed under another tree bridge and headed farther into the realm. It felt odd to be here without Lorn. Like I was trespassing. Over the years, the tree roots were nurtured and grew into the archways for homes. I passed Lorn's, but the lights were dark within. *Where was he?*

One by one, as others peeled off and headed to their own trees, I turned to head into the smaller tree next to Lorn's that had always been assigned to me when we passed through. I slowed to turn up to the path to my room and called out.

"Einan, there's something I must speak to you about. It's about an attack not far from here."

"We've received word about the werewolf attack already, as well as others. It is quite troubling," Einan responded, his brows lowering. "We believe the leader is the son of Allemar."

"How? I mean, who told you?"

"I did." Percy stepped out of the shadows, and my heart skipped a beat. His arm was dressed, and I could see blood marring the fresh bandage. "I felt it imperative to return and warn them."

I nodded. Of course he would have notified them. He may not have been a scout anymore, but his training and loyalty were still evident.

"We are already adding more troops to our borders," Einan said. "And Lorn has gone to seek council with the elders."

"What is to be done?" I asked.

"Honor, this is not an elven matter. We know better than to interfere where we are not welcome, nor invited, because it can be seen as starting a war. But it is a growing concern, nonetheless. I will speak with the council and discuss our further actions regarding this threat."

"What about Lorn? We must get word to him."

Einan bowed his head. "I will see to it that your guardians are notified right away so they know that you are safe here with us."

Guardians. A strange word indeed. Even though they were not married, I did consider Lorn to be my father, and Lorelai was my mother. I watched them fall in love, knew they cared for each other deeply, and wondered what held them back from declaring their love for each other.

"Thank you once again for your hospitality," I said to Einan. "I will stay through the Affinity Ceremony, then be on my way. You can tell them that."

Einan didn't say goodbye—elves never did. He turned on his heel and headed to speak with the elven council. I knew they didn't make decisions hastily. It could be days or weeks before they agreed on what the course of action would be regarding this new menace. They may not concern themselves at all. It was a human matter, for elves could not be turned into werewolves.

When Einan left, I was left alone with Percy.

"Honor," he called my name softly. "I'm sorry I left. I had to return and get word to my brethren."

"You don't need to explain. It's your duty as a scout. I did the same. I never looked for you, either. I took care of Polina and her family."

Percy took a step closer to me, and we could almost see eye to eye. I was tall and almost as lean as some of the elven women. If it weren't for my ears and unassuming hazel eyes, I could probably pass for one.

"We did our duty," he said, as if trying to convince

himself, but I could hear the guilt in his voice. He fidgeted with the leather bracer he wore on his right wrist as though it were uncomfortable. It wasn't odd to see elves with bracers, except Percy and Ardax always wore them.

"We did," I agreed. "That is the scout's code. Duty first."

He blinked, and I could see his inner frustration that he had fallen into his scout training even though he had stepped away from them.

There was an awkward pause as neither of us spoke, unsure of how to mend our friendship and wondering if we could. I chose the elven way of ending our conversation abruptly. I stepped into my assigned room and closed the door behind me.

I leaned my head against the door and waited for the sound of his footfalls as he left. I didn't hear any, which for an elf didn't mean anything. He was probably long gone.

My room was simple. The beautiful knotwood bed had a soft green coverlet, and a single candlestick holder on the bedside table. There were no personal effects because I didn't own any other than the spare clothes in my satchel. I laid Rumple against the wall by the only wooden chair and dropped my bag on the floor. Sprawling out across the bed, I stared out the window that had been opened to let in the night air. It was never cold nor windy in the elven realm. It didn't snow or rain unless the elves wished for it, for they controlled the elements.

During the affinity celebration, I would watch with hundreds of others as the youngest elves presented themselves and the magic chose their new vessels and recognized the elves' gifts.

Gazing through the glass pane, I stared up at the stars.

They weren't real; instead, they were a shimmer of veil that reflected the constellations. For this world existed within the seven kingdoms and was virtually undetected. After all my years of training with Lorn, I had never once been asked to watch the affinity celebration. This would be my first time being invited, and I prayed to the stars I wouldn't mess it up.

CHAPTER SIX

"I want to come," Rumple whined from his spot, leaning against the wall, while I pulled on my leather boots.

"There's no need for you to be with me. Plus, you'll just pick a fight with every elf you see." I stood and adjusted the strap, tying it around my calf.

"Not every elf. I was on my best behavior yesterday," he said demurely.

"I'm not lugging you around. This is supposed to be a holiday." I sighed in exasperation and gave myself a final look in the mirror. My hair looked almost black, as it was still wet from the bathing pools. It was slicked back into a braid, and my cheeks were flushed pink with excitement. I turned, opened my door, and was surprised to see Percy there with his hand raised as if to knock.

"Good morning, Honor." He leaned in and glanced at the axe. "Rumple," he addressed the axe, which surprised me.

"Hey, longface. Tell her I want to party too. She's too lazy to carry me."

I ground my teeth in irritation at the insult.

Percy's eyebrows raised for only a split second. "I'd be happy to lug you around."

"See? Longface is willing to—wait, did you say *lug* . . . why, I ought to—"

"Rumple!" I snapped. "Behave."

I was trapped between Percy—who seemed to be trying to get on my good side—and a petulant dwarf who was determined to poke the bear, and by bear I meant elf. "Fine, you can go, but the first time you insult someone, you are banished back to the room." I glared at the immobile axe.

"I'll swear. I'll even pinky promise."

"You don't have pinkies," I countered.

"Caught that, did you?" Rumple chuckled. "I was lying anyway."

"Rumple!" I growled out his name in warning.

He fell silent, and I just waved Percy into my room as he picked up the leather holster and adjusted it to fit his wide shoulders.

I looked up at Percy and his unreadable face. "You're in charge of babysitting him. I'm not in the mood to deal with his antics today."

Neither one of them said anything. As I left the tree room, I headed down the path to the main courtyards where the eternal banquet of never-ending food was laid out.

Long tables made with living wood, sprigs of fresh green popping up around a plethora of plates filled with food. The eternal banquet was a feast that would go on without stopping, another aspect of their magic. Food was always available for anyone anytime of the day, and it would never spoil.

This was one of my favorite treats about the elven realm.

Although it was eternal food, it was usually the same dishes over and over, but I didn't care as I took a roasted pear, fresh bread, and honey butter. Simple fare. Lorn taught me to eat light, never overindulging because it would slow my fighting and I never knew when a battle would be upon me.

Percy picked up the same items as I made my way over to a large root in a hidden alcove. It made a perfect bench, and it was my favorite spot to eat growing up. I hopped up and Percy casually took the spot next to me. Without asking, he reached for my pear and began slicing it up as I took his bread and spread honey butter over both of our pieces. When he sliced one pear, he handed it to me, and I placed it on the warm butter and waited until he was done with the second. In perfect accord, we made breakfast and when he'd cleaned and put away his knife, I handed him his bread.

I took a bite and savored the juices of the fresh fruit mixed with the sweet honey spread. This had been my favorite breakfast ever since I was a child.

Percy watched me eat, holding his own bread in his hand. He was studying my exuberant expressions. He always did it—watched me with fascination—and would frequently ask about what a certain expression meant. He was curious about my humanity, just as I was curious about his own race.

I elbowed him. "It's rude to stare," I said with a mouthful of food.

"It's rude to talk with your mouth full," he retorted.

I rolled my eyes.

"That one." He pointed toward my face.

"What?"

"That thing you did with your eyes. Which one is that?"

"It means exaggerated annoyance. My sisters do it all the time."

Percy then spent the next few minutes trying to roll his eyes in the same manner, but it only looked like he was having a seizure.

"Stop it," I laughed. "Maybe leave it for the human."

He gave up, and his shoulders slumped a bit in an imitation of me. There it was again. Just like the day he'd found me in the woods, Percy looked broken.

I finished my breakfast and licked the honey butter off my fingers.

"Wait," he said as I was about to stand up. Percy reached out his hand very gently toward my face.

I froze as his thumb brushed softly across my bottom lips. I inhaled and looked into his green eyes, my hand reaching up to grasp his hand to stop him. His lips parted, and I quickly pulled away.

"Honor," he said. "What's wrong?"

"Nothing," I replied, backing away, trying to put as much distance as I could between us. Internally, I was screaming.

Everything.

Everything was wrong. It wasn't supposed to be like this. We were supposed to stay friends. I had to keep my heart under control and not be swayed by emotions. I had a duty. A duty to myself.

And I couldn't tell Percy, or he would spend his whole life trying to help me because that's the kind of friend he was, and I would not burden my friend with my problems.

"Percy." Rulah came up to Percy and stood very close to his side. "I need to speak with you."

I didn't wait for Percy's response, and I took off down the stony path heading down a tunnel of willow trees toward the lake.

I'd traveled with Lorn for two years before he'd first brought me to the Northern Woods. I was six years old when I'd first crossed the realm. All of the elves were beautiful, but at the same time terrifying. There were very few children, and Lorn made sure to keep me far away from them in case I lost control. We were loners in the elven kingdom, keeping to ourselves in the training hall that happened to be built right over a ley line. There I practiced fighting, knife throwing, and archery.

Life was hard as the only human girl being trained by a former scout commander. It was said that Lorn was the greatest scout commander they had ever had, and everyone wanted to be trained by him—but he wouldn't take on any more trainees.

The day he'd walked in with a human girl and declared that she would be his only pupil was the day that sealed my fate. I was the most hated and ignored person in all the Northern Woods. I'd heard rumors that Rulah had even gone before the elven council and tried to get me removed from their courts. The rumors were that she thought if she could get me kicked out, then maybe Lorn would take on other students. It didn't work. Apparently, being the adoptive daughter of Lorelai Eville held weight. The elven council knew to keep my mother on their good side. It didn't help with me being ostracized.

When I was sixteen, Lorn brought in Percy, who was

already a few years into his scout training. Lorn announced he would be my training partner.

At first, Percy was cold to me. Indifferent. He didn't want to train with a human girl. I could tell he didn't think I was worth the effort. He wouldn't talk to me or address me. When he did, he would call me 'Girl'. He ignored me unless we were fighting, and as soon as the weapons were down, I was back to being invisible.

Then that coldness turned to hatred, and the next few months were a living hell as he relentlessly beat me in every single drill.

Knives, he would easily disarm me. Staff, he would knock me on my back. Hand-to-hand combat, I'd be face down, kissing the mat with a knee in my back. He was a firsthand witness to my tirades, temper tantrums, and all of my very human emotions and frustrations. He was years ahead in training, and I hated losing. My mouth was a waterfall of colorful language that he had never heard.

"Why?" I had cried out to Lorn in private. "Why are you making us work together? He despises me and doesn't want to train with me. Why can't we go back to training just the two of us?"

Lorn had quietly rebuked me. "Do you doubt my methods? Have I ever led you astray before?"

"No," I'd said quietly.

"Then you will continue to train with Percy." He had turned his back on me, ending the discussion, or so I thought. He'd slowly turned and called out over his shoulder. "Maybe this lesson isn't just for you, but for him. Have you thought about why he doesn't like training with you?"

"It's because I'm human."

"Really? I wouldn't be too sure of that. Do you know Percy's affinity for magic?"

"No," I'd answered. "He also doesn't talk about it, either."

"Then you don't really know your opponent, do you?"

"Will he tell me if I ask?"

"No." Lorn's eyes had twinkled with mischief. "He won't tell you. Maybe if you beat it out of him." Lorn's announcement about Percy had puzzled me.

After their affinity ceremony, most of the elves had some token or dressage that announced their gift. It could be a necklace with a sun, or a blue scarf symbolizing water. The scouts and soldiers' uniforms were designed to showcase their affinities. It was an honor.

Percy had been way past the age of acceptance of his gift, so he should have been displaying his affinity. But his clothes were always the brown training uniform with no frills, complete with his leather bracers. There hadn't been a single clue as to Percy's aptitude in magic. Instead of focusing on him, I'd tried to change my perspective and focus on my own weaknesses.

I knew it had annoyed Percy. Seeing my emotions displayed so openly on my face and he would fight harder against me, showing no mercy. Month after month, it continued, and then one day, I'd stopped my meltdowns. I'd changed. I didn't speak of my pain. If I was angry, my face was a blank slate. I'd buried my emotions deep and kept them locked away. My snappy comebacks fizzled down to nonexistent. I became a coldhearted soldier with no feelings. Like an elf.

I could feel his confusion in the change of my demeanor. I hadn't cared. I'd wanted to be the best. To survive. I'd fully expected Percy to continue to despise me forever.

Then one day it just stopped.

Lorn was in another meeting with the council, and it was just Percy and I in the training hall at sunrise. Battered and bruised from the previous day's exercises, my eyes had been red from lack of sleep because I'd spent the night going through my fighting forms. There was a bruise on my face where I hadn't ducked in time and had connected with Percy's elbow. I'd had a slight limp from a swollen ankle.

Percy had seen my disheveled face and the change in my gait. "Why don't you give up?" he'd challenged. "Why do you subject yourself to this training? It's obvious you are still lacking."

I was surprised when he'd addressed me. He *never* spoke to me.

I'd picked up the wooden short sword from the wall of weapons and moved to the middle of the mat.

"I have to learn control, and train to live by myself."

"Why?"

"Because I don't want to hurt the ones I love ever again." I'd said it with vehemence and had immediately pictured my parents and those I'd accidentally hurt with my curse. "I don't belong out there," I'd said, pointing with the practice sword toward the veil.

"And you don't belong here." He'd watched my face closely.

"I know," I'd said sadly, then dropped my arm. "I have to learn to live in a world in-between." I'd held up my training sword and beckoned him to do the same.

Percy blinked at me, and I had known the subtle nuance of their culture to read his confusion again.

"You're hurt." He wouldn't raise his weapon.

"I'm always hurt, or haven't you noticed? My body isn't as hardy as the elves. You never cared before." I'd settled into my fighting stance.

"You should rest."

"I don't have time to rest. Come on," I'd demanded again, shifting my weight to my non-injured foot.

Percy then dropped his sword on the ground.

"This isn't fun anymore." He'd turned his back on me and walked away.

"Don't you dare!" I'd screamed. "Get back here, and finish what you started."

He'd stopped. "What did I start?"

As quietly as I could, I'd charged, knowing that he would react. He'd deflected my sword, swept out his foot, and knocked me to the ground. I'd hit the mat with a thud and gasped in pain as the wind rushed out of my lungs.

Usually, I'd always pushed myself up off the ground in disgrace, but that day there had been an outstretched hand.

"If you are so insistent on being beaten up, then it is my duty to oblige."

Our training changed from then on. When Percy disarmed me, he would whisper a correction in what I had been doing wrong. When he flipped me to make me hit the mat, he would catch me by the back of the uniform and soften my blow to the ground.

Lorn never said a word about the change in Percy. Although, I could tell he was pleased.

The real change was when it came to mealtimes. When Lorn was too busy to eat, I would sit by myself in my little hidden alcove away from prying eyes and the table filled with the other scouts. I thought I was invisible to the other elves and would be ignored as usual.

"She's a waste of training, isn't she, Percy?" Rulah had said in an offhand comment. "We should speak to the council again. They have to see that it is wrong for an elf to train a human in our ways. What could be Lorn's reason? He must have gone mad."

"She's so strange. Look at her eating by herself," another scout had added. "It's disturbing. Where is she going to get assigned? It's not like she can ever truly become a scout. She can't enter any of the elven realms without help."

A loud scraping followed as Percy had pushed the bench backward, startling those sitting next to him. He'd grabbed his plate filled with half-eaten food and marched diligently across the hall and sat by me. Without a word, he'd lifted his plate and ate. He'd chewed silently while staring straight ahead, not even acknowledging my existence. But I knew then. That was our truce.

I'd never sat alone since. I didn't know what had changed between us or how. All I knew was that from that day on, Percy distanced himself from the other scouts, and over the years we became friends. We learned to adapt to our favorite spot, eating without a table, passing the food between us, learning each other's habits. We'd worked as one unit, and I began to depend on his friendship.

Until Lorn pointed out that it wouldn't last. It couldn't.

It was last fall when I'd come back from dinner with an impish grin. I had convinced Percy to help me dump all of Ardax's winter gear into the lake after he had been particularly nasty to me. It was dark, after hours, and I was sneaking back into my room. I remembered it like it was yesterday.

"Honor," Lorn said my name from the shadows and my back stiffened. I was caught. He knew. He always knew when I'd done something terrible.

"Yes, Lorn?" I turned to face him. His face was inscrutable. His eyes never flinched, and I couldn't tell if he knew to the extent of my prank.

I focused on the spot over his shoulder, my body rigid and at attention as I waited for the rebuke.

There was the slightest exhale. He was mad.

"It's getting worse."

"What is?"

"I had hoped that you'd have picked up Percy's better traits, but it seems in doing so, he's picked up a few of your more notorious ones." He turned and raised one eyebrow. "Ardax's gear in the lake . . . Have you no honor, Honor?"

His words were like a branding iron that burned into my heart. I hated disappointing Lorn.

"There's something you need to know about Percy."

"I know. He's going to be a scout commander one day."

"No, do you really know who he is?"

"He's Percy."

"Again, you seemed to have missed the purpose of your training completely. You still don't know your enemy." Lorn rubbed his forehead.

"But he's not my enemy."

"Everyone is your enemy. That is the point. The Northern Woods are neutral territory. We are the very best fighters; it is our duty to train our brethren from all the elven clans."

"*Even the southern elves?*" I asked, raising my lip in disgust, picturing an ugly dark elf.

"Yes, sometimes we get elves from Thornhaven, but sometimes there's an expectation of our scouts after graduation. They can't all stay here. They must go back home, and many will leave with an understanding in place of future alliances between clans."

"They aren't here just for training, but political courtship," I said.

Lorn sighed. "Yes, and your friendship with Percy complicates things. You're—"

"In the way," I finished.

"No. It's just that . . .You and Percy can never be more than friends."

"I know that," I said heatedly. "I never asked for anything else. Not once. Not ever."

"I know, but lately there's been a change in Percy, and I see it in you as well. Others are noticing, and they are starting to ask questions. Rulah's family is very vocal about your perceived closeness. And I know that they're hoping for a union between the two."

Pain pierced my heart. "Are you saying we need to stop being friends?"

"I'm saying it would be wise, but I won't force your hand. You knew this day would come. To Percy, you are a mere distraction from his duty."

Now the tears were burning in my eyes, and my vision blurred as I held them back. My hands balled into white-knuckled fists. "Then why did you make him train with me? You would've known that we would've become friends one day."

"You needed an ally close to your age, and Percy was

also an outsider. He may be an elf, but he doesn't know the customs. I thought you two would find a common bond. But now. . ." The pause was deafening, and dragged on to the point where I was scared to inhale. Lorn sighed. "I think I made a mistake. He has become overly fascinated with humans; did you know that?"

I shook my head and wiped at the tears with my sleeve.

"Last night, he snuck out of the woods, and I found him in a human tavern." He sounded so distraught at the thought. I tried to hold in my smile. "I dragged him back, and it wasn't just the one time. He's become a liability. His focus is not where it should be, and that can have a much larger impact on not only our realm, but others." Lorn's eyes met mine.

There it was. The warning. I released my fists, lowered my head, being careful to hide my trembling lips. "I understand."

"Tomorrow is the day where the trainees are sent out on their final test."

My head shot up, and I pleaded with Lorn. "Please, can I try? You know that I would do anything to become a scout. I would die to protect the elven realms."

Lorn shook his head and handed me my pack. It was heavy and filled to the brim with supplies, which only meant one thing. We were leaving . . . again. I wouldn't get to see if Percy passed his final test.

"Can I say goodbye to Per—"

"No. Elves don't care about such necessities."

"But I promised I would tell him if and when I left again."

"Honor, that is precisely the reason why you can't say goodbye. You must break it off."

Lorn and I left in the middle of the night and didn't return until months later. I had heard that Percy passed with the highest of marks.

I was proud of him. How could I not be? When we returned to the Northern Woods months later, I dropped my pack and ran to congratulate him, only to find him and Rulah together by the lake. Hanging back, I watched their interlude through the bushes.

"Are you excited?" Rulah asked.

"I suppose." Percy didn't sound excited. He sounded bored.

"I mean about coming to visit the Lightwood elves?"

He said nothing.

"What's wrong, Percival? What happened to the man who dreamed of power?" Rulah grabbed his hand and forced him to look at her. "I know of your secrets, and I don't care. Why can't you think of me as more than a friend?"

Her voice, once full of hope, broke as she struggled to contain her emotions. She leaned forward and her brow touched his as she lightly caressed the side of his arms. It was a symbol of greeting between lovers.

He pulled away and Rulah became distressed. "Our families have already approved the exchange. Why can't you agree that this is the best course? So much can come of our union. The daughter of Arielle and the son of All—"

"Stop!" Percy shook his head. "I'm nothing like my father. I want nothing to do with any of his schemes, including marriage."

Rulah stilled. Her eyes narrowed in suspicion. "It's the human girl, isn't it? She's the one distracting you, holding you back. She's not one of us. She will never understand our kind or our duty to our realms and each other." Her hand dropped to her side. "We don't love the way humans do. Our flame is eternal. It is a slow fire that burns for centuries. You may not love me now, but one day, when she is no longer of this world, you could. You could learn to love me." She reached up on her tiptoes and placed a gentle kiss on his lips.

From a distance, I saw the surprise on his face; the way his shoulders stiffened and held back, but then slowly sank into her kiss as he returned it.

As I watched, I was overcome with remorse. They were a perfect match; tall ethereal beings, from similar backgrounds and training, destined to bring realms and clans together. I should have retreated. Instead, I watched what I could never have.

Percy's hands grasped her shoulders, and when they broke their kiss, he looked up, and our eyes met across the river.

His lips formed my name, but nothing came out.

I didn't try to hide that I'd been spying. I turned on my heel and left. Not wanting to hear his reasons for kissing her. He didn't need to explain; I understood. It was his life and his duty.

My brain understood duty, but all my heart understood was pain.

Lorn was right. Percy was trouble, and it was best if I ended things quickly.

Later that evening, Percy knocked on my door, but I never answered. He waited by our spot for dinner, but I ate in my room. When I went to train, he was already in the training room, warming up and waiting for me. Everywhere I went, he was there.

And my poor, human heart couldn't handle seeing him

everywhere. knowing that we couldn't be together even as friends.

Then it was I'd who begged Lorn to leave. It didn't take much convincing, especially when I'd felt Rhea's magic. I'd heard her call, and knew I needed to go to her. I'd packed my bag and headed to Kiln.

I was so lost in my daydreams of the past that I ended up at the edge of the lake again.

I stilled, staring at the sun reflecting across the surface, speckled by the leaves sailing across the water. It was the same lake that Percy and I had dumped Ardax's gear in almost two years ago and where I had watched him and Rulah kiss for the first time. A rueful smile tugged at the corner of my mouth as I remembered. There were so many memories, good and bad, that plagued me whenever I came back.

"You're back without your guardian," a gravelly voice said from the copse of trees.

I spun, not at all surprised to see Ardax. I tensed, my hand going toward the hidden knife on my hip.

"Relax, Honor. I'm not here to harm you. I had hoped we could come to an arrangement."

"I don't make deals with the devil," I said.

Ardax grinned, using charm that could easily disarm many women. Me . . . never. I had been the brunt of too many of his verbal attacks to be swayed by a debonair smile.

He let out a quick huff, showing his amusement. "Normally, that's what I say about you."

I snorted, and allowed myself to be at ease. It helped that Ardax wasn't making any sudden moves. His eyes watched me as closely as I watched him.

"The affinity ceremony is upon us. For those that care about such things," he said.

"I know."

Ardax straightened his shoulders, his eyes looking past me, not at me. "I would like to escort you."

"Why?" I asked, taken aback by his sudden interest.

"Don't confuse my intentions. I don't like you," he added.

"No."

I turned away, but he followed.

"Listen, Honor. I'm doing this for Rulah."

"Then my answer is most definitely no."

"Why do you have to be so stubborn?" he called out after me. "Do you not understand all of the problems your presence has caused?"

My anger rose, and I spun on him. "Maybe I'm stubborn because you force me to be."

Ardax backed away a step. "Or maybe it's because everyone sees you as a threat to not just one realm, but two."

I opened my mouth to retort, but stopped and waited for him to continue.

"I take it that you know about Rulah and Percival's understanding."

"I do."

"Then you'll see that I'm doing what I can for the good of our realms. If you go with me, make it known that you *chose* to go with me, then Percy will be free to attend with Rulah. He won't feel like he has to be your protector from the big bad elf." He pointed his thumb at himself.

I studied Ardax's posture, the slender tightness in his lip. "You're in love with Rulah," I stated.

There was a sudden flare of Ardax's nostrils, and I waited for him to deny it, but he didn't.

"I am. But she doesn't care for me. She only has eyes for Percy. So I will do whatever I can to make her happy." Ardax turned slightly. He closed his eyes and raised his chin toward the sun. "I had hoped that if you felt the same way about Percy, that you would understand my plight."

"I don't have feelings for Percy," I blurted out quickly. Too quickly.

"That's good. Then can you put aside your hatred for me and help me do a kindness for someone I care for?"

I thought about what he was asking. Trying to see past Ardax's thorny exterior to see the elf with an unrequited love. What I agreed to . . . And no matter what I'd just lied about, I wasn't doing it for Ardax or Rulah.

"As long as you can keep the stabbing comments down to three for the night," I said, giving in.

Ardax's eyebrows rose in surprise. "Only three?"

"And you need to provide me with a dress. A nice one."

Ardax laughed. "I think those arrangements are agreeable. But you need to be the one to tell Percy that your escort has been taken care of and that his services as the human bodyguard will not be needed tonight."

"Me?" My voice rose in pitch.

"Yes, and the sooner the better. Rulah and Percy's relationship is already strained because of you."

I opened my mouth to argue, but he raised a hand, silencing me.

"A courtship of realms requires delicate maneuvering, not a sledgehammer—which tends to be your way." Ardax crossed his arms and gave me a look begging me to disagree.

"Okay," I acquiesced.

Ardax nodded. "Thank you, Honor. I'll be by your room this evening with everything you require." He marched off up the path and passed Percy on his way.

The two exchanged words, but I was too far away to hear what they said. I could read the distrust on Percy's face. He adjusted Rumple on his back and his hands gripped the leather holster.

A moment later he nodded, his face grim, before he turned and came down the path to meet me. "Ardax annoys me so much. I think it's time we take him down a peg. How about you and I get out the poison oak and rub it on his clothes—"

"I have to go," I rushed out, retreating up the path after Ardax.

"Go? Go where?" Percy asked.

"I need to get ready for tonight." This was proving to be harder than I had originally thought. I didn't know how to break it to Percy that I wasn't going to attend the ceremony with him.

"Relax, we have plenty of time before the ceremony. We can—"

"No, we can't. I mean. You and I can't." I was fumbling my words horribly. My hands gripped the sides of my pants, and I dug my nails into the cloth.

"Honor, what's wrong? You seem upset."

"Upset? I'm not upset. I'm just excited for the ceremony." I forced a fake smile.

"Oh, well that's understandable."

"I'm going with Ardax." I forced the words out, and it felt like sandpaper across my tongue.

"Ardax?" Percy's smile fell.

I nodded. Scared to say anything else, less he read the lie on my face and the panic I was holding back.

"This is a joke . . . right?" Percy's gaze narrowed as he watched my expression carefully.

My breath hitched. "Ardax and I are attending the ceremony together." My words were strained but even.

"Fine." Percy smiled too easily. He leaned back, his head cocked to the side and shifted his weight onto his back foot away from me. "I see how it is."

"Do you?" I asked truthfully, wondering if he could hear my anguish.

Percy spun, his feet carrying him swiftly away. When he was out of earshot, I spoke softly, barely a whisper. "It's not the way it is. Just the way it needs to be."

CHAPTER SEVEN

When I returned to my room that evening, there was a package waiting on my bed. A white box tied with a gold ribbon. My fingers trembled as I pulled it apart and opened the box to reveal a dark green dress trimmed with gold thorn filigree. Alongside it were two golden combs in the shape of thorns. They were beautifully realistic, as if broken off a thorntree.

When I'd asked for Ardax to provide me with a dress, I expected a simple wool gown, instead of my normal pants, tunic, and belt I always wore. This was above and beyond my wildest expectations. As I lifted the dress out of the box, I was pleasantly surprised to find that it was the perfect length and he had provided slippers to match.

It didn't take me long to get ready, and the dress fit me like a glove, except I would need a hand in lacing the back up. No matter how much I twisted and torqued, I was unable to fully lace it. Feeling slightly defeated, I finished brushing my hair and securing the sides up with the golden combs. I didn't have any makeup, and the elves didn't need any. I knew that even though I was wearing an elaborate dress, my beauty would always wane in comparison.

"Well, this is as good as it's going to get," I breathed

out, tucking the last stray hair and securing it with the comb. It seemed like the only chance I would get to wear it.

A knock came at my door, followed by Ardax's voice.

"Honor?"

I relaxed, but only slightly. I slipped the shoes on and cracked the door open to see Ardax dressed finer than I had ever seen him. His long black hair practically shone in the candlelight as it cascaded down his back, his golden eyes looked molten, and his skin looked even paler in his matching green ceremonial clothes. The gold filigree of thorns running along his cuffs and neck matched my dress.

He pushed the door open, and I backed into the room, revealing my attire. Instantly, I glanced to the floor, feeling suddenly self-conscious in a gown made for an elven maiden. I grimaced, waiting for his rebuke about my looks.

Silence followed.

I slowly dragged my eyes up, glancing at his freshly oiled boots to his pressed pants, and up the long jacket with golden closures, to his strong jaw, thin lips, and angled nose. Then I met his eyes, and they were *lacking* contempt. Ardax blinked multiple times and cleared his throat before reaching out to touch a finger under my chin, raising it up from the floor.

"Don't look down." His gentle rebuke surprised me. Then he opened his mouth again. "For tonight, you will shine like a star because you are on my arm."

I snorted. There was the self-righteous jerk I remembered. I turned around, and he saw my attempts at lacing myself.

"Halt."

I froze.

"Do you have no women to assist you with getting dressed?"

I spun angrily. "No, for if you remember, everyone here hates me, thanks to you and Rulah. No one dares to speak to me except for Percy for fear of your wrath."

Ardax blinked in surprise, taken aback by my verbal attack. He took a slow breath. "Then it falls to me. Turn," he ordered, and I glared at him. "Turn," he repeated. "Or you can go the whole night undone, and that will cause a scene."

I would rather have walked into a pit of Sion adders than have his hands touch me, but he was right. I turned and carefully lifted my dark hair exposing my back.

Ardax was very careful to only touch the laces, and he made quick work tying the dress, giving it a gentle tug only when needed. His hands reached for mine, and I released my hair as it fell down my back.

"I didn't realize it was so long. You always keep it braided."

"I never have a reason to wear it any other way."

"That's true. For you also don't wear any other clothes than your hunting gear, which makes you look like a boy."

"That's one," I bit out.

"What?" he said.

"You only get two more insults."

Ardax laughed in surprise. "You were serious."

"Deadly. You don't even want to know what I have strapped under this dress."

"I can guess." Ardax glanced down, and I saw his keen eyes pick out the shape of Rhea's enchanted throwing knife strapped to my leg.

I whistled and snapped at Ardax, gesturing to my face. "Eyes up here."

My sassy words shocked him. His brows shot up, and that stony face cracked into another smile. "You are full of surprises."

"Get used to it," I said. "You ready?"

Ardax nodded and held the door open for me. Side by side, we walked in silence through the trees and across a wooden bridge. Evening had come, and with it, the trees were lit with glowing flowers and fireflies. The ceremony always took place in the middle of the night, for that was when the magic pooling from the sacred hollow was at its strongest.

I knew the way to the sacred hollow. Lorn had taken me there on occasion, as it was a mass of unfettered magic and heavily guarded by the Denizen. Twelve elves that had forsworn all worldly pleasures and titles vowed to give their life to protect the sacred hollow.

As Ardax and I approached the sacred hollow, we had to pass the closest Denizen. His armor was a pure white, a silver staff in his hand; his eyes never flinching as he manned his post, facing away from the sacred hollow. In the past, I had tried to make the Denizen laugh with silly faces, antics, and even bribed them with food. They never lost focus or even moved.

Lorn had explained that nothing I could do would sway them. They had taken a magical vow.

"It's the highest honor to be chosen as a Denizen," Lorn had said. "The ruling families in each realm chose their fiercest and finest warriors, and they were sworn with a magical vow to protect the hollow."

The Denizen lifted his spear, unblocking the way and

allowing us passage into the sacred hollow which was surrounded by willow trees. As we walked under their wispy branches, we passed through another veil of magic. As I slipped through, I could feel the same sensations wash over me. I could feel my heart flutter, my skin grew warm, and my eyes turned glassy with unshed tears again.

Ardax noticed my emotions at passing through the veil, and he seemed stunned by the tears I was trying to blink away. "Does our magic really affect you?"

"It's beautiful, Ardax." I nodded. "Your magic is the most beautiful thing I have ever felt. It's like a song in my soul and it weeps with joy."

He shook his head in disagreement. "No, not my magic."

"All magic," I answered.

He became quiet at my admission. I waited for him to come back with a retort, but he didn't. In fact, when we came to a slippery part of the moss-covered stairs, he took my elbow and braced my back in support.

"Why are you being so attentive?" I asked suspiciously.

"Because tonight you are my guest, and I will treat you with respect," Ardax said.

"But only tonight?"

"Yes."

"I'm half expecting you to push me down the stairs."

Ardax paused, then looked around. "I'm waiting for when there are more people watching. It will make a better spectacle."

I narrowed my eyes and watched his lips. There; the slightest twitch. He had made a joke. But it had almost been lost because his expression didn't match.

"Oh, you don't have to worry. I'm sure I will do something absurd and accomplish that all on my own. You don't even have to get your hands dirty with the human girl."

Ardax blinked, and the hand on my back stiffened. *Had I offended him?* His pacing became off, and I looked up and saw what caught his eye.

Rulah, her red hair flowed down her back with a simple silver braided band around her brow. Her pale skin looked like moonlight as she was dressed in a beautiful, sleek silver dress. Percy stood by her side. He looked fierce; his blond hair braided into one plait, his ears accented with gold and emerald studs. He wore a matching gold braided circlet, and it was the first time I saw *him*. Not Percy, my friend and comrade in mischief, but Percival, a beautiful and eternal elf.

Rulah slipped her hand through his arm, and she practically glowed with happiness at being at his side.

My mouth went dry. Even from here, the couple radiated power, and I could feel it reverberate throughout the clearing. Or maybe it was the ire that was directed toward me. I could feel the coldness as soon as his eyes met mine. I didn't dare smile, not even when his lip raised in the slightest disdain as he saw Ardax's hand still on my back.

I tried to take a step, but my legs trembled. Ardax's grip tightened, and his hand slid around my waist as he steadied me.

The chill grew, and I could feel the coldness seep through my skin.

"Steady," Ardax whispered as he helped me down the final steps into the courtyard.

"I'm trying."

"I was talking to myself," he countered. I looked up, and Ardax's eyes were glued to Rulah, who was leaning close and speaking to Percy—while Percy was tracking my every move. His eyes narrowed at the sight of Ardax's hand on my arm.

My mouth went dry, my heart fluttered, and I had to look away or be burned by the searing intensity of his gaze.

We walked to an open area that looked down on the ceremonial platform. It was a stone circle engraved with the symbols for air, earth, fire, and water. Rethulian, the current elder of the council of elves of the Northern Woods, stood in the center, his iris no longer silver but a pure white.

"It is time," Rethulian's voice echoed into the glade, "for the ceremony of gifts. Today we thank the earth for her magic as she bestows her gift upon our children. Let us welcome, Paris." All the elders gathered together around the platform and a young elf child dressed in white stepped forward, her hair braided into knots on the crown of her head, flowers threaded throughout.

I had only seen Paris a few times in passing. Since my life was spent between training and being on the road, I had very little interaction with the other elves. Paris stood in the middle of the stone platform, with each of the runes and symbols for the elements surrounding her. I could feel the hum of the ley line under the platform and could see the magic seeping through and floating away like ashes after a fire. I was grateful for the magic being so near.

Having never been witness to the affinity ceremony, I had only been told what would happen. The elder would greet the child and each of the elements would pay her greeting in turn. The strongest element would not just greet her, but claim her. All elves had elemental magic, but they were strongest in one area and that would become their identity. I wondered what it was like to be claimed by magic?

Rethulian raised his hands and spoke in a voice that commanded respect. "Paris, the earth welcomes you."

As he spoke, the symbol representing the earth glowed brighter, and flecks of gold flickered up from the earth before dissipating and fading.

"Paris, water welcomes you." Like before, the water symbol glowed, and blue droplets of water rose out of the ground in greeting before falling like rain onto the stone.

My fingers fidgeted as I looked beyond the stone circle and saw the veil of magic above the willows flicker ever so briefly. As if a rock was dropped on the veil and the magic ebbed out from a central point.

I grasped my chest in fear, feeling my heart thudding loudly. *Was it me? Was I doing something to the magic of the veil?*

Air was next to greet Paris, but I was no longer watching the ceremony below. I was staring with narrowed eyes at the spot across from me. I didn't know it at the time, but I grasped Ardax's hand and squeezed.

"What's the matter?" he grumbled, but stiffened when he saw my fearful expression.

"There," I whispered and pointed with my chin. "Across the sacred hollow. Do you see it?" Ardax wasn't the only one watching me because Percy turned to follow my gaze.

Nothing happened. Long seconds ticked by, and I thought I was going mad. Seeing things. I could feel Ardax's frustration at my distraction, but then he tensed when a flicker came across the veil again.

"Something's wrong with the veil," I said.

"Nothing's wrong with the veil," Ardax argued. "It has never failed."

I gave him a look. "Trust me. Something is wrong."

Fire was the next to greet Paris, and this time, the symbol glowed, and fiery embers rose up. The symbol ignited and fingers of fire raced across the ground as if drawn to her, and flames ignited her dress. Paris cried out in fear, but instead of burning her, the flames tickled as they danced across her skin and settled into the palms of her hands.

A chorus of excited voices rang out, for it was said that they needed more fire users. They were considered some of the strongest. It would be years before she could call it freely or branch out into what area of fire magic she would study. But from now on, her clothes would bear the mark of fire.

"Paris, tonight fire has claimed you. Welcome," Rethulian called out, and the elders clapped.

The flicker on the veil came again, and this time I reached for the enchanted knife on my thigh. Rheanon had crafted it for me. It struck true, never missing its target. I slipped behind the group of elves and made my way around the platform. It would be faster if I ran straight through, but I couldn't interrupt the sacred ceremony.

Ardax didn't need any more prompting. We silently moved our way through the mass of people, slipping between the crowd. I tapped Einan and Taris as we passed and signaled with my hands the word for *trouble*. Soon the signal had made its way around the circle, and almost all the scouts were on alert, but none knew why. My gut instinct told me that something was trying to break through the veil. I could sense it. The darkness, the hunger for magic. I had felt it before. Deep inside of me.

As soon as I stepped in front of the veil, a blast sent everyone flying backwards as the veil ripped open and magic burst through, knocking half of the bystanders out cold.

"We're under attack!" I cried out as the first monster slipped through. It was a four-legged beast that moved like a cat, but instead of fur, it was covered in black, shimmering scales that flickered with burning flames. With yellow eyes, its face was long and narrow like a lizard.

I put myself right in its path, but it flew over me with a mighty leap and ran straight for the center platform, directly toward Paris.

The child screamed, and her hands flickered with untamed fire magic, but it wasn't enough. I flung my knife, and it struck the demon beast in the base of the neck, burrowing deep into his skull. Instantly, he fell down dead, his giant maw open, only inches from Paris.

Rethulian looked up in surprise as more of the four-legged creatures plowed through the veil. "Hellhounds! But how?"

The pack of hellhounds attacked, aiming for the unarmed elves. The Denizens appeared in the sacred hollow, a blazing fury of white metal armor, but then they froze, weapons held in the air mid-strike, as if controlled by an unseen magical force.

"Fight! Protect the people!" Rethulian commanded, but the Denizens lowered their weapons and one by one they collapsed to the ground, unmoving like a puppet whose strings were cut. Dead.

Panic increased at the sight of the protectors falling, and the people screamed and tried to run for safety.

The hellhounds continued to pour out of the veil.

Einan intervened, placing himself in front of the magical opening. He took down the next hellhound that jumped through, but the next one slipped past him and was racing toward me.

"Honor!" Percy called my name as he kicked a hellhound in the face. I looked up just as a glorious double-headed axe flew through the air toward me.

I caught the handle and adjusted to the weight of Rumple.

"I'm so glad to see you," I said.

"So, you did miss me?" Rumple quipped.

Swinging him in an arc, I took down one of the beasts. "Less talking and more—"

"Chopping!" He laughed, and I dove into the fight headfirst, rolling to avoid being taken down by a hellhound, then coming up swinging to cut through the jaw of another.

I felt an attack coming and turned just as a hellhound lunged for my throat. My stomach dropped. I wasn't fast enough and tried to raise the handle to block it, but a body stepped in front of me and caught the hellhound midair before tossing it away. It had been stabbed multiple times in successive hits before it touched the ground. Ardax's attack was so fast that I didn't even see it.

Ardax turned and gave me a nod. "We don't have enough weapons, and it's forbidden to use magic in the grove unless you're part of the ceremony."

"I think the elders would forgive you just this once," I said, ripping the hem of my dress, giving me room to run and fight. I was secretly mad at myself for even asking for a dress. I should have come in pants.

A scream of terror followed as another hellhound attacked an elf and he fell from the steps.

Ardax was hesitant. I looked around at the scouts who were fighting with small knives, makeshift weapons, or using hand-to-hand combat against much larger creatures that were made of magic. I could feel it. This night, a night meant for celebration, was one of the few nights a year where our scouts and soldiers weren't allowed to come armed with anything other than ceremonial weapons for dress. It wasn't a coincidence the attack happened during the ceremony, where magic was also forbidden.

I swung the axe, keeping my back toward Ardax. Even though we had never trained together, he was still a scout, and our training kicked in to cover each other's back.

"Duck," I yelled, and Ardax stooped as I swung over his head and took down a hellhound that came from above.

"Thanks," he gasped. "There's no end to them."

"You *have* to use magic to close the veil and stop those things from coming through."

Ardax nodded. "I don't like it, but you're right."

"What was that?" I called out over my shoulder as he moved toward the tear in the magic veil. "Could you say it again, louder this time?"

"Never," Ardax yelled. The stoic elf slashed his way toward the veil. His arms were bloody, and I could see his face was void of emotion. Ardax was earth magic; I could feel the rumble of the ground rising to his call, the ley lines moving, shifting to feed him magic as he prepared to mend the veil. A hellhound lunged for him, and before I could even raise my axe, Rulah launched onto the hellhounds back and with the end of a fallen Denizen's spear, stabbed it into the back of its neck. I looked up to see her eyes filled with fury.

"Protect Ardax, you idiot!" she screamed.

"What do you think I'm doing?" I hissed and turned to one side while Rulah took the other. Side by side we fought, cutting down every hellhound that was now rushing and targeting Ardax as he attempted to close the veil.

Percy was working his way towards us, but he was protecting a group of women. He tried to move them back up the hill, but was constantly getting cut off. He, like Rulah, had taken a spear from the downed Denizen. His fighting was beautiful; graceful like a deadly dance, and anyone that came too close was cut down and knocked out cold.

I grimaced as a hellhound got too close, his claw slicing my bare arm. It burned like fire as its flames and claws ripped through my flesh.

I was slowing down. I could feel my reaction times getting slower.

Focus, I told myself, and zeroed in on watching the hounds. They would bend low, their eyes narrowed, then launch into the air only to be cut down by Rulah's spear or my axe. But I was making more mistakes. Mistakes I shouldn't have been making. Then I felt it. A surge as my body reached out.

Ardax grunted as his magic suddenly left him. I felt my body gaining speed and strength as I began to draw on his power. It was so easy. He was connected to the ley line, and he was the closest to me.

"I can't close it. Something's blocking me!" Ardax cried.

I knew it was me. I knew my curse was draining him. They wouldn't be able to close the veil if I didn't get away.

I gripped Rumple in my hands and looked through the torn veil to the other side. It was dark, but I could see the outline of a lone figure in a gold mask. Was that him? The son of Allemar?

An eerie sound echoed, coming through the tear in the veil. A haunting melody.

"Ardax, close it!" Rulah screamed. She wavered and fell to her knees, suddenly a victim of my leaching.

"What do I do?" I muttered. I looked over my shoulder toward the stone center, down at all the lifeless bodies—both hellhounds and elves combined—and more of the demon beasts kept pouring through like a rip in a grain bag. They had to close the veil, and I was preventing them. I needed to get as far away as possible.

Percy sliced through a hellhound and looked up at me. His eyes filled with fear as I lowered my axe and hesitated.

I knew he couldn't possibly hear me, but I mouthed the words, *I'm sorry.*

"Honor, what are you doing?" he cried out and ran toward me.

I turned, hefted Rumple, and raced toward the opening. I passed Ardax, swung the axe, and impaled another hellhound as I jumped through and into the veil. Raising my weapon, I focused on the man in the gold mask on the other side.

I would end this once and for all if I killed the sorcerer's apprentice.

Pressure surrounded me, and my body was pulled in a

hundred directions. A scream ripped through my throat, and I felt the snap as I broke the connection from Ardax and Rulah.

A backlash of power whipped out at everything around me. The veil suddenly closed, and I was trapped in darkness.

CHAPTER EIGHT

My lungs ached. My skin burned like it was on fire, and then I was shot out of the darkness and landed face first in the dirt. I rolled over and stared up at the night sky.

Where was I?

The moon was waning, and it gave enough light to see the surrounding landscape. I was in a small glade next to a troll's head rising out of the earth. My breath caught in my throat until I saw it was only a trick of the light.

The monstrous head was made of stone. Surrounding the troll head rock was a grove of fire elm trees, whose ever-changing leaves transformed colors like the flames in a fire. I only ever saw the fire elms in the Sion region. I studied the sky, but the stars were wrong. I was farther south. Pushing myself to my knees, I took in more of my surroundings. I was encircled by a dozen black piles of ash. As I drew near, one disintegrated, and the wind carried the disturbed pile away. Were these the remains of the hellhounds that had passed through the veil?

When I was ripped from the ley line, did my curse snap back and attack these creatures? I trembled at the thought. I got to my feet and saw the wounds on my arm were no longer bleeding, but had begun to clot and already heal. How long was I knocked out for and where was the figure with the golden mask?

Whoever was on the other side had summoned these creatures or controlled them, and they were long gone. As I walked the glade, I studied the ground and could see nary a hint of any disturbance.

I had more questions, and I didn't see a way to get answers any time soon. The first problem I had to take care of was what would happen now? I cradled my injured arm and looked around the glade.

"Rumple!" I called out, but didn't hear a reply. "Rumple! Answer me, you stupid pain in the axe!"

Silence followed, only punctuated by the restless wind over the grass.

I bent over and rested my hands on my knees as I focused on breathing and not panicking. I was in a strange place, without any supplies or weapons, and I had lost Rumple.

"Get it together, Honor," I chided. "You're trained to handle any situation. Even this."

That was when I noticed the fresh boot prints on the earth and the trampled grass of where a horse had been tethered to a nearby tree. From the single tree, a trail headed south. It must have rained not long ago, and since then the earth had dried and caked, preserving the prints, leaving a telltale path to follow. Someone stole Rumple and left me for dead?

I spun while searching, but I found no one watching me. There was nothing except the horse tracks. I studied the depth of the treads and the length of stride and discovered that it wasn't a horse, but a donkey.

I should turn north, toward home, find a homestead, and get ahold of my mother, alert Lorn, get reinforcements. Or I could follow the tracks to find Rumple. He would know what had happened once I crossed through the veil. He may be the only witness to the massacre and the after-effects. He may know where the sorcerer went.

Images of the dead flitted across my mind. I shook my head. I had to follow Rumple.

As I limped along the path out of the fire elms, the sun rose and I could feel my body begin to weaken. It wasn't the same as when I needed to get to a ley line. I was just exhausted and dehydrated. My lips were cracked, and I could feel my eyes begin to play tricks on me as pools of water floated just along the horizon.

The woods faded, the trail disappeared onto the hard-packed earth as I came to a road. I looked at the other side and saw no other tracks. The animals and rider either turned north or south.

I cursed under my breath and tried to decide where to go, but before I could make a decision, I saw a dust cloud on the road from the north. It would disappear into the horizon and minutes later I would see the hazy outline as it appeared again. A transport.

The transports were coaches that frequently traveled between kingdoms for long journeys. They would have a banner posted on their door of which kingdom they were currently on their way to and would pick up fares accordingly. This transport wasn't barring any flag, which meant he was between jobs.

The driver, a friendly man with a red mustache and

mop of hair, hopped off his bench and came to stand next to me.

"You alright, Miss? You look like you might need some assistance?"

I could only imagine what I looked like from his point of view. A ripped dress, covered in blood, my hair tumbling about my shoulders. I had lost all but one of my golden combs.

I nodded numbly.

"Where to, Miss?" the driver asked.

"Have you passed anyone on your way? Maybe a lone traveler on a horse, perchance?"

He shook his head. "No one for hours, Miss."

"What is that way?" I asked, pointing south, toward the other possible route.

"That be the city of Marinall."

"Are there any other towns or homesteads nearby?"

"No, Miss, that's why I stopped. There's nothing out this way within a day's travel other than the city. Too far for you to make it by foot in your condition." He pulled the rim of his hat down, and I knew he was referring to my torn dress and fancy slippers. Even now, I could feel the sun's rays burning my skin.

I licked my cracked lips and tried to think where I should go. Training would tell me to return to the Northern Woods, or even to the town of Nihill to find Mother.

A sour pit hit my stomach. No. That wasn't right either.

South.

Everything in my gut told me to head farther into Sion,

and as soon as I made that decision, the stomach pain lessened.

I had traveled to Sion before, but always along the borders. I'd never been that far south, where magic ran far more rampant and out of control because it was closest to the southern elves and their sacred and tainted hollow. Here, the beasts were far more dangerous and unpredictable. It was rumored that the evil sorcerer Allemar himself came from Sion. That was enough of a reason to stay far away from this kingdom.

"I'll go there." I reached up and pulled the comb out of my hair and felt the last curl come free. I placed it into the driver's hands, and his eyes widened in surprise.

"This is real gold," the driver said.

"Yes." I was too tired to argue. I really didn't have anywhere to go, so it didn't matter. I was putting my future into the hands of a friendly transport driver.

"Very well. I don't know if I can make change exactly, but I will do what I can for you."

I nodded as he opened up the door and I stepped up into the empty transport. I folded my body up on one of the long, cushioned benches, and promptly closed my eyes before falling into a deep sleep.

When I opened my eyes a few candle marks later, I realized I was no longer the only passenger in the coach. A very short person sat across from me. Their brown, knotty hair was tucked under a red felt stocking that covered small impish eyes. They wore a brown woolen tunic with a leather belt, and striped wool socks with pointed shoes. The transport went over a bump, and they reached up a hand to steady themself on the sideboard. That's when I noticed they only had four fingers on each hand, so definitely a fae, possibly from the goblin family.

They didn't quite look like Clove the brownie, or either of the goblins who tended our gardens and animals. She or he? It was hard to tell, but from the twinkle in their eye, I think they wanted it that way.

Sitting up, I apologized for not being awake for their arrival.

"Niff," they replied, crossed their arms, and stared out the opened flap of the transport. They must have rolled it up when they boarded, and I saw the scenery hadn't changed much.

I wasn't sure what to make of their reply and decided to sit and wait patiently until I was addressed in person.

They wiggled their feet back and forth on the bench seat the way a child would. I started to second guess their age. Maybe they were younger than I originally thought? Every once in a while, I caught them watching me before turning to stare back out the window.

The transport stopped around midday, and I wasn't sure why, until the driver hopped off his bench and opened the door.

The fae across the bench squinted and pulled the hat over their eyes, and I thought I saw a hint of light reflected in the pupil.

The driver reached in and handed me a wrapped item. "Sorry, it's not much, but since we are still a ways out from the city, I hope it will tide you over. My wife made it." He didn't even make eye contact with the other passenger.

I took the wrapped cloth slowly and even cocked my head toward the bench seat, and the driver didn't notice.

"Thank you for the food. *We* appreciate it," I said, emphasizing and acknowledging the other guest.

The driver's brows furrowed, and he added slowly, "Okay . . ." He closed the door and a few moments later and we were moving again.

"He can't see you," I surmised, pointing to where the driver was sitting above its head.

The fae nodded and grinned, revealing short, even teeth.

"But I can?"

Another nod, and I could tell I was playing a game, and they were waiting eagerly until I put the pieces together.

"Hmm, then that would make you a Nisse or Tomte?"

The fae nodded again, and I felt relief in identifying the elusive fae that was part of the four-fingered gnome family that could go invisible at whim.

I unwrapped the cloth and revealed a pastry filled with jam. It was a day or so old, but still smelled good. My stomach growled, but I knew it was always better to share. I leaned over and handed the gnome the treat.

They bobbed in their seat happily and took a bite of the pastry again, gazing out the window.

"Must be nice to be able to go about without being seen. Have you been traveling long?"

Juices dripped along the gnome's palm, and they licked up the side of their hand while nodding.

"I'm sure you pick up on a lot of gossip."

The gnome bobbed their head again. Gnomes weren't ones to travel or leave their homes.

"Have you heard tales of strange creatures, or any word of villages being attacked?" I described the thing that attacked and broke through the veil in the Northern Woods.

The gnome froze and faded out, and then I was sitting in an empty compartment. But I knew I wasn't really alone. I listened and could hear the soft breathing. If I could sense an elf hiding in the woods, the gnome in a small transport was as loud as a fox in a chicken coop.

I turned away, keeping my distance, and waited for the gnome to reappear. I could still see a faint flicker, as their magic didn't really hide their aura. But they weren't in the mood to reveal to me again.

I retreated and leaned back against the sideboard as we continued on.

By nightfall, we had reached the bustling city of Marinall. The horses' hooves were no longer padded by the earth, but clopped along the brick-paved street. Spiral-shaped lanterns sprang up out of the ground, alighting along the roads like glowing beehives. Though it was night, the air was definitely humid. Without a cloak, I still wasn't cold. What a complete change in weather compared to the north. I pulled up the window cover and stared at the city in awe.

In the northern kingdoms, most of the buildings were either made of brick or wood. In the south, they were clay, stone, and homes were white or cream in various domes or spiral shapes. I had never traveled this far into Sion and was amazed at how some of the buildings looked like seashells sprouting up out of the ground.

Even the locals' clothes were exotic, with wrapped pants and vests in bright golds, blues, reds and yellows.

The driver slowed outside of a three-story sandstone

building decorated with blue and gold pennants. I recognized the stitching on the pennant as an inn.

The gnome chose that moment to reappear and pushed back their hat revealing more of their face. I saw the hint of a beard tucked beneath a scarf.

He pointed out the window, and I followed the stubby fingers to multiple white spiral turrets that surrounded a central building with a golden dome. Even at night the light of the city reflected against the gold.

He trembled in fear as he pointed.

When the driver opened the door, I made a motion and asked him what it was.

"Oh, that's the summer palace of the King of Sion. They're preparing for the council of kings."

"That's not for weeks."

"No, Miss, it's in a few days," he corrected.

Long ago, King Leonel had been engaged to my adoptive mother, Lorelai. It was said that it was his breaking of their engagement that sent my mother into her spiral of hate toward the seven kingdoms.

But over the last few years, I'd learned that her anger may have been justly due, for indeed there was much corruption sitting on the thrones of each kingdom. Her revenge brought justice and enlightenment and also exposed many of the lies. Lady Eville, labeled a villain because she was a powerful and feared woman, also worked for the good of the seven kingdoms—although her motives may have been a bit selfish as well, considering her adoptive children were all settled into royal marriages.

"How many children does the king have?" I asked. I knew that King Leonel had been married a few times and was once again widowed.

"Twelve."

"And how many are sons?"

The driver rubbed his hand across his forehead and looked uncomfortable. "Uh none, much to the dismay of His Royal Highness."

I smirked. I had no doubt that his quest for sons may have been hampered by a curse from my mother. But that also meant the streak of her daughters marrying a prince or royal would be broken. There was no foothold to be gained in Sion from a daughter of Eville.

The driver pressed on quickly. "With what you have paid me, I can guarantee you lodging at the Silk Slipper, and I know the owner. She'll make sure you have everything you need. If you give me a few candle marks, I'll return with Sion credits for you as change for the comb you paid for your passage."

"How many credits will I have left over?" I asked.

"About thirty."

"Can you deduct the travel for two passengers?"

"Two?" I had stumped the driver with my question. I looked back at the bench seat and saw the slight wrinkle in the padding of where the gnome was sitting and had hidden himself once the driver came up again.

"Yes, two."

"Are you sure? I mean, it was only a day's journey and—"

"I'm sure."

He nodded, and headed into the inn to speak with the owner. I waited around till we were alone and spoke to the gnome. "Thank you for your company. I hope to see you around again."

A faint shimmer followed, and he was gone.

"Saphira will see to your needs." The driver inclined his head toward the inn, signaling for me to enter. "Go on in."

I entered the Silk Slipper and saw a woman who I at first thought was speaking quietly to herself. She was staring intently into a bowl of water. I saw a faint flicker within the reflection and knew she was communicating with someone through a pool of water.

"Yes, more have disappeared without a trace. The family members are worried, but the palace is covering it up, but I don't know why?" she whispered.

I assumed the woman speaking was Saphira. Not wanting to eavesdrop, I waited silently by the door.

The woman turned and looked down at the floor as if something disturbed her, and then her head snapped up at me, seeing me for the first time. Her bright eyes widened; her red lips pulled back into a knowing smile. She nodded as if listening to the other speaker. "I will look into it. It seems that help has arrived in the most unlikely fashion, and you don't have to worry about the other issue. All is safe."

She dipped her hand in the bowl of water and the image flickered out.

"Sorry for the delay. I didn't hear you come in, which is odd, because I have the most excellent hearing." She extended her hand. "I'm Saphira." An elegant scarf covered her head and ears. Despite the intense sun this far south, she had perfect skin, keen eyes, and a simple beauty mark on her upper cheek.

"My driver sent me inside. He said he would return to settle up and bring me change."

"Yes, Amar has been a faithful driver for us for years.

Come, come, let's get you taken care of, and he'll return shortly."

I let the hospitable Saphira lead me down a hall to a private bathing room with a large built-in bathing tub below the floor. She pulled a lever on the wall and hot water poured into the tub filling it full.

Saphira kneeled, adding various oils and petals to the water. Immediately I could feel myself begin to relax as the scents of spearmint and lavender filled the air.

She laid out a robe, and more jars of oils and soaps.

"This is for your skin; the other your hair." Saphira pointed to the scrapers, ladles, and combs left out for me as well. "I will see to your nourishment."

She backed out of the room and closed the door after me.

I stared at the pool of water filling and wanted to dive headfirst into it, but forced myself to take my time. I used the copper ladle and took care of washing the dust and dirt from my feet and body and added bathing salts before entering the bathing pool.

Exhausted, I sighed and leaned my head against the rim of the tub and waited, letting my muscles soak in the heat and relax.

I could feel my eyes growing heavy, and I slowly dipped below the water to wake myself up. I counted to ten and listened to the beating of my heart as I tried to sort out my thoughts. As I came up for air, I brushed my hair out of my face and saw a tray of food had been brought while I was underwater.

There was something odd about the setup, and I noticed that one of the biscuits had a bite taken out of it.

My eyes narrowed, and I looked among the steam and saw the culprit hiding in the corner.

It seemed that the gnome had an affinity for the sweet treats and had taken a nip of one. I carefully sorted them out and placed the sweet biscuit on a plate and pushed it toward him.

A whoosh of steam rose as the invisible gnome moved toward me, then the biscuit was gone in a flash. I smiled and sank below the water, somewhat grateful for the quiet company of the elemental fae.

CHAPTER NINE

More importantly, my room had an angled view of
the front door to the Silk Slipper, and I was taking
note of the coming and going of the patrons. As I watched,
a gold-trimmed carriage pulled up. A footman appeared,
opening the door for the extravagantly dressed young man.
He stepped out of the carriage and looked around at the
street filled with unwashed children with disdain. A
wagon pulled up behind him, and I heard him give orders
for all of his trunks to be unloaded in his room.

He pushed a servant that wasn't moving fast enough,
and I instinctively reached for my dagger that wasn't there
anymore. It wouldn't do me any good to interfere in
matters that didn't concern me.

Instead, my hands found the pouch of gold that Amar
had left me. The driver kept his word, sold the comb, paid
for the room for the night, and left me with the change—
minus fare for two passengers. From the weight of the
coins, I knew it would be enough to get me supplies. The
dress I had was torn and stained, and it would only cause
me to stand out. I needed to blend in.

A loud crash drew my attention back to the street
where an elderly servant had lost his hold on the trunk and

it crashed to the ground, spilling the wealthy man's clothes onto the street.

"By the stars, Bredlin! You dropped my trunk. You no good rotten!" He turned and grabbed a whip laying across the driver's bench.

I didn't think before I reacted, moving on instinct and leaping out the window, onto the canopy, and dropping to the street in front of the terrified servant. My forearm came up to block the downward strike of the whip.

The leather struck me painfully, wrapping around my arm. I felt the sting as the tail nicked my neck, leaving a burning sensation.

I gritted my teeth, snarled, and wrenched the whip out of the rich man's hands. He was taken aback at my sudden appearance out of thin air.

"You have no right to interfere. This is between a master and servant," he said.

I slowly unwound the whip from my forearm, an angry red welt already forming. I ran my palms along the braided leather and grasped the heavy handle, testing the weight of the whip. I took a step forward.

"Master and servant?" I said, flipping the whip out to the side, letting it snap in the air. "All I see is someone who abuses their power too easily."

I don't know what came over me, but I didn't like this man, or the way he treated people.

"How dare you? Do you know who I am? I'm Lord Rasmen of Balendale." The man puffed up his chest, making him seem even more intimidating, but I didn't back down.

"There is no reason to beat your servant. It wasn't his fault." I used the whip to point toward the trunk and its broken handle lay in the dirt. "As you can see, you've grossly overloaded your trunks where they cannot latch correctly, and your clothes have now paid the price."

"I would never . . ." the man stammered and looked at the broken trunk. I had heard enough. I tossed the whip to the ground, and over the man's shoulder, I could see city guards coming our way.

"A good washerwoman could get them cleaned in no time." I took a gold coin out of my pouch and tossed it into the air.

Lord Rasmen snatched it out of the air like a frog catching a fly.

"For the trunk, and your forgiveness toward your servant."

The servant had slipped away into the crowd. I hoped he wouldn't return, using this time to escape this horrid man, but I had a feeling old Bredlin would be back and would be treated worse because of my interference.

Lord Rasmen's eyes narrowed, and he rubbed his fingers along the coin's ridges, probably trying to see if it was fake or real.

"I will stay my hand," the Lord said. "But who are you, that you meddle so easily in the affairs of others?"

"I am called what you lack." I lifted my chin and adjusted my stance as another carriage came toward me. I took my chance to abscond, and leapt onto the footboard as it passed, letting it carry me away in a crowd of people and horses. With nimble footwork, I slipped onto the back of a second carriage and crouched low as I quickly sped away from the spot where city guards had descended.

I rode for a few city blocks before I crawled to the top of the carriage and leapt onto a nearby stack of crates.

After hopping down into an alley, I hid behind a barrel and waited to see if anyone had followed. The alleyway remained empty. But I knew better than to expect an easy getaway. I ran between the buildings, crawled up a wooden trellis onto the nearest roof, and made my way across the buildings, and circled back around to the Silk Slipper Inn roof.

I was right. Lord Rasmen was speaking to the city guards and pointing at his trunk, then waving frantically. I took advantage of the commotion below to slip back into my room, swinging from the roof into the open window. The sun was so bright, my eyes couldn't adjust, and I entered the room blindly.

As soon as my feet landed on the stone floor, a shadow moved toward me, and I reacted. I spun, bringing my foot up and around. It was blocked midair, and a wrist wrapped around my ankle. With strong, deft movements, I was forced down into a crouch to avoid breaking the bone.

"I think you are just the person I'm looking for," a feminine voice chuckled. She released my ankle and stepped back, pulling the shawl from her face. Saphira grinned at me.

"I'm so sorry." I bounced up to my feet in horror at having attacked the owner of the inn.

"Don't be. I saw what happened on the street. I would have intervened if you hadn't, but then I would have lost my mark. By stepping in, you protected the servant, and I get to keep Lord Rasmen close."

"Your mark?" I asked, watching Saphira with new eyes. She had a crossbody satchel that was probably filled with weapons. Her footsteps were muffled by the silk slippers she wore. The way she moved with purpose, her toned and muscled arms, and the calluses on her fingers . . . There was no mistaking it. I could see the trained assassin hiding behind the silks and perfume. "You're a trained spy."

"Sometimes," she said with a smile. "Other times I just happen to overhear things. For instance, you are the one called Honor, are you not?"

"How do you know my name?" I asked suspiciously.

Saphira pulled her scarf back to reveal her ears and elven heritage. I had already suspected from the way she blocked my attack, but she confirmed it.

"I know of you, Honor, because I'm friends with Lorn. Long ago, he trained me, and I've turned those skills into a thriving business. Sometimes he comes and visits me and shares tales of your travels and escapades. I had heard you were lost in the battle of the Northern Woods. Many believe you to be dead."

"Dead? But how did the news travel so fast? That was just a day ago."

Saphira shook her head. "That attack was over three weeks ago."

I sat down on the bed in disbelief. "How can that be? I remember . . . well, I don't know what I remember. My brain is a bit foggy."

Saphira went to the side table and took a water pitcher, poured me a glass, and handed it to me. "Here. Drink."

The door to my room swung open a few inches as if caught by the wind. I followed the slight shimmer of the invisible gnome's glamour, and never let my eyes stray from him for fear I would lose him.

"You *are* good. You've even spotted my elemental." Saphira snapped her fingers, and the gnome appeared on my bed.

"We've already met," I said, realizing now how she knew so much about me.

The little gnome from the transport raised his hand and waved merrily at me.

"Nimm is quite impressed with you, and he was the one who figured out that you were the Honor of Northern Woods who'd disappeared."

"Ah," I replied, understanding now how she had gotten her answers. Nimm was her spy. "I don't understand how I've missed such a large passage of time."

"You jumped through a veil near a sacred hollow. Magic is fickle, and time passes differently. We may never know, but what I can do is catch you up on what has happened in the last few weeks."

I sighed and settled onto the bed, not sure if I was ready for what she was going to tell me.

Saphira spoke slowly, as if not wanting to startle or overwhelm me with news.

"The attack was three weeks ago. I can tell you that the kingdoms are up in arms, news is traveling fast, and the world is in turmoil over where these attacks will happen next. Not to mention that each of the kings are already on their way here for the high council, and their queens have been banned from coming."

"I expected they wouldn't be allowed," I said, thinking back to my conversation with Rosalie.

I was impressed by Saphira's information and her willingness to share it with me. But I was still suspicious of her reasoning for doing so. I stayed silent and waited for Saphira to continue with her discussion.

"I know you overheard my conversation in the water

bowl." She crossed her arms and expected me to deny it. "How much did you overhear?"

"That people are disappearing, and you think it's being covered up," I answered.

Saphira nodded. "Yes, large groups of townspeople and servants from the palace are going missing, and I believe the king is covering it up."

"Could they just be running away?"

She frowned. "It could be, but I don't think so. There's something else at work here, and I'm going to find out."

"You sure do know a lot."

"It's my job to know."

"Who do you work for?" I asked.

She smirked knowingly. "I work for whoever pays the highest." In an instant, her demeanor changed, she sighed, and her shoulders dropped. "But right now, I hear a lot of fear and worry, and it's emanating from those within the palace. Coin isn't as important as answers are. But that is not your concern, nor your problem."

"I'd like to help. Is there anything I can do?" I asked.

Saphira studied me for a long moment. "Yes, maybe there is something you can help me with." She reached into her satchel and pulled out a map that had been folded and refolded many times. She laid it out on the small side table, and I saw all the candle wax and ink stains from hours poring over it. "I don't think the attacks are random. But I can't figure out how they are connected. Look at the locations of each attack and tell me, what do you see?" Saphira pulled out a folded map of the seven kingdoms: Baist, Candor, Kiln, Isla, Florin, Rya, and Sion.

I leaned over the worn map and studied the various markings, seeing the faded X of attacks and the darker marks of the most recent. At first, I didn't see any connection.

"I don't see anything."

Saphira bit her lip. "Look closer, Honor." She placed her hands on either side of the map and waited.

Not wanting to give up so easily, I leaned in and tried to see a hidden connection between the attacks. "They're not connected by main roads or rivers. The attacks aren't linked by densely populated cities, either. Most attacks were in the capitals, but others were in small farming communities. There seems to be no rhyme or reason for any of the attacks, nor a hint of where they're going to strike next."

"I had feared as much." Saphira leaned back, and I felt like I'd disappointed her. I stared at the map and tried to look at it through a different set of eyes. Ones not marked by buildings, human icons, and names. I went back to a much older map.

"Wait!" Quickly, I traced my fingers along invisible lines on the map. Ones buried deep in my memories. Ones I knew because they were important to my survival. "The ley lines. Each of these attacks is where one of the ley lines intersects with another ley line. The convergence of the two powerful lines of magic is what's drawing the attacks."

As soon as I said it, I knew I was right.

Saphira's blue eyes widened in surprise. "You're right. I don't remember where all the ley lines are, but I'm sure one converges here." She stabbed her finger at a small village in Kiln.

"It does," I said.

"I don't remember where the others meet."

"I do." I closed my eyes and ran my fingers over the

map, seeing gold lines light up in my memories as I traced all of them and began counting how many times they overlapped and converged. It was like running along a rabbit tunnel, going down hundreds of dark passages that broke off, but knowing that eventually, if I kept searching, the tunnels would converge into one main warren.

"Here." I opened my eyes and stared where my finger had pinned a place on the map. "It's where they all converge, and the most magic line trickles down to . . ." I moved my finger to see that it had a blurry section on the map that seemed to move.

"Where is this?" I asked.

My eyes met Saphira's, and she nodded. "That is Thornhaven sacred hollow"

I sucked an angry breath between my teeth. "Then we need to go there."

"Impossible. That realm is beautiful and deadly. The veil of magic protecting it is too strong. No one has been able to find the entrance in years."

I crossed my arms, thinking of the veil protecting the Northern Woods. There were many ways to enter. "We look for a back door."

Saphira smiled. "Yes, there are always many ways in, but few ways out. The next closest convergence of ley lines is . . ." she pointed at the palace. "Right next door."

We looked up at each other, then glanced out the window toward the palace. My heart thudded in excitement, and I could see her mind working and cranking out a plan.

"If we can find the point in the palace where the ley lines cross, we should be able to use it to gain access the sacred hollow."

"What do we do?" I came right out and asked.

"I need you to get inside," I said.

"Why me?"

"I've tried. King Leonel's paranoia has reached a new high. He has heavily warded certain areas of the palace. Nimm won't set off the smaller wards as a low-level fae. The king still employs house-elves. But Nimm accidentally set off one of the larger wards."

Nimm shuddered and pulled down his scarf down to reveal a jagged white scar on his neck.

"He barely escaped with his life," Saphira said. "But you are the daughter of Eville with no magic. I have to assume that you're the only one that can get past the wards."

No magic wasn't exactly true, but I hoped my curse would nullify the wards enough to not stop me.

"But how exactly do you plan to get in? With all the kings coming, the guards will be doubled or tripled. I can't just walk in the front door without an invitation. I'm not a noble."

Saphira grinned and leaned out the window as another commotion came from the streets. I followed her gaze when a colorful wagon came to a stop in front of her inn. A man with a black mustache in a bright red and blue vest and puffed pants stood on the bench and joyfully waved his hat at us.

She waved back and her smile turned up slowly as she looked from me to the colorful man in the wagon.

"Leave that to me. I've already thought of a plan. It's the one group of magic users that are welcomed anywhere."

"Who?" I asked, leaning out the window to see a caravan of wagons and vardos.

"The Magical Menagerie. How do you feel about small spaces?"

"Not great." I worried at my bottom lip and wondered what in the stars she had gotten me into.

CHAPTER TEN

C old fingers brushed against my bare skin, causing me to jump in surprise.

"*Ouch!*" I hissed, wincing in pain as a needle jabbed me.

"I warned you, don't move, or you'll get pricked," a voice shot out.

"Are you sure you only have a needle?" Keeping my head straight, I saw the top of Amaryllis's blonde head. She turned me around and adjusted the back of the leotard. She was in the process of altering one of the troupe's performer costumes to fit my lanky frame.

"A needle can be a fine weapon; one for sewing up injuries, making clothes, and also . . ." She tucked the fabric under and pinned it causing the costume to creep up my backside, exposing my cheek. I tugged it down to cover more of my bottom. Amaryllis used the needle and pricked me. " . . . teaching young girls patience."

"Yeah, that's because you gave me half an outfit." I swallowed and looked at how little clothing I was wearing. This time I tugged up the front of the leotard to cover more of my chest.

A hand snaked through the air and slapped my wrist. "Stop that," Amaryllis warned.

I never imagined that Saphira's plan to get me into the palace included the traveling Magical Menagerie. It was owned by my sister Eden's birth parents, Bravado and Amaryllis De Ella. If I looked past the discomfort and thought about it, it was the perfect cover.

Lorelai Eville had traveled with the Magical Menagerie for years, using her fortune-teller's booth and scrying abilities to spy on the kingdoms. There she became friends with Bravado and Amaryllis, the owners of the eclectic show which included many unique acts and fae animals. In truth, they were spies under the guise of performers, using their gifts to get into places no one else could, and then keeping Lorelai in the know with updates on the seven kingdoms.

It was pure coincidence that the Magical Menagerie had been commissioned by King Leonel himself for the next few weeks, including private shows and tours for the royal daughters themselves. Saphira had even traveled with the menagerie once as a contortionist. She used to squeeze herself into impossibly small spaces. Saphira introduced me to Bravado, and explained her plan to get me into the palace.

Bravado was immediately on board with the charade, and Saphira was convinced I could do her old contortionist act. She proudly brought out a box the size of a small dog and set it before me.

"I can't fit in that," I exclaimed.

"Nonsense. In our line of work, we have to squeeze into small spaces to avoid detection. You should easily be able to handle this."

"Maybe if I didn't eat for a week. And you're an elf. I think your bone structure is different."

"Try it." Saphira pointed at the box.

"I'm not going to fit."

She tapped her foot. I rolled my eyes and stepped into the box and tried to sit. I felt like an oversized toad squatting on a small mushroom.

"No, you need to sit, then pull your leg over your head." She pushed my back down, and I slipped into the box, my hips barely squeezing into the sides.

"I think it helps if she's double-jointed," Bravado said, as Saphira tried to lift my leg above my head.

"Ouch," I hissed. "I'm stuck."

Saphira grunted as she let go of my leg, obviously out of shape as she tried to make me her protégé. "I don't know what else she can do."

"Let me help," Amaryllis said. "First, we need to make her look like one of us, then we will figure out her act later."

Except the costume was not what I was expecting *at all*. If they had shown me the skintight outfit first, I would have run the other way. But now I was committed to the plan and excited about learning a routine. I wasn't scared of hard work or a few bumps and bruises.

Amaryllis was almost an exact replica of Eden, except with more smile wrinkles around her eyes. Just being near her made me homesick for my sister.

Amaryllis's mouth was full of silver pins, and her hands flew with practiced ease, tucking, pinning, and adjusting. "Eden could use glamour to change her appearance into another, or transport using a fire circle. Can you do that?" Amaryllis asked. She removed one of the pins and adjusted the fabric, taking it in and pinning it even tighter than it was before.

"No." I sucked in my breath.

"What about reading minds like Aura?" Bravado called out from behind the colorful partition between his half of the room and ours. Eden's father was a talented glassmaker who could enchant memories into glass. "That would give you close contact with each of the nobles? Madam De La Cour would even be willing to help you."

"No." I winced as I felt another prick of a pin. How much tighter and shorter can this costume get? I wondered. I pulled on the back of the hem, trying to tug further down over my backside.

"Stop fidgeting," Amaryllis said.

"And before you ask, no, I can't shapeshift like Maeve, or control water like Meri, or charm objects like Rhea, or be all powerful like Rosalie." I could feel the bitterness build within my heart after I spouted off each of my sister's names.

"Then really acrobatics is your only option," Bravado called out. I could see his shoulders shrug as the sun high-lighted his figure on the other side of the screen. "In fact, it's the only option for you."

"But does it have to be so tight?" I pulled at the fabric again and winced in anticipation of the slap.

"Done." Amaryllis got up and turned me to face the full-length mirror in the tent.

Immediately I reached to cover my chest as every curve of my body was outlined by the tight-fitting and colorful material that left very little to the imagination. The leggings were red and white stripes, my leotard was covered in skintight shimmering blue, red and yellow triangles, and my arms were bare.

There was nowhere to conceal a weapon that didn't involve swallowing it. If I thought swallowing swords would work, I would try it, but it was nothing more than a glamoured blade.

"Oh, I almost forgot the jacket." Amaryllis dug through a trunk, and I felt a sigh of relief until she pulled a mere scrap of material and slipped it over my arms. The jacket was just a vest with puffed sleeves.

After the jacket came a pair of slim boots with the thinnest layer of leather on the bottom.

Bravado came around the screen and looked me over from head to toe. He nodded and rubbed his chin. "She looks the part, but now can she act the part?"

"I can do whatever needs to be done," I promised. "As long as it's not being shoved into small boxes, apparently."

"We will see." He grinned, and I didn't trust the twinkle in his eye. "I have another idea."

Bravado led me out of the tent and into a small clearing just outside of the caravan. The rest of the troupe had gathered there, and they were rehearsing until it was time to go to the palace. Thirty or so wagons had circled up, and I could hear the squalls, growls, and cries from some of the larger wagons that were holding animals.

As we walked through the camp, a female ogre gave me a wave before heading into a larger tent. I craned my head as we passed the tent opening.

"That's Ogress, our seer," Bravado spoke up.

"I know," I said in awe, slowing to take a closer look at the tent. "She works out of the tent that my mother enchanted."

Bravado called out. "Keep moving. There's no time for gawking."

As I walked, I could feel the material sliding up my back cheek and I pulled it down, walking awkwardly. "Are you sure I couldn't just get a job taking care of the animals?"

"No, the menagerie and workers are confined to the grounds and are not allowed into the palace. The troupe has more freedom as we are doing shows throughout the palace and can be called upon at any moment for private bookings."

Sorek, a heavily muscled man with a bald head, was working a winch and clamp and had two sets of striped wooden poles set up in an X, and a thick rope was strung between them about four feet off the ground.

"Up you go!" Bravado tapped one of the poles.

I jumped up between the poles with ease and settled my weight on the thick cord. Now I understood the need for the soft leather shoes as I felt my feet form around the two-inch rope.

Without being told, I started to walk the tightrope. It was actually easier than walking along the tree branches when I trained with Lorn, where one end was always weaker. When I got to the other side, I raised one hand in the air.

"Well, she's got balance," Sorek commented. His voice was deeper than I'd expected.

Bravado's mustache twitched, and he reached into his pocket and pulled out a weighted ball. "Catch!" He tossed it to me, and I easily caught it. Rapidly firing, two more came my way. He made a motion with his hands. "Now juggle."

"Juggle?" I moved carefully to the middle of the rope and attempted to toss the first ball into the air, followed by the second. It wasn't pretty, but I could make a few rotations before the balls were in the dirt.

I hopped down and picked them back up. "I can do it," I said. "I just need time."

"We don't have time. The king's jugglers can juggle eight."

Amaryllis tapped Bravado's shoulder, and she leaned over and whispered to him.

"I see. Yes, that could work." He turned to his strong man. "Sorek, get the silks and rings out of the supply wagon."

"What's going on?" I asked.

"You said you would do anything, right?"

"Yes."

"How do you feel about heights?"

My mouth went dry at the mischievous look in Bravado's eyes.

A candle mark later, Sorek had scaled a tree in the clearing and hung a giant ring and two silks from a high branch.

"What are we doing with this?" I asked suspiciously, running my fingers along the material.

"Amaryllis reminded me of a dancer who performed with us once. She is no longer with us, but her equipment is."

"Danced?"

"Like this." Amaryllis wrapped her upper arms around the silks and then lifted her feet off the ground, then she slowly spun in a circle. She stood, and I watched as she carefully took off her shoes and climbed, wrapping the silk

116

around her feet and waist. I memorized each placement, and she climbed up the silk till she was several feet in the air. "If you place them right, you can unwind." In slow motion, she released and unwound one full rotation before stopping.

"I can do that," I said confidently.

"But can you do it thirty feet in the air?" she asked.

"Thirty feet?"

Bravado nodded. "The higher you climb, the more dangerous."

I grabbed the silks and climbed, spending the next few minutes under the careful direction of Amaryllis.

After trial and error, and a few tangles, I was able to figure out the pattern and mimic Amaryllis's earlier stunt.

When I was done, I released the silks and did an awkward bow.

Sorek snorted.

"That'll do," Bravado said, triumphantly. "We can't teach fearlessness, but I can teach showmanship. There may be hope for you yet. We've got four days to turn you into a performer."

Four days. So much could happen in four days.

My saving grace was that the caravan had camped right over a ley line. I was almost buzzing with energy and intensity, and I threw myself into training. I had missed the routines of fighting and working on a mat. This time, the routine was different.

From morning until night, I trained. Rising before the sun was up, I spent hours conditioning my upper body strength and working on my flexibility before I even reached for the silks. Then I spent midday to evening working a few feet off the ground, practicing holds, grips, various knots and securing myself, just figuring it out as I went. Survival training had taught me knots and ties, and I was thankful I could pull that from memory. It was one less thing to learn. I knew how to tie a slipknot, hammock knot, and even invented a few on the fly. But it was the drop that was the scariest. I had no problem climbing high into the boughs of trees, wrapping the silk around myself into a cradle and leaning back, dangling above the ground. I didn't even have a fear of hanging with a silk wrapped around my wrist as Sorek gently swung me in a circle. It was the controlled drop. That was the scariest move, and one I hadn't quite mastered. I was a little apprehensive to go higher than a few feet above the ground.

But Bravado didn't think I needed to do it. I could possibly get away with swinging, spinning, and sitting in the air if I added a little flair to my performance.

"Flair?" I asked as I sat rubbing down my hip. I had ugly welts and bruises on my legs. The muscles in my arms were trembling from strain and overuse, and I knew I needed to get into a hot bath and treat them.

"Yes. Flair." He jutted his hip outward, flung his hand into the air and spread his fingers wide and grinned. His mustache twitched with mirth, his thick hips bounced, and he tried to walk on his toes, swaying comically until a few of his laborers shot whistles his way.

Bravado stopped mid-flaunt, coughed into his hands, and blushed.

"I'll just . . . um . . . get my wife to show you."

Amaryllis then spent countless hours working on my body positioning, the flair of my fingers and hands, and showing me the correct way to drape my hand over my head and give a coy look at the audience.

"Remember, you are beauty and grace in the air. From up there, you want to seduce everyone with a look. The men will want to marry you, the women will want to be you."

I tried batting my eyes, throwing an arm above my head, flaring my fingers and pursing my lips in what I thought was a seductive pose. Amaryllis groaned. "You look like you're constipated."

I dropped my arm. "I can't help it." I sighed. "I fight with weapons and my fists. I can knock a man down and kill him with one blow. I wasn't trained to be feminine."

"Then your training was severely lacking," Saphira said as she stepped into the glade to join Amaryllis. "You've trained your whole life to use man's weapons. Now it's time to learn the weapons you were born with."

My head snapped up, and I saw the conspiratorial smile pass between the two women. "It's our turn to teach you how to wield the most dangerous weapons of all."

"I'm not going to enjoy this, am I?"

"Oh, probably not, but we'll have fun teaching it to you." Amaryllis laughed.

CHAPTER ELEVEN

The city was alive with celebration in anticipation of the council of kings. Nobles from all the kingdoms were coming to court, which also meant that the streets were packed with citizens readying their own celebrations. Musicians, dancers, and vendors worked late into the night, all trying to appease the rich and fill their own pockets with coins as everyone prepared for the high council. I even gave up my room at the Silk Slipper and had taken to sleeping in a Magical Menagerie tent so I could learn the troupe lingo and better blend in with the others.

It was odd to be around so many people. It felt like I was starting to fit in. With the elves, it was obvious I was an outsider. Every single day, my ears set me apart.

Here, I felt like I could belong.

"Come along," Saphira said, pulling me after her as she wound through the streets, following a route only she knew. So I wouldn't trip, I picked up the hem of my borrowed dress and followed her. Amaryllis was close behind me, and I could feel her fingers playing with the curls of my hair. She had spent the last few candle marks primping my hair, pinning it up and applying lots of makeup to accent my eyes, making them look exotic.

Even the dress was exotic. It was a deep red with off the shoulders sleeves, and a split skirt which gave the illusion of a dress but had puffed pants underneath. I felt beautiful, and it was interesting to note how a bit of rouge brushed on my cheeks and color on my lips brought another layer of confidence. It was like another coat of armor I didn't know I needed.

"Alright, Honor. Here is your first test." Saphira waved her hand at the young men wandering around the streets. "You need to get one of them to approach you."

"Easy enough." I raised two fingers to my mouth and let out a high-pitched whistle. Every head turned my way, and I waved my hand in the air and beckoned the closest man to come toward me.

"Are you in need of aid, Miss?" the sandy-haired man asked.

I heard Saphira's audible groan, and I looked behind me as Amaryllis was laughing hard behind her hand.

"She's fine. Thank you!" Saphira grabbed my shoulder and pulled me away from the worried man. "What were you thinking?" she chastised softly.

"I did what you asked, and in record time too." I grinned triumphantly.

"Okay, that is not what I meant." Saphira ran her hands down her dress, and I could tell from what she was *not* saying that I had irritated her. "Watch me."

Saphira unpinned part of her shawl and let it dangle off her shoulders. When she walked, like a dancer, and it made her hips sway.

Amaryllis narrated softly to me. "The trick of picking a mark is to make him approach you. You never want to approach them. This way they feel they're in control, and if you can do it without speaking a single word—all the better."

"I take it you have done this before?"

"How do you think I got Bravado to fall in love with me?" she laughed softly; her joy evident.

Saphira passed an older gentleman, and she slowed, gave him a wide innocent look, and then very carefully let a silk scarf slip from her fingers, and she carried on.

The man swooped down, picked up the scarf, and gently tapped her on the shoulder.

"Don't overdo the look of surprise," Amaryllis said, still narrating. "Be coy, but innocent."

Saphira looked surprised and carefully took back the scarf, running it through her fingers. As she brought it up to her hair, her finger brushed her lips before they parted and she inhaled.

The man froze, his eyes never leaving her face.

"And then draw attention to one of your best features. She is drawing attention to her lips. Now watch. He's ensnared."

Saphira leaned forward and whispered in his ear. The man turned red and nodded.

We waited until Saphira came back, and I asked what she'd told the man.

"I said the Silk Slipper is famous for our sweet and sumptuous desserts which can be attained at all hours of the night," she answered.

The innuendo wasn't lost on me, and I stuttered. "But that makes it sound like you offer. . ."

Saphira cackled. "The best desserts in the city, and we do offer them anytime, day or night. Never mind that they are also delivered by Trask, our male bouncer. That lord will have checked out of his current in and be in the Silk Slipper before the night is over. I didn't lie, but I did poach a nobleman. Remember, I deal in secrets, and the more powerful men I have in my inn, the better the secrets."

Amaryllis was laughing, and I couldn't keep my own smirk hidden.

"Your turn." I turned to Amaryllis.

"Oh, no. My days of wooing men are over. I wanted to be here to watch and coach you. I find it incredibly brave what you are doing, and I think your mother would be proud of you. I know I am."

"Thanks," I said.

"Okay, your turn," Amaryllis said softly.

I steeled my nerves, stopped biting my lip, and started walking. At first I tried to walk like Saphira had, but I heard another audible groan. *Okay, too much.* I closed my eyes and focused on my training. Walking softly on the balls of my feet muffled the sound and gave my hips a smaller sway. It felt more natural.

But what was my greatest asset to draw attention to? My hands were my first thought because I was a fighter, but that wasn't what the two women were trying to teach me.

I was raised by a male. I was most comfortable with weapons and blades. I didn't learn needlework or knitting like my sisters had. The only needle I used was to stitch up gashes on the field.

I didn't use makeup. I used salves to prevent scarring. My knowledge of flirting was nonexistent because I never needed to. The only person I was close to was Percy, and he mostly tolerated me.

A young man stood in front of a weapons vendor's

table full of blades and knives. I felt intrigued, my attention going to a small throwing knife. I wanted to immediately grab it and test the weight in my hand. But that wasn't the weapon I was learning to use.

I turned around, casting a helpless look at the two women who were watching from the shadows. Saphira crossed her arms, her mouth pinched, while Amaryllis was all smiles and shooing me on.

The task was to get them to come to me without speaking, but how did I gain their attention? I reached up and patted my curls and felt awkward. I couldn't do this.

Quickly, I scanned all of my exit routes. I had three. One was in the path of guards; one was over the roof and then a quick jump over the wall. One was the fastest, but would cause the biggest commotion.

I turned, intent on abandoning the quest and giving up, when I saw him and did a double take. It was impossible to miss him among all the others. He stood out a head above the rest because he was the finest specimen there. He was polished, sharp, and attractive. Only a fool would walk away now.

My hands trembled, and my heart ached. I missed the sound of his voice.

Rumple.

He was hanging on a hook on the back wall of the vendor stall. Then a middle-aged man in a green jerkin and cloak blocked my view and pointed to Rumple. "I'll take that one."

"No!" I panicked. "That's my axe."

The vendor brought over the double-headed axe, and I couldn't help but stare at Rumple . . . Who was eerily silent.

The man turned and gave me a disbelieving look. His face was tanned, his brown hair was long, brushing against his collar, and he had deep green eyes. I could tell he was part of the blacksmith guild from the hammer and anvil pin he wore on his cloak.

"Your axe? I find that hard to believe," he scoffed.

"It's true," I blurted. "It's my axe. I lost it."

"Then how did it end up here?" the buyer asked.

I turned toward the vendor and he offered up a shrug. "Don't quite remember. Some farmer traded the axe to me a few weeks ago."

"It can't be your axe." The guild member reached for his leather pouch and pulled out coins to pay for Rumple.

"You're wrong. It *is* my axe. My sister forged him in Kiln. She even put runes on the side of the blade."

The guild member was quickly losing his patience with me. "I find it hard to believe that a female crafted this fine work of art. And again, I think you're mistaken. This is not your axe."

"No, it is. I can't explain exactly how I lost him. *But the axe can speak up for himself and prove it?*" I gritted out to Rumple.

"That's enough." The guild member turned and grabbed Rumple, who was missing the leather holster.

"I'll buy him from you!" I slapped all the coins I had left on the counter, and the guild member just snorted. "I paid three times that."

"Rumple!" I cried. "Please, Rumple, say something to prove that I'm not lying."

"My name is Randolph, not Rumple," the guild member snapped. He turned and walked down the street, carting away my axe.

I cast a look over my shoulder and saw how worried Amaryllis and Saphira were. This was not going how I thought it would. Randolph got into a carriage with a guild mark. The door slammed behind him, and I had a few seconds to decide.

"I'm sorry!" I called out, running after the carriage and jumping up onto the back. Crouching low, I waved cheekily after the two ladies as I rode away.

CHAPTER TWELVE

R andolph Greenfield's carriage pulled up to a grand two-story stone house on the edge of the city. The iron gate was marked by the same guild symbol he wore on his cloak. When the coach approached, the gates opened, and I slid from the back and hung beneath the carriage, holding onto the frame, my skirt dragging along the gravel.

The carriage slowed at the front of the manor, and a footman came to open the door for Randolph. I slipped out the other side and ducked behind the nearest row of hedges. My adrenaline kicked in; my heart was racing, but my hands never trembled. This is what I lived for. This used all of my training as a scout, except I didn't have any weapons . . . yet.

Peeking between the bushes, I stared up at the manor house and studied all of the various ways I could get in. The easiest would be to wait for everyone to fall asleep for the night, and then sneak in, but my problem came when I didn't know where Randolph would place his newly acquired weapon? What if it was in a cellar, or a locked trunk? I didn't have all the time in the world to search every nook and cranny for Rumple. And I hated waiting.

When the driver took the carriage to the carriage house

and the last servant followed Randolph inside, I ran for the side of the house, staying low to the ground, pressing my back to the wall. I went from window to window, peeking inside, searching until I found Randolph in the main hall.

He was showing off the axe to one of the servants. When the servant tried to take the axe, Randolph shook his head and headed up the main stairs.

Backing up, I studied the stone wall and plotted my route. Stepping on the window ledge, I pushed up and grabbed onto an ornate stone that jutted out farther than the rest. The muscles in my arms screamed as I once again put them to the test, but I was getting used to using my arms to climb. Reaching higher, I felt along the stones until I found another handhold.

It was slow going, hand over hand, but I wasn't going to give up until I reached a second-floor balcony. Slipping over the railing, I crouched just outside the double doors and waited. A match flared to life, and then one by one the candles were lit within the room, revealing a lavishly furnished bedroom. An elaborate four-poster bed with blue velvet curtains, a tufted chair, and a gilded mirror that ran the length of the wall filled the space. Above the stone fireplace were hooks where other blades hung in honor.

Randolph took Rumple and hung him next to a beautiful two-handed sword and a deadly mace.

Now, I needed to pick the balcony doors lock and wait till he was asleep.

Randolph came toward the balcony. I leapt to the side ledge, pressing my back to the cold stone and prepared to jump down to the ground, but I heard the click of the key, and he opened the door to let in the night air.

Well, he just made that easier for me.

When Randolph retreated into the room, he started a fire in the fireplace and settled into a chair while he stared up at the wall at his new axe.

I waited outside in the cold until the fire burned low. Randolph never got up to restock the fire or move to his bed. I had to assume that he fell asleep in the chair.

I had to take my chance. I tiptoed into the room, only slightly saddened that I didn't get to use my lock-picking skills. My feet moved silently over the floor, light like butterfly wings, barely putting pressure down on the wood, testing to make sure there weren't any loose floorboards.

When I came to the rug, it muffled my steps even further, and I craned my neck and glanced around to the front of the chair.

Sure enough, Randolph had fallen asleep. His eyes were closed, his chin had dropped onto his chest, and his hands clasped over his belly. Soft snores punctuated the night, along with the crackling of the dying fire.

The huge fireplace was going to be a problem because I could barely reach the end of Rumple's handle, and I had to stand on tiptoe to raise him high enough to unhook him.

"No," a harsh voice said.

I spun, thinking I was caught. But Randolph was still asleep. Although he opened his mouth and let out a yawn.

I waited a few terrifying, long seconds, and looked back up to Rumple. "You decided to talk, after all," I whispered.

"You abandoned me," he pouted.

"I didn't abandon you."

"You did. I came through the veil and was all alone."

"Did you see the apprentice who cut through the veil?"

Rumple fell silent again. I took it as another chance to reach up and unhook him from the wall.

"I said no. I want to stay here."

"Why?" I asked, wanting to know his reasoning.

"Because it's warm here and . . . I'm appreciated. The whole carriage ride, he marveled over me. Said nothing but good things about me. Where all you do is insult me."

"I don't *always* insult you," I said.

"Yes, you do. I'm staying here."

This wasn't working out how I'd planned. "Look, I came to rescue you."

"Does it look like I want to be rescued?" Rumple's voice grew loud.

Randolph snorted, and I jumped back behind the chair, crouching low and waiting until he fell back asleep completely.

I waited until my legs began to cramp, and then I made my way back over to Rumple. "What do you want me to say? I'm sorry, I made a mistake. I'm here now. We can make a great team again. Plus, Rhea will miss you."

Silence.

I was being ignored.

"Fine," I spat. "Stay there on the wall and rust away, where you can be admired by firelight, but won't have any enemies to vanquish. I doubt you'll ever see battle again. You're too high and lofty for that."

There was the slightest noise from Rumple, which could've been the hint of a whimper. I decided to play hard to get. I backed away toward the window and continued to whisper. "Yeah, I'm sure I'll encounter that pack of hellhounds again, and I'll make sure to take all of them down by myself with a knife. Not just any knife, but a dull knife."

This time, a snort came from Rumple.

"Yeah, I'll take a table knife. Because they never get to see any action and will appreciate cutting into things besides butter. They never talk back, unlike some weapons I know."

"You wouldn't," Rumple whispered.

"I would. Besides, if I lose one, there are a million others just like it, ready to take its place. But you can stay here and dream about all of the battles of old and not take part in anything new. I'm sure you'll become a family heirloom, and sit on that wall for hundreds and hundreds of years."

I had made it out onto the balcony and was about to close the door.

A great caterwauling ensued.

"No, take me with you! I don't want to sit here forever! I'm a dwarf! I'm destined to fight!"

I froze as Rumple's screaming woke up Randolph, who was looking around the room in a terrified frenzy. The knife from his belt was already in his hands as he prepared to attack.

I groaned.

"Honor, don't leave! Take me with you. I can't stay with this big ogre anymore!"

Randolph stiffened, turning slowly toward the fireplace, his eyes wide with terror. His mouth dropped open when he heard Rumple continue his tirade.

"Y-you t-talk?"

I bolted straight into the room, forgetting about being quiet. I tried to get the surprise on Randolph. When I got to the fireplace, I jumped straight up, knocking the handle up in the air, jostling Rumple enough that he unhooked and fell forward.

I reached out to grab the handle at the same time Randolph did, and we both locked onto Rumple.

"You!" Randolph growled when he recognized me. "You dare to steal what's mine?" With all of his weight, he swung me around, but I didn't let go.

"He's not yours. He's my friend," I gritted out as I was outmatched with bodyweight. I swept my foot, hooking him behind the knee, hoping to knock him off balance and he'd let go, but he fell, taking me with him. I used his falling momentum and jumped, flipping to the side and wrenching the axe from his hand.

"Yeah, what she said!" Rumple yelled. "Wait, did you just say you're my friend?"

I landed awkwardly on the floor, Rumple resting safely at my side. This was not the time for reunions.

"Sometimes you are," I muttered. I jumped to my feet and ran toward the door.

"Wait. You can't go." I paused as Randolph struggled to get up from the floor. He held out his hand. "Do you know how much a talking blade is worth? We could be rich. I'll split the profits with you."

I waited on the balcony and pretended to consider the offer. "How much are we talking about?"

"You wouldn't dare!" Rumple growled. "Rhea and Kash wouldn't like it if you sold me."

"Quiet, the humans are talking." I held back my smirk. "Remember, you could have saved me the trouble of stealing you if you had spoken up at the market."

"But you told me to stay quiet in public or you were

going to drop into a lake," he whined. "You know how much I fear water."

"Of all the times you disobeyed and got me kicked out of pubs and bars because you couldn't shut your trap, you chose *that* moment to obey?"

He was silent.

I sighed and addressed Randolph. "I'm sorry, but as I said before, he's my friend, and I can't explain the reason I came to be without him, but I'm thankful to be reunited." As I spoke, I retreated until my backside bumped into the balcony railing.

"I'll call the guards," Randolph threatened.

I leapt onto the railing, holding the axe in my hands. I turned to face the guild member. In his beefy hand, he held up a silver whistle.

I let a smile of pleasure creep across my lips. "I'm counting on it. Otherwise, this escape would be too easy." I stepped backward off the balcony.

As I fell, I swung the axe and let it fly until it sunk into the wooden support beam under the balcony. It slowed my fall and dropped me a few feet closer to the ground. With a mighty swing, we dislodged and dropped the last twelve feet to safety.

I heard the whistle, and the lights in the guardhouse flickered on as candles and torches were lit.

"After her!" Randolph bellowed. "I want that axe."

The baying of hounds followed, and now I felt a moment of fear. I knew I was fast, but could I outrun scent dogs?

"You better get moving," Rumple encouraged.

"I thought you wanted a fight?"

"I want to fight, not become a chew toy."

I laughed and ran hard. Letting my training kick in, I stuck to the rocky path and not the soft earth. I used the blade of the axe to cut off ribbons of my dress to make scent strips and tie them to tree branches and bushes in an attempt to slow the dogs.

And as I ran, I couldn't help but feel the elation as the adrenaline rush raced through my body. This is what I was made for. This is what I enjoyed more than anything. The freedom to run and hunt and be chased, and I looked forward to running the maze of the city streets as I evaded my hunters.

CHAPTER THIRTEEN

R umple was quiet as we headed to the small blue and cream striped tent that had been given to me. It wasn't grand, had a few holes that needed patching on the roof, and a few others where it was wearing thin—but I loved it. It was a roof over my head, and it was mine. Whereas I'd spent most of my life sleeping beneath the stars and or under a lean-to canvas that all scouts carried, this tent was a more permanent structure. I pulled the canvas flap back and slipped into the darkened interior.

"Where have you been?" Saphira yelled, appearing out of the shadows of the tent.

It was a few hours till morning, and I thought everyone would have been asleep. I was wrong. My disappearing and taking off in the middle of the city to jump on a strange carriage had clearly caused them concern. With the exception of Lorn, I was unused to having someone worry about me.

A finger snapped behind me. The enchanted glass wind chimes that hung in the tent glowed, illuminating the colorful canvas in an array of purples and yellows.

Bravado stood next to the chimes. It was his magic that

caused the chimes to glow. Sitting on my bedroll was Amaryllis, her face filled with tears.

When she saw me, her hands flew to her mouth. "What happened to you?" she cried out. "Are you hurt?"

I then realized the image I was presenting them. I was dripping wet, my dress was torn to shreds, and all the beautiful curls in my hair were now a sopping mess of tangles down my back. But I had a wicked gleam in my eyes as I held a golden double-headed axe above my head.

"I got the pain in the axe back!" I yelled in victory.

"Stop it!" Rumple bellowed, and I enjoyed the moment as everyone's faces turned to a look of shock as they encountered the talking weapon.

"This is Rumple, as in Rumple Stiltskin, the great dwarf protector of Ter Dell," I added.

"It t-talks," Bravado stuttered.

"And cuts and chops and is great for beheading." I sounded like a vendor trying to sell them the latest knife ware.

"Is it cursed?" Amaryllis asked. She had stopped crying and looked at the axe in wonder. I had forgotten that she'd spent most of her life trapped as a bird, cursed by Allemar.

"It curs—es," I quipped, trying to lighten the mood. "But I don't think he can become a dwarf again. His soul was trapped in cursed gold, and Rhea forged the weapon, but managed to also preserve his memories."

"You shouldn't have run away." Bravado changed the subject. "We were worried."

"I'm sorry for worrying you, but as you can see, I'm fine." I patted my chest.

"I knew she would be," Saphira huffed. "She *was* trained by Lorn."

I pointed my finger at her and nodded. "Exactly. No harm came to me. I just had to get back what belongs to me."

"And how did you do that exactly?" Amaryllis asked, her eyes narrowing and once again taking in my appearance.

I crumpled under the look only a concerned mother could give, and the truth came flying out of my mouth. "I broke into a manor, confronted a member of the blacksmith guild, and stole Rumple . . . which also meant avoiding the guards and getting chased by hunting dogs."

Bravado's mustache twitched and I could see the look of pride he was trying to hide.

As they continued to grill me, the sun's rays slowly lit the canvas tent, and I knew I'd have to start training again. But I also desperately needed sleep. I looked longingly toward my cot, my feet and joints aching. Outside the tent, I could hear the rest of the troupe rising and talking loudly.

Bravado read my mind as he ushered the ladies out of the tent.

"Sleep, Honor. I'll wake you in a few candle marks before we pack up."

"Pack up?" I asked.

He grinned. "It's time. The gates are opening. We are heading into the palace. Our first show is tonight."

"I'm not ready," I said, my body tensing.

Bravado grasped my upper arms, giving them a slight squeeze. "Don't forget your purpose. We have spent our lifetimes hunting down the evil of the kingdoms, being spies, trying to right wrongs. I know of what you faced in

Ter Dell; a horde of goblins and the entity known as Greed. The darkness that's within this kingdom is far more dangerous and is only bolstered by Allemar's apprentices. You've felt the backlash of what we hunt, and you know it cannot go unchecked. You can't let another Northern Woods happen again."

I took strength from his words. "But how do we know that it's the same evil?"

"We don't, but it's darkness all the same, and you are a bringer of light. Lorelai foresaw all of this long ago. Believe in yourself. This is your path."

My hands trembled as I clutched the collar of my destroyed dress. Bringer of light? I wasn't so sure about that. My curse said otherwise. Bringer of death and loneliness was more like it. But I couldn't share my fear with Bravado.

My eyelids grew heavy and my knees weak. Bravado left me alone as I collapsed on the cot.

"What have you gotten yourself into?" Rumple asked quietly, but I didn't answer, as I could already feel myself spiraling into sleep. I clutched the handle of the axe and was out in seconds.

Adrenaline coursed through my body. I balanced on the threshold of feeling like I could run a hundred miles . . . or maybe throw up. It was a tossup. I was praying it wouldn't be the latter. I bounced on the balls of my feet, wearing another ridiculous skintight outfit. My hair was slicked back into a high ponytail on the top of my head. It hung to my hips and felt heavy, like a whip.

I couldn't even recognize myself with bright red lips, and all the glitter and heavy face paint that created an alluring eye mask of white and blue whirls.

The caravan was lined up in a specific parade order, with the performers at the front and followed by the colorful vardos. Even the horses were decked out with brightly colored straps and bells.

At the back were the supply wagons, followed by the tail end of acrobats. The entrance through the city was supposed to be a spectacle; a parade of entertainment for the children and patrons before they headed into the palace.

"Consider this your dress rehearsal. All you have to do is walk and smile," Bravado encouraged.

It should be easy. I wasn't hanging on a silk, but I did have one in my hand.

I watched nervously as Bravado went to the front of the line, pulled the whip from his hip, and with a mighty twirl, swung it over his head and jumped in the air. Letting it crack, the sound echoed, and people backed up. He began his march. Every few feet, another jump and a crack straight above his head, and the path cleared.

A troupe woman wearing bells on her hips held a tambourine up in the air. She began to rattle it as a young man started to pound out a rhythm on his drum. Bryce played a jig on his flute, while Whitney filled in the music with his guitar. The jugglers started letting their balls fly as they walked, and our parade moved forward through the city. Kids rushed to the sides of the roads and waved at all the people. Amaryllis was graceful in her flowing skirts as she spun and danced, tossing out small hard candies to the children. Sorek flexed his muscles, showing off his tattoos, and held his knives above his head.

Kline, one of the other performers, gave me a nudge in the back as I'd forgotten to move with the group. I gripped my silk and walked, letting it drag awkwardly along the ground as I struggled to deal with so many people staring at me. I wasn't used to being the center of attention, and I felt myself freeze up.

Behind us, I could hear the crowd gasp as Ogress sat upon her wagon. Her green skin looked pale in the light, while her hair was adorned with colored moss and beads braided into the long, thick strands. She had a gold hoop on her ear and her smile was hidden behind two pointy teeth that shot up from her underbite, giving her a frightening appearance. She was quite a spectacle as eight oxen pulled her wagon. Then came the menagerie of animals, and more screams followed. This time the screams were of delight as children saw a unicorn for the very first time.

Amaryllis dropped back next to me and whispered words of encouragement. "Relax. Wave your hand."

I had forgotten how to use my hands. I lifted up the silk and waved at a young blonde-haired girl leaning out of the second floor of her house. She disappeared and reappeared seconds later with her own kerchief, and waved it back at me enthusiastically.

I spun in a circle, and she mimicked me waving the silk. I laughed, and her smile grew bright.

That was all it took to ignite the fire within me.

I *could* do this.

I pretended that the silk was at the end of a weapon, and I knew how to do forms. I'd spent countless hours running fighting drills, tucks and rolls, and as Lorn had once said—fighting was a form of dancing. I listened to the beat of the drum and began to *dance* with an unknown opponent. Sweeping my foot behind me, holding the silk above my head, swinging it out and around, jumping over an imaginary staff coming for my head, I tucked and rolled along the street, easily coming back up to my feet. I ran a few feet and did a cartwheel, followed by a backflip, and heard the cheers follow.

Adrenaline kicked in and I continued to perform various jumps and flips. I slayed a hundred bad guys with my silk. All through the streets I danced, my heart pumping, my breath catching, and my cheeks hurt from smiling. I didn't even notice when we passed through the golden gates of the palace. The ground had become firm, shifting from packed earth to stone.

The wagons slowed and pulled to a stop before the front door. The performers continued their parade right up to the steps where King Leonel stood with his many daughters.

Twelve daughters, dressed in pastels, the oldest appeared to be in her late twenties, the youngest in an indigo dress looked no more than fourteen.

"Get ready for the big finish!" Amaryllis called.

Bravado called out a crisp shout and I could feel the drum and flute pick up to a crescendo, and I knew a finale was coming. He cracked his whip, and the pure white horses that normally pulled the supply wagons were untethered. They pranced and flick their heads and neck back.

"Up!" He cracked the whip, and they rose high on their hind legs, their front hooves painted gold glimmered in the sunlight.

The jugglers tossed their knives high, and as I prepared to do a final somersault, I saw one of the king's daughters slip from the top step and tumble down the stairs, right into the path of the show horses' hooves.

The oldest daughter gasped and made to run down after her. "Grace!"

I acted. Running toward her, I dove, landing on top of Grace. I grabbed her and rolled as the horses came down. One clipped my hip, but I kept rolling, bringing her with me until we were out of harm's way.

The flute, drum, and tambourine stopped as we lay on the stone, my side burning with pain. I helped the princess up and saw blood splattering her dress.

"Are you okay?" I asked, leaning back, checking for wounds. I met hazel eyes and a face that mirrored mine. Princess Grace had her hair in unique braids and curls that flowed down her back, and her hands were soft and uncalloused. Thankfully, my face was disguised by heavy paint, and I didn't think she could see the striking resemblance between us.

Her hazel eyes welled with frightened tears, and I was terrified that she was hurt.

Rough arms seized me, pulling me from the princess, and I was flung out of the way as the guards surrounded her. A circle of bright yellow and silver uniforms blocked my view, and King Leonel rushed to tend to his daughter.

Amaryllis knelt by my side, her quick hands feeling along my hip, searching for the wound.

"You'll be fine. You just need a few stitches," she concluded.

"How is the princess?" I asked. "What's going to happen?"

Her face was pale; lips pinched together with worry as her terrified eyes flicked toward her husband. "I don't know."

Bravado, as the leader of the troupe was imprisoned, two guards stood on either side of him, holding his upper arms in place.

"Your parade endangered the princess," the captain of the guards yelled into Bravado's face. "You will be punished severely."

"No!" a voice called out from within the circle of the guards. "It wasn't their fault." A princess with almost black hair pushed her way between the guards and moved to stand in front of Bravado, her hands held wide as she turned to address her father. "It was an accident. Grace slipped and fell. Nothing more."

"Isn't that right?" The oldest princess cast a pleading look toward Grace.

There was the barest flicker of accusation from Princess Grace toward a younger blonde sister with a knowing smirk. As if she didn't truly believe it was an accident, and the young sister who played innocent knew it. Grace nodded her head. "It was an accident. Please, don't punish them." Her pure voice and angelic eyes were almost impossible to ignore as she pleaded with her father. King Leonel's face crumpled beneath the magic of her innocence.

"You're right. It was not as if they planned to endanger you." King Leonel waved toward the guards, and they released Bravado.

I heard Amaryllis's quick intake of breath as she tried to hold back her sobs of relief. The once merry moment was gone as the troupe stood in the courtyard surrounded by guards, unsure of their welcome and whether we would be allowed to continue with their show.

I hadn't moved from my spot on the ground, my hand covering the wound on my hip.

King Leonel walked toward me, and I stared up at the most intimidating man I'd ever met. He had long black hair and piercing dark eyes; his stony expression made more daunting by his intricately styled and angled beard. He was dressed in cream-colored robes, with a red garnet stone on his crown.

"Are you well?" He glanced at my wound.

"Nothing serious. I'll be fine," I assured him and proved it by getting to my feet. My hip was sore, but I knew I would recover. The bleeding had already stopped, and I knew my body healed faster than normal.

"Good." He turned to Bravado, ignoring me completely.

Bravado bowed, getting low to the ground, his face touching the stone. "I am sorry, Your Majesty. It was not our intention to put the princess in harm's way. Please accept our most gracious apologies."

The king stared at Bravado's prone back, and I feared he had changed his mind about punishing us.

"Up," he commanded, and Bravado raised but still bowed. "You may have unintentionally put my daughter at risk, but at the same time, a member of your troupe saved her at the cost of her own safety. I thank you, and look forward to your shows. This time, I expect any dangerous acts to be performed *without* audience participation."

Amaryllis had grabbed my elbow for support during the king's speech with her husband, and I could feel her tremble. When he turned to head back inside, she went weak-kneed and I had to grab her to hold her up.

"It's fine. He's safe. We all are," I said.

She was still shaking. "Thanks to you." She grabbed my arms. "If it wasn't for you, Bravado would've been killed. We might *all* have paid the consequence for the death of his daughter. But you saved her . . . and us."

I didn't realize how deep-rooted the terror of the moment had been. As I looked down the line of performers, Amaryllis's relief was mirrored on everyone's faces.

We were given orders to continue on and set up within the palace grounds. Like worker ants scattering, everyone quickly jumped into the wagons. Within seconds, they were moving . . . except Madame Ogress. She sat on her wagon behind her eight oxen and with narrowed eyes, watched the youngest princess as she joined her sisters and headed back into the palace.

"Ogress, we need to move," I said. She was blocking the path and stalling the wagons behind her.

Madam De La Cour shook her head and leaned down toward me. "That was no accident," she whispered.

I gasped. "What do you mean?"

"She didn't slip. She was pushed."

"Why would someone try to kill the princess?"

"Why indeed?" She gripped the reins of her oxen. "That is the question, isn't it?" Madam De La Cour suddenly stilled. Her eyes narrowed again, and I heard a slight growl from her throat. I followed her line of sight to the flurry of pastel dresses heading up the steps and into the palace hall where Princesses Grace and Lisbelle were speaking.

CHAPTER FOURTEEN

"Let me," I demanded of Amaryllis, who was attempting to thread a needle to stitch my wound. Her hands were still trembling as she struggled to find the eye. I sat on the back of a flatbed wagon while everyone else had started setting up the tents. In the main gardens, a giant tent was being constructed with all of the magical animals. Most of the acts would be inside the palace, but the rest of us would be confined outside the palace itself, unless we were performing.

She passed the needle, and I found the eye and measured out the thread. When I leaned back in an attempt to stitch myself, she spoke up.

"We should wait for Bravado." She sniffed and wiped her eyes.

"It's not that bad. It has already stopped bleeding. I can do it," I said. With a few quick motions, I had stitched the wound closed. I was thankful that it was just skin. No muscles were injured, so it would be quick to heal. I was more bruised than anything.

Bravado raced to us while clutching a round tin. "Here is the numbing ointment."

"We're done," Amaryllis said.

Bravado looked confused. "You didn't wait for the salve?"

Amaryllis shrugged. "Honor was impatient."

If I had known there was a numbing agent, I would've waited. Instead, I played it off. "It was only a few stitches."

"Still, I don't think you should perform tonight." Bravado placed the tin on the wagon bed.

"I can bandage the wound. It won't tear." I slid off the back of the wagon and raised my arm to show full motion and how secure the stitches were.

"No, there will be plenty of performances over the next week. But tonight, you will rest here and get better. That's an order." He rested his arms on the side of the wagon bed.

"But that means I can't get into the palace or snoop around."

"Exactly," Bravado said. "Everyone knows you're the one who saved the princess. If you show up, all eyes will be watching you. You have made yourself a hero. There will be no sneaking around for you. Let the gossip die down."

"But I was wearing face paint. That's like a disguise."

"He's right," Amaryllis said, tucking the thread and needle into a sewing box.

"What am I supposed to do?" I scanned all of the troupe members that were hard at work. Sorek pounded heavy tent stakes into the ground. Humperstink gave orders to much taller men. Even Ogress hauled over the largest center pole off one of the wagons, and with her mighty strength, shoved it into the earth without even needing a shovel. I felt the impact reverberate through the ground.

Bravado tapped his finger on the side of the wagon.

"Stay here. Help with set up, but don't go where the crowds are, and stay away from the princesses. We will do our best to investigate any rumors ourselves."

"Fine," I said.

Bravado's eyebrows shot up as if he wasn't expecting me to agree with him so easily. "Honor," he warned.

"You gave me an order. I was trained to obey orders," I said simply, raising my hands in surrender. He shot Amaryllis a wide-eyed look, and she shrugged.

Bravado brought over the evening schedule for the first group of acts that would perform for the king, his daughters, and his most esteemed guests.

I stood, slipped off the back of the wagon, and made my way toward Sorek to help with setting up the tents.

Amaryllis and Bravado departed, splitting up and each heading to a group of people to prepare the rest of camp.

Sorek finished with the tent stakes, came over, and reached for the first canvas roll. I stood to help him lift, and he gave me a stern look.

"What kind of man would I be if I let you help when you're injured? Not a good one. Go see if Humperstink needs help. I think the unicorns have been unsettled since the commotion."

I knew they were probably fine, and he was trying to find something for me to do that got me out of the way, and unicorns were an excuse. I reached under the driver's seat of the wagon and pulled out Rumple. His dangerous edges were covered with a thick leather pouch. His handle dropped out the bottom of the bag, and I had fashioned straps to wear him on my back. It didn't seem as intimidating walking around with a leather bag on my back compared to an axe.

I knew that Rumple and the dwarf Humperstink got along great. As I was heading to the far back tents, a trumpet of fanfare gave me pause. An esteemed guest must have been arriving, and I felt a pull. Without thinking, I found myself walking toward the main entrance to see who garnered such a welcome.

Just as I stepped past the bushes, a retinue of elven soldiers entered through the palace gates. I frowned as I tried to figure out what court they were from.

I moved closer to watch the entourage arrive. In two long rows, the elves rode through the gates. Their leather armor was black with silver accents; their mounts were strange beasts taller than any steeds from the northern realms. It took a few seconds for me to comprehend they weren't horses, but bear-like creatures.

The elven riders were silent. Their eyes were vacant and uncaring, as if they saw nothing, felt nothing—but I could feel the darkness within them. The fractured magic.

Southern elves. These were not the kind, loving elves of the Northern Woods. These were purveyors of dark magic. I stepped away from the gardens, and as soon as my foot touched the paved road, the air around me shimmered as another elf on a bear appeared before me.

How had I missed his glamour?

A sword touched my chest in warning. I looked up into the silver eyes of a southern elf. He didn't say anything, but I could feel his ire; his warning to back away. His bear mount shifted, and I glanced down.

I couldn't pull my gaze away from the size of the bear's massive paws, and the deadly claws that were only inches away. I missed it when the soldiers had spread out, and someone had dismounted from the largest of the bears before heading into the palace to be greeted by the king himself. With the black thorn crown, I knew it had to be Allrick, the current elder of Thornhaven Court.

"Thank you, Allrick," King Leonel said. "I see you brought your finest warriors. I know with you protecting the princesses, Lorelai Eville and her adopted daughters won't be able to lay a hand on my children or kingdom."

Allrick bowed his head in acknowledgement, but it wasn't a full bow. "We are here to serve and protect you as long as our agreement still stands. When the council of kings is over, you swear by your—"

"Yes, yes," King Leonel interrupted, looking uncomfortable. "I will keep good on my promise. You just need to make sure. . ." The king's voice trailed off as Allrick headed into the palace.

I tried to step closer but was met by a second elf guard. He raised his bow and pointed a black arrow at me.

The same kind that was found lodged in my mother's chest.

Murderers.

I backed away, slipping into the gardens and away from them with an uncomfortable realization. Their magic *was* broken. It had a funny taste to it, and I found myself stepping back not from fear, but from the desire to draw closer to their magic.

No. I should stay far away. It was safer for me—and them. It seemed my curse found them extremely interesting, and that worried me.

By nightfall, the menagerie tents had been raised, and the first night of performances were well underway within the palace. Music was wafting out of the open terraces and into the gardens. I could hear the troupe's musicians begin their melodic intros for each of the acts.

I stood on top of a stone bench on my tiptoes and was straining to catch a glimpse into the hall, but all I could see was the ceiling and the beautiful crystal chandeliers.

"Need a lift?" A deep voice came from behind me, and huge hands lifted me straight up into the air. I wobbled, and then found myself sitting comfortably on Ogress's shoulder, my hand bracing against her moss-covered head for stability.

"Thank you," I said.

"You're welcome." Ogress's voice reminded me of stones tumbling down a mountain. The ogre and I watched as the jugglers were the first act up, followed by the acrobats. "When your sister, Eden, was with the troupe, she was the real showstopper. People came from miles to see the father-daughter duo. There was no other act like it."

"I bet." I smiled, remembering the poster of Cinder De Ella, the magical girl who disappeared into cinders before your eyes.

"And now she's Queen of Candor," Ogress said.

Between the performances, the orchestra played music. A low rumble came from the earth, and I felt a shaking sensation. I was prepared to jump, thinking there was an earthquake except it wasn't. Ogress was growling in disapproval. I followed the direction of her glare. In the palace, I saw the blonde princess on the dance floor. She was the one that Grace had glared at earlier on the front steps. The young blonde princess was dressed in pale blue, looking as beautiful and just as angelic as ever. The other princesses followed, and each one was quickly claimed by one of the many gentlemen who came to the palace for a chance to woo a princess.

"Not right," Ogress growled out.

"What's not right?" I asked, adjusting my posture to try to see who was the suitor that was dancing with her. It looked like Lord Rasmen, the man who'd beat his servant in the streets.

"The stars are not fortuitous. I foresee death this night."

"I've already saved Princess Grace's life. She's safe."

"It's not her I'm worried about." Ogress sighed.

"Who then?" I asked, but she fell silent.

With a furrowed brow, I tried to crane my neck and get a closer look. Frustrated that I was not allowed into the palace, I vowed that I would be performing tomorrow, no matter how injured I was. I would get stronger, heal fast, and get inside the hall. I wanted to see the southern elves, follow that princess. There were too many secrets, and I was so close.

Even as I watched with envy, I could feel my body start to quicken with adrenaline.

The dance was over, and the crowd parted as another group of acrobats came onto the floor. The show was just getting good when Ogress turned and headed back toward her tent.

"Wait, I'm not finished watching. There's more I'd like to see—"

"You are done for tonight. You're very draining," she said.

"I'm sorry, I'll stop talking. I—" I paused and felt how *not* tired I was, and knew the ogre was not referring to exasperation. "How did you know? I mean, I didn't mean to."

"You think I don't know about your kind? I may be old, but I'm not foolish." Ogress reached up and pulled me off her shoulder, very carefully putting me down on the ground.

"My kind? What do you know of my kind? What am I?"

"It's not my place to tell you. The time is not right." Ogress stopped outside of her tent and gestured for me to go inside. "This tent was made by Lorelai before she ever adopted any of you. Before you, dear Honor, were even born. It was warded with her magic to amplify the gifts of whoever is inside. She may not have foreseen the true purpose of creating this tent, or its future purpose when she imbued it with magic and wards all those years ago, but I've foreseen it. It was not made for me, or for Bravado's fortune-teller. It was made for you."

"Me?"

"Sleep, Honor, and you will understand." The ogress pushed me inside her tent, and I tripped onto the giant velvet pillow inside—the one she sat on and told fortunes.

I sunk into the softness, and as soon as I did, I felt my body tingle as I began to absorb the magic that was spelled within the canvas walls. It was the same as touching a ley line.

As I lay there, a warmth touched my hip, and I knew

that my body was healing. I could feel the aching leave. It was the same as when I passed through the veil of the elven realms. Tears filled my eyes as I stared up at the top of the tent. But this time, it was for a different reason. It wasn't because of how the magic made me feel, but for what was hand-stitched onto the canvas tent roof. Lorelai was preparing for me; protecting me before I was ever born. The stitching faded with age, and a few threads had broken and were dangling from the top. But there was no mistaking my mother's handiwork, or her familiar script.

Another tear slipped down my face as I read aloud the two words stitched in canvas.

ABOVE ALL, DO IT FOR HONOR

Whether it was her mantra to bring honor to the kingdoms and right wrongs, or if it was for me. I didn't know.

I slept like the dead, and when I awoke the next morning, it was to see that the stitches had already healed themselves. The bruises had faded to a yellow as if they'd been healing for weeks.

When I stood up, my body was vibrating with pent-up energy, and I knew I may need to run a few miles to burn it off.

The tent flap opened, and a morning breeze tickled my skin before the flap closed. I knew it wasn't the wind.

"Nimm?"

The terrified gnome appeared in the middle of the tent, waving his hands and pointing outside.

As I stepped out, it was to the array of frantic troupe

members. I saw the ogress come out of my old tent and I asked her, "What's wrong?"

The palace guard was speaking with Bravado and Amaryllis. At least it looked like neither of them were being arrested, just informed. When they were done, they came to me.

"It seems Lord Rasmen is missing," Bravado said, carefully hiding his worry by clasping his hands in front of him.

"Missing as in kidnapped, or missing as in he went for a walk and didn't return?" I asked.

"No one knows," Bravado said. "It seems that Lord Rasmen and all of his servants have disappeared into thin air, leaving all of his trunks and belongings behind."

"I find that hard to believe," I said loudly. "That man was too full of himself to leave a stitch of clothing behind."

"Hush, Honor," Bravado warned, his voice dropping low as more guards went past us into the palace. "It's best to keep a low profile. Head down, don't ask too many questions. Remember, we are *the help*, and those in authority will talk freely around us because they believe we can't think for ourselves. But I agree, I don't think they just disappeared on their own."

As he spoke, the flame from the nearest campfire turned blue and flickered as it grew in height and temperature. A spark of paper shot out of the flames and floated right to Bravado. He snatched it out of the air.

Bravado held out a scrap of paper with burned edges. Even as he held it, the parchment crumbled away to ash. I recognized it as one of my mother's spells. As she scried the kingdoms watching through her magic mirror, she would often send messages to Lorn through the fire. It was an enchantment that could send a few words, a message, or a phrase. She'd toss it into the flames and it would burn up. Then it would fly out of the fire nearest the one to whom it was addressed before quickly crumbling into ashes once the message was read.

In the past, it had always been directions toward trouble within the towns, or a warning of rogue beasts that were causing problems, so I knew it would be similar.

"There was another attack by the son of Allemar." His voice was grave.

"When? Where?" I asked.

"Last night. There was an assault on the peaceful centaur herd near Vailhaim. Just like before, the attack came out of nowhere and disappeared just as fast."

Immediately, my mind was filled with visions of the hellhounds in the Northern Woods. "What kind of creatures attacked?" I asked.

"Brackenbeasts."

"Brackenbeasts," I breathed out. They were the legendary creatures of Sion, with the head of a lion, horns of a bull, and the strength of a bear—one of the things that formed from the tainted ley line of the sacred hollow of Thornhaven. If it wasn't for the southern elves, there wouldn't be an issue. "Werewolves, hellhounds, brackenbeasts, omnis." I ticked off the creatures that had been sighted at the attacks. "None of these species would ever work together on their own. Not unless they were controlled by someone."

Bravado nodded. "I agree. It really does seem to be the work of the son of Allemar."

Humperstink and Sorek had made their way over to us, the former walking with a limp.

"And all of these creatures originated because of the

deviated ley line of magic in Sion. I have to think that the disappearances, the arrival of the southern elves, the attacks, the entrance to the sacred hollow, and the son of Allemar are all connected," I said.

The clatter of armor made my heart jump as another retinue of soldiers marched past us heading toward the palace.

Bending low to adjust the slipper I was wearing, I whispered, "What do we do?"

Amaryllis wrung her hands and looked up at the palace. "The show must go on. We get inside and continue to gather information. We map the halls, escape routes, take notes of guard rotations, find the access points for attacks, gather any news from the servants about Lord Rasmen's disappearance, and track the movements of the southern elves."

"They are going to be locked down pretty tight to outsiders," Bravado said, rubbing his face in thought. "More dignitaries are arriving every day. Humperstink said he only marked one wing. Guards almost caught him. Luckily, he was able to use his earth magic to give them the slip, but he set off a ward."

"The wailing would not stop," Humperstink said as he pulled up his pant leg and I saw a burn across his skin.

"This is too dangerous for you. I should be the one marking the wards and searching for the son of Allemar. I can do it. Just let me perform tonight," I said.

"No," Humperstink and Bravado both answered at once.

"I'm fine, really. I'm healed." I pulled open the edges of my ripped fabric, and Amaryllis's face paled at seeing the almost perfect skin.

"How?" she asked in disbelief.

"Long story, but believe me, I think I'm the one that needs to do this job. I think my mother knew."

Bravado and Amaryllis exchanged a long look before agreeing. "We've always trusted your mother, and now we trust that you know what to do."

CHAPTER FIFTEEN

The metal ring sparkled as it was being hoisted high above the chandelier in the center of the ballroom. It was dizzying watching it slowly spin. I'd never performed at that height, but it didn't matter. If I was ten feet off the ground or thirty, it was all marble below me. I watched as Humperstink pounded the ring's fasteners into the stonework.

"Are you sure this will hold?" I asked, my voice echoing in the empty ballroom.

"It will hold. One thing I pride myself on is knowing rock." As a dwarf, Humperstink had an affinity for earth magic, and he was the one who had found the strongest part of the ceiling and had scaled the ladder supported by Sorek.

Humperstink released the silk, and it fell in a cloud of red toward the marble floor.

"Give it a swing," he called down.

I wrapped the silk around my upper arms and lifted myself into the air, hanging a few feet from the ground. "Seems okay. Sorek?" I turned for his opinion.

Sorek waited for Humperstink to descend the ladder. Then he grabbed the silks and did the same thing, pulling

159

harder than I had to make sure that it would hold someone of his immense weight.

"It's sturdy," he admitted.

"See?" Humperstink said proudly.

"Don't gloat. It's not becoming for a man of your age," Rumple said from within the backpack that was leaning against the floor.

"My age? You're the youngin'. You need to respect your elders."

"Elders?" Rumple argued. "I'm over two hundred years old."

"You can't count how long you were imprisoned in rock, you idiot," Humperstink challenged.

"Can too."

"Not."

I chuckled and allowed the two to bicker back and forth. It seemed like it was what dwarves were meant to do. It reminded me of a small dog I had seen once in a village. The smaller dog always seemed to bark and challenge any dog larger than himself. Rumple—well, he liked to challenge everyone.

A ruffle of color in the hall caught my attention. I moved from the ballroom to the double doors and peeked out between the crack in the open door.

It was two of the princesses, Lisbelle and Grace. "You need to be more careful, Lisbelle. It's not safe to wander about . . . alone," Grace said softly.

"It's our home. How are we not safe within our home?" Lisbelle taunted.

"That's not what I mean, and you know it."

Lisbelle spun and grabbed Grace's arm, digging her

fingernails into the flesh. "I don't have to listen to you," Lisbelle snapped.

"Stop, you're hurting me." Grace tried to pull away, but Lisbelle wouldn't have it.

"Lisbelle, if you won't listen, then it will be *you who pays the price*." Grace's voice dropped so low that I wasn't sure if I had heard her right.

As if on cue, Allrick came up behind the princesses, his aura intimidating.

Lisbelle's face drained of color. She backed up a few steps and her head dropped toward the floor. There was a whispered response, but it was beyond what I could hear. Allrick nodded and moved away, and the princesses retreated down the opposite hall. I stepped into the hall and watched them turn the corner.

I followed, but was stopped by a guard.

"Only royals beyond this point." He held out his arm, blocking my path. I watched helplessly as the two princesses continued down the hall.

"Yes, sir," I said, and headed back to the ballroom. It was the only room we were allowed access to for the time being.

Who were they referring to? Allrick? Someone else?

"Can you follow them?" I whispered under my breath.

Out of the corner of my eye, I saw a flicker and then nothing as Nimm took off, slipping between the guard's legs.

By nightfall, the palace ballroom was packed with nobles from all across the kingdom. The white marble floors were polished so smooth they gleamed in the candlelight.

Creeping roses covered the columns almost to the ceiling, filling the room with a pleasant aroma. Stained glass windows depicting even more flowers turned the ballroom into an indoor garden. Enchanted chandeliers hung around the room and flickered with glowing light.

Even though I hadn't been in the palace long, I caught a glimpse here and there of a house-elf appearing to bring out food or replenish drinks before disappearing into the walls as if they walked through them.

I had long ago learned from Eden that many of the palaces had secret compartments and hidden passages that led from the lower kitchen to the dining rooms, where they would bring up food on a pulley system. If a fae disappeared, it was usually into a hidden door, cupboard, or behind a painting. Already, I had taken note of where these hidden passageways were.

There were two in the ballroom. One behind a tapestry of a man with dark hair, possibly a young King Leonel, sitting on his throne. With the speed at which drink trays were being brought up and replenished by human servants, I assumed another was hidden behind a painting of a fountain.

A soldier wearing the yellow and black colors of Sion came down the hall, and I retreated into the room, closing the door a few more inches until he passed. Then I flung it open and stared across the hall into the ballroom as the king's steward, Wentworth, an elderly man in yellow robes with diamonds on the collar, spectacles, and a mustache, announced the arrival of the princesses in order from oldest to youngest. Analisa, the eldest, followed by Karisa, Louisa, Marisa, Risa, Therisa, Grace, Annabelle, Clarabelle, Lisbelle, Mirabelle, and Willabelle.

The moment Willabelle's violet dress slipped off the last carpeted step as she descended from the upper balcony, eager men swarmed the twelve daughters of Sion like greedy vultures circling their prey. When one suitor stepped away from the pearl and silk adorned princesses, another took his place. From across the carpeted hall, I hovered in the doorway, watching the men with suspicion. Each one could be here under false pretenses. One of them could be a secret sorcerer, weeding his way into a princess's heart and into the throne room with the sole intent to kill and destroy in the name of Allemar.

"They have to be here," I whispered under my breath as I watched the nearest man. He looked heavenly in a green suit with a black cloak, but I searched for any hint of malcontent in the way he moved or skirted the room with his eyes. He could be one of Allemar's apprentices. Then I saw his gaze rest longingly on the banquet table full of finger foods.

Eh. Probably not.

"Excuse me," Sorek mumbled as he shuffled past me in the cramped storage room. It was all we were given as a staging area for all the props and performers needed for tonight's performances.

Bravado paced the floor while Humperstink scrambled around gathering up the basket of spilled juggling balls.

"Why are they acting this way?" I asked Bravado, watching as the princess with dark red hair waved off a handsome suitor. She didn't seem interested at all in any of the attention bestowed on her, but it didn't deter him.

"The king has no male heirs." Bravado was watching the same thing I was. Men strutting about like peacocks trying to impress the young ladies who didn't even seem interested.

I frowned as I quickly counted out each of the daughters. With them having three different mothers, their looks varied from blonde to brunette, and two had red hair. "Well, wouldn't Princess Analisa be first in line for the throne as the oldest?" I asked, angling my chin to the tall brunette in a red dress.

"You would assume, but again, that's not how the law of ascension works in Sion. King Leonel is determined it must go to a male, and since he was cursed to bear no sons, it has been a bit of a stalemate." Bravado's mouth went up in a smirk. "Cursed by your mother, by the way. It will have to go to the next in line for the throne."

I hadn't kept up with the lineage of the king of Sion, unlike my other sisters, who treated royal gossip like it was dessert. "Which is . . ." I tried to think of the various land-holders, and how they were related to the king.

"Lord Rasmen," Bravado said softly.

"But he's—"

"Disappeared? Dead? Exactly. And the next in line with the biggest land holding is Lord Dyer." Bravado gestured with his chin, to the man who was as tall as he was wide. Dress in red velvet and a green hat with a feather, he resembled a bloated tomato. "I can only assume that he may be next to wind up the same as Lord Rasmen."

I watched the burly Lord Dyer waddle onto the dance floor and place himself right in front of Princess Grace, making it impossible for her current suitor to dance around him.

A few words were spoken, and the man abandoned the princess to Lord Dyer. He bowed and reached for Princess

Grace's hand and pulled her into a dance, much to her dismay. Her eyes went wide, and she kept craning her neck, looking for someone to help.

Grace's dark curls were pinned up with pearl pins, and her soft green off-the-shoulder dress made her look young, but I suspected she was around the same age as me.

Bravado twitched his mustache and pointed to Princess Grace. "Have you noticed that the one in the green dress looks a lot like—"

"Me," I finished. "I know."

"How odd. Now I understand your choice of attire. It would definitely draw unwanted attention."

I adjusted the silk ties on the mask, making sure it wouldn't slip down my face during my performance.

Bravado moved away from the door and was back to pacing a wear pattern in the fancy rug. He began going over the order of performances, which included jesters, more acrobatic tumbling, and ending with my aerial silk routine.

I waited until there was a lull in the orchestra music, then Bravado pointed to me. "It's time."

I pulled at the bottom of the skimpy leotard and grinned in triumph knowing Amaryllis couldn't slap my hand away. I knew I was a mesmerizing sight. Dressed in silver and blue, my silver-painted mask was adorned with small clear crystals gently glued around the eyes. Even my nails were painted blue.

I took a deep breath, cocked my hip to the side, and raised my chin. It was time to become someone I was not. I rose to my tiptoes and walked barefoot across the hall on the arm of Bravado.

"You really did well during the parade," Bravado whispered under his breath.

"I was fighting my enemies," I said, smiling as the crowd parted before allowing us inside the grand ballroom. All eyes were on us as we stepped to the center of the room. I could either tremble beneath the scrutiny or use it to my advantage.

"There are plenty of enemies to slay in this room," Bravado chuckled. "Knock 'em dead." Bravado motioned to the drummer, who began a drumroll. "Ladies and gentlemen, we have a stunning performance for your enjoyment tonight," Bravado called out, his voice raising to a crescendo. With a twirl, he released me, and I spun, lifting my hands, trying to be as graceful as I could, and then slowed in the direct center of the room.

He nodded to the palace servants, and they snuffed out the candelabras and lowering the chandeliers, casting the room into darkness.

Gasps of surprise followed, and I smiled as the flutist from the troupe began a well-known song. One that I had practiced a routine to.

The silk drop into my hands and quickly I climbed up, as if I was scaling the vines on the cliffs of Craeton. Silent and with purpose, I counted down how long I had as I prepared myself. Bravado snapped his fingers and the glass chimes that hung from the ceiling came to life, illuminating the silver tones of my leotard as I hung suspended thirty feet in the air, silk wrapped around only one arm.

More gasps of surprise followed when Sorek stepped onto the floor, grasped the silk, and began to spin me. I arched my back, elongated my arm, and looked up at the ceiling as we went faster and faster. I closed my eyes and focused on riding out the wave until he slowed.

Now came the next part of the show, where I formed knots and swung as if on a swing. Then I wrapped them around my feet and ankles, balanced in the air, slowly lowering myself into the splits, while grasping the silks with my hands.

With each stunt, I could hear the princesses gasp, and the danger of what I was doing only fueled the adrenaline within me. I wanted to do more. Crazier stunts and faster. I slipped down the silks to the floor, wrapped them around my upper arms, and took off running in a circle to the closest edge of the crowd, which quickly backed up when they saw what I was doing. I leapt into the air and flew like a butterfly, my toes pointed, the red silks flowing behind my back.

I laughed as I touched down again and ran faster, as the desire to fly higher overcame me. As I passed an intimidating group of men, I felt my stomach drop. It was the southern elves. Dressed in midnight jewel tones, they were just on the edges of the shadow, not lit by the enchanted glass circle of Bravado's magic, which created a lit ring on the white marble floor. As I took a second pass and flew near the elves, I felt a pang. A familiar warning of danger.

I slowed, tiptoeing to the center, my heart racing as I stared out into the sea of shadowy faces. My gut was telling me danger, but I didn't know what or where the threat was coming from.

I stalled in the middle of the floor, scanning the room, my chest rising with each panicked breath. Something was wrong. I caught the barest glimmer. Someone was using glamour magic and hiding among the crowd.

Was I being paranoid?

Then another flicker and I saw the tapestry move, and I sighed. It was only the house-elves. The fae were using their magic to keep out of sight.

Bravado caught my eye. He was watching the crowd and trying to judge my expression. He mouthed the words, "Are you okay?" He started to move to the center of the room, and I had a feeling he was going to stop the performance.

I shook my head and plastered a fake smile on my face. I had to keep going. I couldn't disappoint the troupe or the king. I needed to do my job. Bravado retreated to the side and gave me an encouraging nod.

It was time for the finale. I gripped the ends of the silks, securing them around my waist and body to form a safety knot. Slowly, I climbed higher and higher, gathering and wrapping myself into a cocoon of red silk. As I reached the hook in the ceiling, I had a moment of doubt at what I was going to attempt but pushed it aside. I trusted myself. I knew I did everything right. The flute solo was rising in pitch and was about to do a dramatic trill, and I counted . . . the moment the melody dropped, so did I.

A feminine scream ripped through the air as the silks disintegrated around me. I plummeted straight for the ground. I reached out for the silks, my safety line, but they were gone. Flower petals fell through my fingers, and I saw the white marble floor rush toward me.

CHAPTER SIXTEEN

Death came for me as a painful black cloud. One moment I was falling, the next, a hammer slammed into my body, and I gasped.

My chest constricted as I struggled to inhale as strong arms held me tight. My face was buried against a muscled chest, my eyes closed in disbelief. Someone had caught me. I still wasn't sure how, except for their extraordinarily fast reflexes. The beating of their heart thudded loudly against my ear. I breathed in the familiar scent of airy pine and a hint of the never flowers, which instantly reminded me of the Northern Woods.

Percy!

He couldn't be here, but yet . . . he was.

With gentleness, Percy let my feet touch the floor as he held onto my waist and spun, giving a bow to the crowd. He held my hand above my head, twirled me before the audience and then lowered me backward into a dip, my hair cascading down, my foot naturally rising into the air.

The crowd came to life with applause at the grand finale.

Bent over backward, I stared up at Percy in disbelief as

he humored the crowd with his dashing smile. He was dressed all in black, his blonde hair pulled back. Easily, I counted the number of throwing knives he had in his vest, the slight bulge on his outer thigh concealing the hidden dagger, and the tenseness with which he held my hand. He had come prepared for war. It was Percy I was sensing, hiding from the audience.

"This time it seemed you fell into my lap," he teased as his eyes scanned the room for danger.

"I sensed you," I whispered out the side of my mouth.

He pulled me back up, his right hands firmly around my waist, his left waving at the crowd. "I knew the moment you did."

I looked up toward the ceiling, at the hook with the missing silks. Red petals continued to fall around me like snow. One touched my cheek and it dissolved, and I felt the smattering of warm liquid.

I flung out my hand with a flourish and pointed to the petals, playing the crowd as if it was all part of the show. But I knew better—someone had tried to kill me and would have succeeded if it hadn't been for Percy.

Percy stilled, his back tensing. I spun, following his gaze, and settled on the corner where the southern elves had gathered around their leader. It wasn't Allrick that caught my attention, but Ardax, who stood at his side.

"What is Ardax doing with *them*?" I hissed.

"The same as I am," he answered.

"What?"

Percy spun me, forcing me to refocus my attention as I had to bow before the twelve princesses and King Leonel. When I glanced up, Grace could not take her eyes off of me. There was desperation in the way she was trying to meet my gaze. Had she made the connection of how close we look even beneath my mask?

"I need to leave," I whispered. Percy held my hand, and in the most unelf-like fashion, jumped and pranced out into the hall. As I tried to match his enthusiasm, I slipped on one of the rose petals and was disgusted to see it turn to liquid.

Blood?

Bravado filled in brilliantly as we made our hasty exit. He began a grand speech, calling attention to not only my aerial display, but the extreme death-defying feat that followed.

The crowd erupted into a grand display of clapping, whistles, and shouts.

"Encore!"

We slipped into the storage room, and I collapsed on the trunk. Immediately, my body betrayed me. I buried my face in my hands, trembled, and struggled to get my breathing under control. Great panicked gasps racked my body as I mentally processed what had just occurred. I had almost died.

Percy dropped to the floor in front of me, pulling me into his lap, placing my face against his chest.

"Honor, you're safe. I'm here. You're safe."

"I-I can't," I gasped as the panic attack continued to grow and my lungs constricted, but it wasn't just the breathing. I could feel my cursed magic grasping out in fear, reaching for Percy. I tried to shove him away, to keep us safe.

He wrapped his arms even tighter around me. "Don't push me away. Not again."

He refused to let me go. I tried, but Percy wasn't going

to let me win. Instead, I closed my eyes and visualized walls to try to control my curse. I could feel it reaching for Percy, as it was triggered by my fear.

Never had I felt fear like that. Even fighting a horde of goblins or being swallowed up by a giant wave in Ter Dell was something I could face because I had a weapon.

There was no weapon to fight this feeling that washed over me as Percy pressed his lips gently into my temple, leaving a soft kiss upon my brow.

How did one fight falling in love?

With each gentle kiss, he chased away my fears and darkness. My hands pressed against his chest, and I could feel the frantic beating of his heart as it matched mine.

My heart raced, my fear edged away, and I was able to put the monster back into its cage as I tried to hold on to this moment.

"Honor," he breathed out my name.

Percy lifted my chin, wiped a tear from my face, and leaned in to claim my lips. I felt myself reaching up to meet his, and then Bravado, Sorek, and Humperstink came rushing into the room. I pulled away in surprise.

"What in the stars happened out there?" Bravado asked.

"The silks just . . . they disappeared," Humperstink said. "The clasps are still secure."

"Someone cast a transfiguration spell," Sorek added. "In front of all those people."

"You could have died," Humperstink growled out.

"I think that was their intent," Bravado said, looking at me. "Do you think it's because someone knows who you are?"

I'd stepped away from Percy, putting as much distance

between us as I could in the small space. "I don't see how they could know. We worked hard to disguise my identity with face paint and masks, plus no one knows what I look like except you and—" My eyes rested on Percy's black doublet, pants, and the intricate silver details that seemed familiar to what Ardax was wearing. "Percy, why are you dressed like the southern elves?" I asked, fearful of the answer.

Percy straightened his shoulders, and he looked me straight in the eye. "Because I am one."

I swallowed and felt my stomach drop. *He knew.* He knew how much I despised them.

"They killed my mother," I whispered in anger.

A flash of pain flickered across Percy's face. "I know that's what you think, but it's not the truth."

"And you never once thought to tell me the truth about who you are?"

"I was trying to spare you more pain."

Sorek's eyes narrowed, his lips pinched, and he rubbed the back of his bald head. "Bravado, should we give them some time alone?"

"No," I said.

"Yes," Percy said at the same time.

I glared at him, and he just glared back. The tension in the room between us grew, and I could see the others becoming uncomfortable with the situation.

I was about to lay into Percy when the king's steward interrupted us with a knock on the door frame.

"Pardon me." Wentworth waved for Bravado's attention. The troupe leader went to the door and spoke in hushed tones with the steward.

I watched their exchange on pins and needles. Bravado closed the door and turned to give me a worried look.

"I'm sorry, but we've been ordered to continue with another set of performances. I'll get another act ready. Will you be okay?" He addressed me, but looked at Percy with distrust.

"I'll be fine. Go," I said.

Bravado and the others left and headed back into the ballroom.

As soon as we were alone, Percy shook his head. "I'm sorry, Honor. I still can't believe you're here and alive.

I shrugged and stood up quickly. "You know, it takes more than a horde of hellhounds and a sorcerer to kill me." My thoughts were still reeling from the almost-kiss and the overwhelming sense of betrayal.

"It seems so." Percy took note of my distance, and there was a tightness around his mouth. "Honor, what happened that night when you went into the tear in the veil? No word, no clue, no sign of you. I begged Rethulian to find you with his magic. All he could tell me is that you were not in this realm. I assumed the worst."

I quickly explained what happened; the piles of ash I awoke to, how Rumple was missing, and my journey to the palace.

He shook his head in disbelief. "How. . ." He rubbed his chin and began to work out the magic. "I don't understand how you survived. That's amazing."

"But why are *you*"—I pointed to him, showing my confusion, and then pointed to the ground—"*here?*"

Percy's look became dark, his brows furrowed. "Immediately after the attack, Ardax and I were summoned to return to Thornhaven Court."

"Why?"

"There's been an issue with the current Denizens of the sacred hollow."

"What's wrong with the Denizens?" I asked, worried about what would happen if the magic of that tainted ley line were to get loose.

"They . . . keep dying." His voice dropped, and I heard his frustration.

"But elves live unnaturally long lives," I said. "Your kind doesn't die from sickness or disease."

Percy's mouth tightened in anger. "I know that. We know that. I have no idea what's going on except that Allrick has made some kind of deal with the king in hopes of gaining power, land and wealth." He raised his green eyes to meet mine, and I saw the weariness. "We are supposed to protect his daughters from evil, but not any evil. The daughters of Eville."

"Me," I breathed out.

"King Leonel hates your mother and believes she's wrongfully stolen the other kingdoms' thrones with magic. It has caused quite a commotion, and he knows there's one more daughter out there." He gave me a sad smile. "If you do try to harm one of the daughters of Sion, I'll be forced to stop you by any means necessary." I was taken aback at the insinuation, my brows furrowing. He subconsciously pulled his sleeve down to cover a mark on his wrist that was visible without his bracer.

I caught the movement, but he crossed his arms, blocking my view.

He studied me and I had a feeling I was going to hate whatever was going to come out of his mouth next.

Percy reached out and grabbed my upper arm, leaning

down, and he whispered to me while his eyes never left the open door. "Honor, you must leave here. I've been hearing things. Whispers about the other kings' arrivals. I can't guarantee your safety."

"And that's precisely why I can't leave. I have to stay to protect my family, *and* the kingdoms. It's my *duty*." I said the word duty with anger and pulled out of his grasp. Knowing he, too, understood the heaviness of the word.

Percy went still, his eyes narrowed in disbelief.

"You would die for a kingdom that doesn't accept you and fears your sisters?"

"Just because they fear what they don't understand doesn't mean they aren't worth fighting for," I said nobly.

"But are they worth dying for?" Percy snarled.

"I don't intend on dying. Just as you will fight for your cause, I will fight for mine."

"I knew you'd say that." His lips pressed together. "I can see by the way you're dressed that you aren't carrying a weapon. Unless you have Rumple stashed somewhere in that extremely revealing outfit."

I crossed my arms over my chest and suddenly felt extremely self-conscious.

"I wasn't sure if he would trip the protection wards in the palace."

Percy's face fell, his eyes cast downward. "I'm not sure. Elves and dwarves have a long-standing hatred of each other. Even though Rumple is an enchanted weapon, his aura still comes across as a real dwarf. It's only certain magic that sets them off."

"He'll be thrilled about that," I said softly. Percy was trying to keep his distance, and I could see the wall close off his feelings, and he buried his emotions deep. I felt I needed to apologize for hurting him with how I'd behaved the last time we saw each other.

"I'm sorry about going to the ceremony with Ardax. I—"

"Honor, stay far away from him," Percy interrupted. "I can't say for sure, but I think it was Ardax who tried to kill you earlier."

"Did he recognize me?" I breathed out, my hand subconsciously touching my face.

"I did, but I could recognize you no matter how much paint you try to disguise yourself with, and no matter the outfits you wear to distract from your face. I will always know you."

He bowed his head, and a group of nobles passed into the ballroom. Percy went with them and blended into the crowd seamlessly, his glamour not affecting any of the wards.

Emotions flooded me. He'd almost kissed me. He'd kept secrets about his origins, never once trusting me to know the truth. Our entire exchange was hot and cold. He'd saved me. Then told me to leave? Telling me he'd stop me by any means necessary? Thinking I would harm the princesses? My hands balled into angry fists, my fingers digging into my palms. Who was this person? This wasn't the same elf I had trained with in the Northern Woods.

I untied the face mask, opened the trunk, and pulled out a pair of pants and a black shirt. Slipping them over my leotard, I tucked a blade into a hidden pocket. I dropped the mask into the trunk and pulled out a pair of boots. No longer did I feel exposed, my armor and weapons firmly back in place, and the dagger tucked away in my pants. I sighed in remorse as I stared at the trunk, knowing what was coming next. I was ready to face whatever danger came my way.

Even if the danger was Percy.

CHAPTER SEVENTEEN

My leg muscles were cramping, and I could no longer feel my toes. Tingling had worn away to numbness. My shoulder was wedged at an odd angle and the darkness was all-consuming as I focused on breathing. Timing each breath in and holding it before releasing it slowly, all while listening for the last of the guests to return to their room.

Bravado and Sorek had returned after the final performance of the evening and had carefully moved the props around the room, positioning the trunk behind a chair and covering it with a blanket.

"Good luck," Bravado whispered, giving the trunk a light tap.

I tapped back once and then began the long wait, judging the passage of time by the breaths I took and listening for the sounds of feet moving down the hall. When all was quiet and nothing stirred for several candle marks, I pushed open the trunk and unfolded my body. I'd been stretching since my first attempt had failed, but I had finally mastered squeezing into the impossibly small trunk.

Saphira would be proud.

My back cracked as I stretched my hands above my

head, and I delicately put pressure on my feet until the pins and needles faded away. It was painful, but I was in the palace. I pressed my ear to the door and listened before pulling the handle, pleased at the silence of the hinges that Sorek had freshly oiled just that evening.

Bravado and Nimm had given me all the information they could about the layout of the palace and had made a hastily drawn map, which I committed to memory. I knew precisely where the royal living quarters and the servants' hall were, but there was one wing that was heavily guarded against magic. Even the house-elves avoided that particular wing.

"There!" Bravado had tapped the map. "There is where you must go. Do you see how that area of the palace is over a ley line; do you see all the wards around it? There must be something hidden there. You must get here undetected. Can you do it?"

"I can do it," I said.

"Then we must practice." He'd unloaded a trunk from the wagon and opened it up, showing the many props within, but then he'd pushed them aside to reveal the false bottom. Just big enough to hold a very small person.

I wasn't worried about making my way through most of the palace, as I easily slipped past the half-asleep guards who were positioned outside of the throne room. Twice I'd scaled a marble column while guards passed by me before slipping down and moving toward the forbidden wing.

I felt a tug on my leg and looked down to see Nimm frantically pulling away from the hall, pointing at the floor and then back at his neck. I gestured for him to wait before kneeling to examine the trap.

A ward was here. That meant magic, which meant I

could either set it off or nullify it. I lifted my hand over it and felt the beginning of an electric shock, and I pulled it back to safety.

I chewed on my lower lip as I leaned close to study the ward. I knew nothing of magic or spells. I couldn't even read the sigils on the ward, or decipher what kind of attack or blow it would do to me. But I had to remind myself, I wasn't like my other sisters. I didn't have magic. I couldn't control it or manipulate it. I just nullified it.

I ran my fingers along the outer edge and felt the hum of magic. Like before, I pulled at it, like tugging on a string of a child's top. Not so fast as to spin it, but slowly as to unwind it without making it wobble. I absorbed the magic, feeling refreshed, and I sensed a hum of energy as the ward slowly died.

I stood, preparing to step over the ward. My hands trembled. Had I done enough? Pushing one foot out, I brushed the edge of the invisible ward and felt nothing. The ward was cold and dead. Confidently, I stepped on it and turned to Nimm, who took more time working up his nerve to cross it. Once he put his boot on the ward, he did a little dance before scooting ahead to scout, disappearing before my eyes. I deactivated two more magical wards and felt full afterward—almost intoxicated and sleepy. I continued exploring the wing, making a mental map as I headed toward the special wing of the palace that was over the convergence of two ley lines.

This is it. The answers I searched for were just on the other side of those doors. A secret back way into Thornhaven. Or maybe I would be lucky enough to stumble into a secret lair of Allemar's apprentices. In Florin, Rosalie had found a dungeon where Allemar had done blood sacrifices to amplify his power. I could only assume that the missing people of Sion were disappearing for the same dark purposes, which meant the apprentices were probably here.

I paused in front of a set of double doors with gold flowers. I kneeled in front of the door, staring into the heavy gold lock. As I was about to pull the lock and pick set out of my hair, Nimm came rushing down the hall, his hands waving in excitement.

"What's going on?" I asked him.

The gnome beckoned me to follow, and we slipped up a set of back stairs used by servants. It took us to a small balcony that overlooked the golden door, just as a retinue of soldiers marched down the hall.

Their captain, a man with a red cloak instead of black like the other seven guards, took out a golden key and unlocked the door, ushering the guards inside.

"Remember, no one leaves or enters these rooms, do you understand?"

"Yes, Captain Lathe," one of the guards said.

"Protect them at all costs," the captain demanded.

"We will," a second guard added.

They saluted, and then the captain sent in five soldiers and locked them inside while two more kept guard outside.

I frowned.

This was an unexpected turn of events.

But now we were trapped. I couldn't head back down without walking in front of the guards. It was time to wait until the guards changed. I curled up and felt Nimm slide into my lap for warmth as we prepared for the long night ahead.

My eyes were heavy, and my back was sore as I waited

for morning. Soon the sun warmed my face, and I yawned. I rubbed my eyes and glanced over my shoulder to see that Nimm had dozed off as well. When I cast a look over the balcony, I was surprised to see the guards were gone. Before I could make my escape down the stairs, the hall echoed with the sound of armor and more guards.

We froze on our balcony as Captain Lathe and the king appeared.

"Where are the guards?" King Leonel accused.

"I don't know, Your Majesty." Captain Lathe turned in a circle, just as confused.

He leaned forward, pressing his ear to the golden door. "It's quiet." He gestured to his men and pulled out a key from his belt. He unlocked the door and flung it open. His soldiers went into the room, and from my perch above, I could see an opulent sitting room with green rugs and an ornate wooden table. I turned my head sideways to see another hall.

They went in quietly, swords drawn and ready to fight an army, but nothing happened. No fighting, no clashing of weapons, and no sounds followed. A grave-looking Captain Lathe came out and bowed before his king.

"How are they?" the king asked, wringing his hands.

"All the princesses are sleeping peacefully."

"And their shoes?"

"Same as before. Destroyed."

The princesses? These golden doors and this heavily warded hall led to the princesses chambers? They weren't in the royal wing with the king?

I chewed on the inside of my cheek in thought. It would make sense that the king wanted to protect his daughters behind multiple magical wards. Maybe that was the reason he moved them to a more protected wing of the palace; for the ley lines to charge the wards. He was really terrified of my family.

But what had happened to the guards that were there last night?

A commotion followed as a young guard rushed out, his face ashen. He leaned over and whispered to Captain Lathe, who in turn addressed the king. His face equally as pallid, a bead of sweat formed on his forehead. "It seems one of the guards has been located in the sitting room, Your Highness."

The soldiers struggled to carry a heavy makeshift stretcher and covered it in a sheet out into the hall. They were rushing, as if scared of being caught within the room.

The king's face drained of color. "Don't tell me it happened again . . ."

Captain Lathe nodded. "Unfortunately so."

The first guard struggled with the corner he was holding, and in his hurry, lost his hold. The stretcher fell, and the sheet slipped off to reveal a dead guard.

"He's been dead for quite some time. His body is cold to the touch."

King Leonel groaned. "Where are the others?"

"No sign of them."

"Then we will say they robbed and killed Remus, then ran away to avoid punishment."

"Very well, my king."

Two more guards jumped in to help remove the dead corpse and haul him away.

"But how do we stop this? Those were my very best guards."

"It wasn't as if my daughters were able to slip past both

of them. New slippers are destroyed, and they sleep all day. This is not normal behavior. I think they're under a spell. The other kings are set to arrive soon. If they find out about what's happening here, it could start a war."

"Are we not already on the brink of one?" Captain Lathe sighed. "I'm doing my best to keep neighboring lords from encroaching on our borders. Since you have no male heirs, the southern elves think the lands should revert back to them."

"I would rather burn my kingdom to the ground than let the fae have it. A decision will be made at the council of kings. I'll beg for one of them to wed any one of my daughters."

"They're all newly married, sir."

King Leonel cursed under his breath. "I'm cursed, I tell you. The whole world is working against me." He paced the foyer in front of their rooms, rubbing his short beard in thought.

"There is someone else you can call," Captain Lathe suggested. "I know you hate hearing her name, but I believe she's a powerful enough sorceress to deal with this."

King Leonel recoiled as if bitten by a snake. "I would never bring Lorelai Eville to fix my mess." He spun and stormed closer to where we were hiding, stopping in front of a younger portrait of himself. The young king was beardless in the painting, which accented his strong jawline, and his eyes were lit with self-confidence. He reached up and ran a hand down the canvas and whispered so softly the captain couldn't hear. "I made a mistake years ago, and I've lived with it my whole life. I can't let her see what I've become."

There was a long pause followed by a sniff as the king wiped away moisture gathered at his eyes.

I leaned back on my heels as more guards took up a place outside of the room and the king left. *Was he still in love with my mother after all this time? Had their broken betrothal not been his choice?*

Nimm pulled on my arm, and I followed his line of sight to watch a servant carry a covered tray down the hall, and when she passed the princesses room, she gave it a wide berth.

There was definitely something strange going on in the palace, and why did the guards pull a dead body out of the princesses' sitting room? What in the stars was going on here?

CHAPTER EIGHTEEN

I t was another few candle marks before I could sneak back out of the palace. Immediately, I sought out Bravado, explaining everything that I had overheard between the king and his captain.

"I've deactivated the magic wards in the palace as requested, but I think the princesses are in danger. They're terrified, and then the guards that are supposed to protect them end up dead? We need to get a word to warn my sisters and mother."

Bravado rubbed the sweat off his head as he was unloading trunks from the back of a wagon. "Well, you see, that is easier said than done."

"Why not? Don't you have a mirror here?"

"Mirrors don't travel well. They always break." He pushed another trunk back and was searching through the wagon. "And we have no one here that can charm one." He shrugged.

"How do you keep in contact with my mother?" I asked.

"We don't." Bravado found the trunk he was looking for, pulled it open, and began to rummage through it. He pulled out an old canvas poster and laid it on the wagon bed. It came undone and unrolled.

"Ever?" I asked, craning my head to look closer at the poster. I saw the words *Dueling Divas* in block letters across the top, and two women in colorful outfits.

"Never." Bravado stood and leaned forward, one foot on the edge of the trunk. His voice dropped to a whisper as his eyes carefully scanned the area for eavesdroppers. "We don't contact her. It's safer that way. She always finds a way of reaching us whenever she needs to."

"I thought you were her eyes and ears for the kingdoms?"

"We are, but that woman and her nosey mirror usually know things before we do." He leaned back and continued to dig through his trunk. "And then she finds ways to get word to us for confirmation or instructions via a fire spell. Or we wait until she sends a vessel—like a sparrow—with a message, and then we use it to reply."

"But she doesn't always know when there's trouble. There's been times when her magic mirror went dark or refused to show her what was going on in the kingdoms. She's had to send my sisters out to investigate on her behalf. That could be what's happening here?" I whispered.

Bravado stood up and grinned. "Why do you think we *are* here, in this kingdom . . . right now." His mustache twitched with excitement. "It wasn't by accident. We weren't scheduled to come to Sion till next year. The other performance troupe that was hired came down with a severe case of pox."

My mouth dropped open in surprise. "No . . ."

He nodded his head. "Your mother is a devious one, no

doubt. I happen to know they received a hexed delivery. As long as they stay far away from the palace, they're fine, but every time they try to head this way, the skin rash comes back fiercer than ever."

I pinched my lips together to keep from laughing. One, it was horrible that my mother hexed them; two, it was a genius way to open it up for her own spies to get into the palace.

She really was the master manipulator.

"It was because of the rumors that the son of Allemar had surfaced that she sent us here, and she knows about your disappearance and sudden reappearance."

"How?" I blinked in surprise.

"Saphira, of course."

"Another one of my mother's spies, I assume." Thinking back to Saphira's connection with Lorn, it wasn't surprising.

"Saphira told me she was in a conversation with your mother when you showed up at her inn. It was Lorelai's idea to get Saphira to convince you to join our troupe since we were already on our way to the palace."

I felt the wind get knocked out of my sails. I had prided myself on being my own person, setting my own quests, and vowed to not be manipulated by my mother. It was why I didn't immediately contact her to tell her I was safe. But it seemed I never needed to. I had plenty of manipulators pulling on my puppet strings.

"You could have told me from the beginning that this was all her doing," I said.

"Ah, but you were doing so well on your own. It was great watching you fly without her hovering and without Lorn's instruction. And then you have to ask yourself,

Honor. Would you really have come if she told you to? Especially considering this kingdom is your birthplace. There are a lot of ghosts from the past you have to face."

I sat on one of the unloaded trunks and stared at the leather sole of my borrowed boots. There was a speck of dirt, and I rubbed it against the grass to try to get it off while I gathered my thoughts. Bravado was right. I may have ended up here on my own, but maybe not as fast or with as much help.

I looked around at the bustling troupe members, all in their colorful garb. Weapons were partially for show, but they were also real. They really were a small, mobile army.

"What's the plan, then?" I asked a tad listlessly. My previous excitement had dissipated, but not by much.

Bravado reached into the trunks and was pulling out wrapped bundles as he continued to search for something. "The palace, possibly because of what you saw this morning, has closed its ballrooms and dining rooms for the day. They're moving everything outdoors, keeping us further at bay as the first king is due to arrive today. So we have to improvise some new acts." He unwrapped a leather bundle and revealed six flat blades. "How do you feel about throwing knives?"

"I love them." I grinned, feeling my adrenaline surge at the idea.

"I thought you would."

Thud! The knife tip stuck into the wooden target, the handle shaking ever so slightly.

"Your aim is off," Rumple said.

"It hit exactly where I wanted it to." I lined up the flat throwing knives in my hand and positioned my feet so I was square against the giant wheel.

"Then your brain is off," he grumbled.

"The goal isn't to hit the center," I reminded him.

"That's just foolish. You always want to hit the center."

I released in rapid fire, and with each one, an outline started to form on the target board. A human outline.

Sorek, who had been leaning against a tree watching me, whistled between his teeth. "That sure is an impressive aim you got there."

"Thank you." I grinned. "Now, I just need you to stand over there and let me throw knives at you."

Sorek coughed and moved away from the tree. "I think I hear Humperstink calling for me."

"Get back here," I yelled after him. "Wasn't there once an act called the Dueling Divas?" I said, referring to the faded poster I'd seen Bravado pull out of a prop trunk earlier.

"There was." Sorek seemed to get a bit misty-eyed. "They were orphans, like you. I took them under my wing. They had practiced for years under me before either of them had ever been allowed to become a human target."

"You're saying you don't trust me?" I scoffed and sent another knife flying toward the target. The thud was satisfying, and so was watching his eyebrow raise even higher.

"I've learned to not trust anyone," Sorek answered, and held out his hand for a blade. I handed him one. "You live longer." He aimed and let go. Sorek's blade landed squarely next to mine, the flat blades butted up next to each other as if they were one.

"Now, *that* is impressive." I whistled.

"I know. Like I said, I've had a lifetime of practice. But I'm not standing against that target."

I chewed on my lip and stared up at the large man. He was still wearing the same vest he always wore, and never seemed to change into other clothes. He certainly wasn't affected by the weather. I sighed as I pulled at the gold leotard and red and gold puffed shorts I was wearing. My red leather mask made my face sweat in the sun, but I had to stay disguised. I'd much rather have a mask I could slip off when I needed to wipe my face than deal with more face paint. If only I could lose the bright red lip stain that made me feel more like a lady of the night than an entertainer. When I first saw my reflection, I thought my lips were the color of fresh blood. But once I got over the macabre illusion, I didn't mind the deep red color on me.

Late risers made their way into the gardens for afternoon tea, and a few milled about. By the afternoon, the space was filled with nobles roaming and looking for entertainment.

Paper lanterns were strewn throughout the gardens on strings, casting more splashes of color and waiting to be lit come evening. Guests came and visited Madame De Le Cour, as much to stare at the giant ogress as to have their fortunes told.

Sorek was busy bringing small groups in through the menagerie tent to see the water sylphs, pixies, and other rare and exotic creatures, some tame, and others quite deadly—like the unicorns.

The unicorns were beautiful, ethereal, and I was thrilled when Humperstink had given me a private tour and let me draw close to a family of unicorns. I'd wanted to reach out and run my hand down the foal's buttery soft hide, but I'd immediately recoiled when I'd felt the familiar darkness within me reach for their magic. I'll never forget how the mother unicorn turned to attack me, her horn missing my face by mere inches. I had fallen backwards onto the floor and backed away, the whole while tears slipped from my eyes.

I couldn't help but wonder why I was made this way. What twisted thing was wrong with me that I couldn't control the drive to possess other's magic?

Since then, I stayed far away out of reverence for these magical beasts. I would never want to unintentionally harm them.

Standing between the ogress's new fortune telling tent, and Bravado's table of magical crystals, I watched a group of the princesses enter the menagerie tent across the way. They had broken off into groups of three and the crowd followed wherever they went.

There was a lag as the crowd of nobles walked around the camp, waiting for the princesses to come out, no doubt so they could swoop in and begin their evening of wooing. The princesses didn't seem to be affected by the fact that a dead guard was found in their room.

Who had killed the guard, and how exactly did he die?

And why was the king worried about their slippers?

A throat cleared, and I turned to see a young nobleman standing in front of my wheel. I had noticed that most of the princesses were avoiding him, despite being of suitable marrying age for any of them.

His pants were nicely tailored; a large gold button on his jacket depicted his family crest, which looked like a buck with antlers with red rubies for eyes. His hair was sandy brown, his eyes a warm hazel, and he had a becoming smile.

"I'm sorry, my lord." I turned and gave a curtsy. "What may I do for you? Would you like to try your hand at the wheel of death?" I pointed to my spinning target wheel. "If you win, you could have your fortune told by Madame De La Cour, the only ogress fortune-teller in all the kingdoms." I waved my hand toward the ogress's tent. "Or perhaps a crystal charm to capture your favorite memories." I waved toward Bravado's table where he was using his magic to instill the memory of an older man's first kiss into a rose-shaped crystal. It was fascinating to watch Bravado pull the memory out of the gentleman's mind. It played above his head for all to see before being siphoned into a crystal.

The young man shook his head. "No, thank you. I've actually come because I recognized you from last night. You are the performer who was on the silks, were you not?"

"I was." I felt heat rush to my cheeks. I wasn't expecting to get recognized or have someone want to bring up that unfortunate accident.

"I have to say, it was amazing." His eyes twinkled. "You were magnificent flying through the air, and that illusion with the silk and rose petals at the end . . . Well" —he lowered his eyes and then brought them up to meet mine—"it took my breath away." The coy flirtation made my heart skip a beat. There was no denying the attraction.

I stepped back, suddenly unsure what to do with the outright adoration.

"I'm sorry, I haven't introduced myself. I'm Nathin Albright of Denford."

"I'm from Denford," I rushed out in excitement, feeling an immediate kinship.

"Really, that is something. Have you ever been to Havrick's Hall?"

"Oh no, I left when I was four," I said wistfully.

"You would have loved it. It's my family home. If you ever come to visit, I would love to give you a tour." Nathin's eyes crinkled when he smiled, making him seem so much more approachable and handsome.

I must have looked a bit shocked by his proposal because he quickly added, "Of course, that also includes the whole troupe. I know my younger brothers would really love to see you perform."

"I will mention it to Bravado."

He dipped his head. "Please do. I can't wait." He grasped his hands behind his back and grinned again, not seeming in any hurry to leave and I wasn't in a position to chase him away either, as I was enjoying his company.

A commotion of squeals and giggles followed as four of the princesses swarmed out of the menagerie tent and twittering laughter filled the air. The men who'd been lingering around for this moment made their way toward the king's daughters.

"I think that's your cue?" I nodded toward the princesses.

"I'm quite happy right here," Nathin said, not taking his gaze from me. "I find you more fascinating than a princess any day."

My cheeks flushed again. "Then why are you here?"

"Why indeed?" Nathin chuckled. "I am here in the interest of politics only. It would be unbecoming for me to insult the king and ignore his invitation. Besides, who am I to turn down everything the palace has to offer? I get to meet interesting people, enjoy fabulous food, and get swept off my feet by the marvelous entertainment." I felt my heart flicker at the compliment. Nathin really knew how to turn on the charm, and I wasn't immune to its effects.

Nathin turned to study the three-legged stool with the throwing knives upon it. He lifted one and gently fingered the blade. "It's sharp," he said in surprise.

"It needs to be, to stick into the target well enough." I pointed at the painted target behind me. A small crowd passed behind Nathin, but I didn't pay them attention.

"Would you do me the honor and show me how it's done?" he asked, handing me the knife.

In slow motion, I made a show of lining up my hips, grabbing the knife by the tip of the handle, and mimicking the proper arm movement needed to make it stick into the wood. I let it fly, and it spun easily, sinking into the target.

"Beautiful," Nathin said, staring at me. I had a feeling he wasn't referring to my shot. He picked up a blade and gave me a questioning look. "May I?"

I nodded and backed away. He raised his hand over his head and tried to copy my stance. The blade flickered as it soared in the air, but as soon as he released it, I knew it was wrong. The handle clattered against the target and fell into the dirt.

"That was embarrassing," he said.

"You'll get it," I said encouragingly. "Let's try again." I handed him another knife, and I went into instructor mode, even going so far as to place my hands on his hips and widening his stance. "You want to release here." I stood to the side, but he wasn't adjusting right. I moved to the front and brought his hand down where he was now reaching over my shoulder, and we stood face to face. He lowered his hand down onto my shoulder.

"You are an excellent instructor," Nathin commented softly.

I smiled, opening my mouth to respond, but an angry voice cut through the air.

"Is that what you call it? I would say this is more fawning than teaching."

I ducked under Nathin's arm and moved a safe distance away to meet Percy's stare, its harshness emphasized by the midnight black uniform of the southern elves. Everything about him seemed cold. Gone was my brother-in-arms, who had laughed with me, protected me, shared meals with me . . . Instead, I faced a stranger.

I didn't like it.

"I'm sorry if I've offended you with my teaching technique," I said, being forced to pretend we didn't know each other.

"And failing miserably," Percy said. His eyes pinned me, and I almost trembled under his gaze. What was this sudden hatred that was directed toward me, and why?

Nathin came to my defense. "I wouldn't say she failed." He picked up the blade and threw it easily, landing inches from the center target.

I glanced between the target and Nathin in shock.

He was obviously only playing me about not knowing how to throw.

Percy stilled, and I knew a dangerous storm was brewing. "How about a contest, then?"

"And what does the winner receive?" Nathin crossed his arms.

"A private lesson from her." Percy tossed his thumb my way, rankling me further when he didn't even ask my permission.

"Deal." Nathin grinned and marched over the target. He pulled out the blades and pointed to three paper targets on the backboard. "First person to hit the three spinning targets wins." He seemed a little too eager as he handed half of the throwing knives to Percy.

I stood to the right of the wooden target and gave it a spin, backing away as Nathin and Percy stepped up to the line. Percy didn't even raise his knives but watched as Nathin threw his three blades and hit two of the three targets.

Percy's mouth tightened in the slightest of grins, as if he knew that outcome was inevitable. He glanced at me and I shook my head, begging him not to outdo the young lord. We both knew he was quite capable of pinning a fly's wing mid-flight. There was no reason for him to humiliate Nathin. The smallest tic in his jaw showed his annoyance at my head shake. With three lighting strikes, he hit the target dead center.

I rolled my eyes and slowed the wheel, pulling the blades out of the target, frustrated by the way he was behaving.

A slow clap followed. "What a wonderful show, but it was definitely lacking the danger aspect."

We turned to see a group of five princesses, which included the eldest, Princess Analisa, and Princess Lisbelle, who was the one addressing us. An honor guard of elves stood to their right. Ardax looked my way, but I couldn't tell if he recognized me.

"If you are going to do it," Princess Lisbelle stepped forth from among her sisters, "why not up the stakes?"

"Up the stakes?" I repeated numbly. I didn't like where her suggestion was going.

"Why, yes. Grace, why don't *you* stand against the target?" Her grin, though shy, was anything but innocent.

"No." Percy placed the throwing knives on the stool. "Our game is over."

"Oh, I haven't even begun to start playing yet." The princess smirked, toying with a knife he'd set down.

My skin crawled with the hidden danger in her tone. She turned to Grace, her eyes narrowed, and I could feel the anger within her. It was matched only by Rulah's.

"Come on Grace, why don't you play *my* game and stand against the target," she gestured with the knives. "Let's see how brave *you* are?"

Grace stilled and her eyes flickered to me and Nathin for help.

"Fine," I acquiesced. "Let's up the stakes." Picking up the blades, I turned, and instead of giving them to Lisbelle, I handed the blades to Percy, my fingers brushing his slightly.

"H—" he breathed out so low that no one else could hear.

I shook my head before he used my name, and he stopped. I moved to stand against the moving target. Stepping onto the footholds, I reached around to tie the leather strap around my waist, and then slipped my hands through the leather cords and wrapped my palms around the hand posts. I raised my chin and looked right at the princess. "I'm ready."

Percy held the knives at his side, unwilling to throw them.

"Well, that's a surprise, but somehow not unexpected. Someone willing to lay down their life for Grace . . . again." She rolled her eyes. "How did she get you—a stranger—to protect her? Did she weave a stupidity spell on you?" Lisbelle asked sarcastically, as she stepped aside to let Percy line up for the shot.

His fist shook, and I knew he was going to back down. Before either of us could react, Princess Lisbelle stepped forward and tossed the knife she was holding right at me.

I stared as the blade wobbled midair and the handle hit my thigh. If it had rotated a hundred and eighty degrees, she would have stabbed me.

"Oh, my bad," Princess Lisbelle giggled. "But really, you should know better than to protect someone like *her*. Ardax, you do it." She made a spinning motion with her fingers toward me.

My gaze shot to him in fear, and Ardax stepped forth, grabbing the extra knives from the table. Before I could pull my hands out of the hand clasps, one of the guards gave the wheel a spin, and I had to hold on for dear life as I rotated quickly. My vision spun. I could see a blur of colors, and I prayed that the princess wasn't reaching for another knife. I heard a thud of the first knife hitting the target near my leg. *He won't hit me. He won't.*

"Ardax, you can get closer than that," Princess Lisbelle said. "After all, she's nothing more than a puppet. Prove me wrong."

Thud. The second knife was near my thigh.

Why did I think an actual human target was such a

grand idea earlier? I wanted to take it all back. It was a horrible idea.

Thud. A third knife near my arm. *Thud.* A fourth near my ribcage. *He hates me, but he wouldn't actually stab me.*

"Last one," she whispered. "Make it count. Then we will know for certain."

Who was she talking about? My heart hammered in my chest. I was going to throw up. I knew it.

The last blade landed with a sting, and I knew it nicked my neck. I bit my lip to keep from crying out as Percy rushed over to slow the target. As soon as it was done spinning, he unclasped the belt and pulled me from the wheel.

My knees buckled; my legs unable to hold myself upright. I collapsed to the ground as the earth moved and spun beneath me. I lightly touched the burning sensation and pulled my hand away to see my fingertips coated with blood.

Ardax! I inwardly fumed. I looked up to see Percy held back by two of his elven brethren, each holding his upper arms. His nostrils flared in fury, but he knew to fight them would be to reveal who I was. Ardax looked uninterested as he put the last knife on the table and turned his back on me dismissively.

"I'm bored." Ardax let out a long sigh. "I'm sure there's better entertainment elsewhere."

Princess Lisbelle looked at me in surprise, her eyes narrowing further in suspicion. As if by my not moving away from being struck, I had proven my devotion to Princess Grace. Lisbelle's face darkened for a split second and the mask was quickly replaced by a fake smile. She gave Grace a jovial wave. "Next time." And departed after Ardax.

I thought all the princesses had left until a rustle of green skirts drew near. I looked up into the relieved eyes of Princess Grace.

The princess didn't speak, but it looked like she wanted to say something. Her eyes flickered to Nathin and the others still lingering about. She clasped her hands and moved away without so much as a word.

"I can't believe he nicked you." Nathin had taken a handkerchief and placed it against the cut. "I thought he would be more of a gentleman than that. Or at least he should have stayed to apologize." He seemed very put out by Ardax's actions.

"It stopped bleeding," Nathin said, and pulled the kerchief away, tucking it into his pocket. "I think you were lucky it wasn't deeper. It just barely scratched the surface."

"Yeah, I was lucky . . ."

I couldn't believe Ardax had done that. He had full control, and still, he nicked me with the blade . . . but then I thought about it. With the bloodthirsty way Princess Lisbelle was egging him on, I had to ask myself, did he have a choice?

CHAPTER NINETEEN

B y sunset, the gardens had come fully alive. Torches and lanterns lit the night, and the glow from the palace even shone down onto the paths. I thought the grounds were beautiful in the middle of the afternoon . . . They were like fairy gardens at night. Near the ponds, frogs croaked out a chorus of greetings, and fireflies flew along the hedges making it look like fairies dancing along the roses. It was wonderful. Not to mention the scent of the roasting meat and the delicacies that were brought out on trays.

I touched the bandage on my neck as I handed another blade to a portly noble, and gave him advice on hitting the target. The knife skidded along the grass.

"I think it's bent," the noble assured me. "That's why it missed."

"I'm sure you're right," I gritted out between my fake smile and handed him another.

The knife handle hit the target but didn't stick.

"That's one," he crowed.

"It needs to stick."

He gave me a disapproving frown and picked up another knife, then sighted along the blade.

I turned my back and fingered the wound and kept watching to see any signs of Percy. I wanted to talk to him. To get an explanation.

I was so consumed with my search that I didn't bother to stop the noble as he gave a gesture to his man, who silently sidestepped to the target, picked up the knife that had landed in the grass, and plunged the knife into the center of the target.

"Aha! I did it," the man lied, pointing his chubby finger. I moved to remove the blades. There was still a clump of grass stuck to the tip of the knife. I was proud that I kept my frustration hidden behind a wooden smile that I'd been using all night.

"Congratulations, my lord. Which prize would you like?" I waved my hand at the table of crystals.

He bowed over the prizes, picking up each one and holding it to the light.

"They're just crystals?" he whined. "Not worth anything."

"Not so. Turn it to the light like this." I mimed turning the crystal. When he did, it came to life, and the little etched figurine of a horse began to run.

"Amazing!" he chuckled and picked his prize.

"All thanks to Bravado De Ella, the enchanted glass-maker." I waved my hands toward the owner.

"Yes, yes. Do you think the princesses will like it?" he muttered.

"I'm sure they will," I lied, knowing that they each already owned at least two bestowed upon them by many other suitors.

Just then I caught sight of Ardax heading farther into the gardens, where the hedgerows formed a bit of a maze.

"Will you excuse me?" I quickly wrapped up the remaining crystals and tucked them away, grabbed the throwing knives and my covered ax, and stormed after Ardax.

"Finally, we are off on a murderous quest," Rumple whispered.

"For once, I'm in agreement with you. I feel like murdering an elf."

"Yessss," Rumple hissed, and I could sense the hum of his excitement reverberating through the backpack. I was grateful that he had been quiet the whole afternoon.

I slipped into the hedgerows, and the farther I traveled, the taller the rows of bushes grew until I could no longer see him. At each junction, I slowed and looked both ways to find where he had gone. I saw the edge of Ardax's black cloak, but then heard another voice.

He was meeting someone.

As I drew closer, I slowed and listened to the muffled voices.

"Uncle, I can't do this."

"You must," a stern voice countered. "No matter the cost."

I peeked around the edge of the bushes and recoiled when I saw the tall, dark foreboding figure wearing a crown made of thorns. Allrick. He was just as intimidating and scary as the stories foretold.

"You say that, but too many have fallen—" Ardax started.

"Silence!" Allrick slashed the air with his hand. "You know that this is the way. We are bound by blood and magic. It is our punishment and retribution. Your cousin understands this. Why can't you?"

"Do not compare me to Percy," he started, but he was quickly shut down by his uncle's hard glare. Ardax bowed his head in remorse, but his hands were clenched into angry fists. He whispered an apology in elvish.

"Our kingdom will grow in greatness because of what you are going to do. Soon we will be stronger than even our northern brothers, and they will bend to our will." Allrick turned to leave but paused and looked back over his shoulder. "Do what must be done."

"How can you trust them? When we both know promises made by human lips are fickle," Ardax said.

"Maybe? But our lives are long and elves never forget."

"That lowlife, fiendish long face!" Rumple growled from my pack. "Let me at him."

Allrick lifted his cloak and when it dropped, he was gone, disappearing the moment he sensed the threat.

Ardax's elven vision wasn't hampered by the lack of light within the maze. He found me in the darkness right away, and I couldn't read his stony expression.

He took a step in my direction, but I didn't stick around. I took off running as fast as my legs could carry me, not even careful about being quiet as I cut corners and crashed into every bush and scattered rocks in my haste.

As I burst out of the gardens, I ran straight into Lord Nathin, almost knocking him over.

"Are you okay?" Nathin grabbed my elbow and steadied me, his brows furrowed in concern.

Ardax stepped out of the maze, his gaze resting on Nathin's hand on my elbow, noticing the he was hovering over me.

"Yes, I'm fine." I pulled my arm away from Nathin, trying to put distance between us. I didn't want poor

Nathin to become a target for Ardax's malicious intentions.

I glared at Ardax, wondering if he recognized me under the red leather mask and bright red lipstick I was wearing.

I didn't get to find out. A palace messenger approached me, and Ardax backed into the maze and disappeared. I turned to see a young boy with a buttoned jacket and gold pin.

"Miss?" The young boy's voice cracked with nervousness as he spoke. "Would you come with me, please?" He nodded in the direction of the palace.

I looked toward the halls and saw a flash of green skirts by the fountains just inside the palace, and then it came again. A tingling sensation of being watched from the shadows crept over me. I had a feeling I knew who it was.

"I'll be back," I said, turning to excuse myself from Lord Nathin.

"You better. It always seems like you're slipping away from me," he teased.

"I promise I won't avoid you during our next meeting."

"I'll hold you to that promise," Nathin said, his eyes soft.

There was a moment when I faltered too long, not wanting to leave. Nathin reached out to touch my neck and pulled down the bandage. "It's healed already?"

My hand flew to cover my wound. Most wouldn't understand how fast my body healed itself.

"Oh, yes, I used an enchanted salve," I lied. "My profession is very dangerous, and we always have to be prepared. Excuse me, I will be back."

Nathin nodded as if he bought my lie. "Very well, then. I'll see you soon."

Nathin waved and headed into the row of hedges, and I took a deep breath and followed the young page. The boy led me into an inner courtyard with a fountain and benches.

I turned to ask the boy who I was meeting, but he was already gone.

The night had taken a chill, and goosebumps rose along my arms, for I was still wearing nothing more than the leotard, shorts, and mask.

"You came?" a soft voice spoke from the darkness. "I wasn't sure you would."

I spun to see Princess Grace standing on the other side of the fountain. She looked exhausted. Her eyes were red-rimmed, as if she had been crying.

"I was summoned." I bowed softly.

She came forward and stood eye to eye with me. Looking me over, she even raised her chin to check our height.

"It is nigh impossible if I hadn't seen it with my own eyes." She seemed in a daze as we stared at each other. "How is it that you look like me?" Grace asked. "Is it some sort of spell?" She pinched my cheek, and I gently pushed her hand away.

"I assure you, this is the face I was born with, and glamour spells wouldn't work on me," I answered, revealing part of my secret.

"Really?" Grace seemed excited at the news. "Are you immune to all spells, or just glamour? What about potions and charms?"

I fell silent, not wishing to reveal more. Grace pinched her lips into a thin line, studying me further. "I would say it's remarkable. We could pass as cousins, possibly even sisters—except for your northern accent." Grace turned and paced the courtyard, chewing on her bottom lip the same way I did when deep in thought.

She looked up at me and reached for my hands, clasping them between hers. That is where I could immediately tell the difference between us. Princess Grace's hands were soft and silky smooth with perfectly rounded nails, whereas my fingers were rough and calloused from hard work and handling weapons, and my fingernails broken and chipped.

"I have a dire problem and need your help."

"With what?" I asked.

Grace shook her head and bit her bottom lip. "I can't speak of it."

I frowned and looked at Grace with frustration. Her head dropped. "I'm sorry. I know it's frustrating, but I'm truly unable to tell anyone . . ." When she raised her eyes, they were glassy with unshed tears.

"You're under a spell that makes you unable to reveal secrets," I said, understanding her excitement at learning my immunity.

She nodded, the tears falling freely now as she used allegory to vaguely explain her situation. "I'm a pawn in a deadly game; where kings are players and pawns always get sacrificed." Her breathing hitched, and I could see the panic rise within her at her hopelessness.

"What happened to Lord Rasmen?"

"A most unfortunate accident," Grace said, her eyes

wide with fear, and she began to babble in a sing-song voice. "Drink the tea and dance until dawn. If you lack the strength, you become a pawn. Sacrificed for the old king's sake, kill the queen and a new world make."

Nothing of what Grace was saying was making much sense, but I could feel her terror. Even now, she kept looking over her shoulder as if waiting for someone to come out of the shadows and pull her away.

There were a hundred scenarios running through my head, and none of them were great. I wanted to protect her, and felt that I was the only one who could help.

"Come with me." I grabbed her hand and pulled her after me out of the courtyard. I scanned the area looking for a place to hide, trying multiple doors until I found one unlocked.

"Where are we going?" she asked fearfully.

"I'm going to help you, but I need you to trust me."

Grace brushed a stray strand of hair out of her face and nodded at me fearfully.

"Get out of your dress."

"What?" She crossed her arms over her chest and looked at me in surprise.

"We're going to trade places. I'm going to be you, and you will be me."

"But if anyone catches you impersonating royalty, you'll be killed. I can't let you do that."

"I know," I said. "It's the only way to find out what's going on so I can help you."

Grace seemed hesitant at first, and I let her eyes roam over us again as she clearly weighed whether this charade would work.

We switched outfits, and I felt awkward. My hair didn't curl the same way as hers, my body was more muscled in some parts and thinner in others because I was a trained fighter.

Grace helped make the dress fit better by adjusting the corset. I gasped as she yanked on the ties. "Have you really never worn one of these before?" she asked.

"Never," I wheezed out, clasping my stomach, unable to control my grimace. Grace grinned and did a twirl in my leotard. Since I wasn't doing aerial work, I had cute, puffed shorts and a colorful blue vest.

When we went to swap shoes, I paused as she rolled down her silk stockings to reveal heavily bandaged feet. Even now, I could see sores on her toes with dried blood crusting to them.

"What happened?"

Grace dropped her head, burying her face into the puffed sleeves of the entertainer vest she now wore.

"It's okay," I soothed. "You're safe now."

She nodded and took the soft leather shoes I handed her. Grace winced as she slipped her feet inside, and then there was a look of relief when she felt the support of the sturdy shoe.

"These are heavenly."

Princess Grace's slippers seemed brand new and ever so soft, with barely a lining for the sole. They felt light and comfortable.

I handed Grace my leather mask, and she seemed hesitant to put it on. "Another mask," she whispered. "To hide secrets and pain."

I was about to pull it back when she slipped it over her eyes, tied it, and looked up at me. Her mouth trembled with fear, but she pulled herself together. She licked her lips and swallowed.

"You look good," I encouraged. "How about me?"

"Here." She pinned up the sides of my dark hair, letting it cascade over my back, then I braided her hair the way mine had been done. We stood back, admiring each other.

"It won't fool your sisters," I said.

"You can. I'm not well-liked among them."

"Why is that?"

"The king loved my mother, whereas the others were marriages of convenience. Because of that, they treat me ill. I've become very good at blending into the background and going unnoticed. It's safer."

I believed her. Had she not been pushed the day of our arrival, I wouldn't have ever noticed her.

"Is there anything you can tell me about tonight?"

Grace tried to open her mouth, and no words came out, so she shook her head sadly. "Just be careful. Whatever you do, don't stop."

"Don't stop?"

"Yes, don't stop," Grace repeated.

A bell tolled out the hour, and Grace panicked. "You have to get back to our room. Follow my other sisters' lead. Just watch, listen, and don't speak. Do you understand?"

I nodded.

Grace looked relieved, until a commotion began in the palace, and she turned away in fear. "And I'm sorry for what has transpired. It's not my fault." Grace backed away.

"Go to Bravado. He'll help you and show you my tent where you can sleep. Tomorrow we'll change places again."

I handed her my pack with Rumple, thankful that he was as quiet as ever while we conspired.

"Thank you." Grace reached out to hug me, and then dashed into the night. I looked down at the silk princess slippers I wore now. Picking up my pace, I proudly walked in the direction of their rooms, thankful I knew where they were.

I felt a tug on my dress and knew Nimm had joined me on my journey. We came to the ward, and I paused. He clung to my leg as I stepped over it. Nothing happened. It hadn't been reactivated. I came up to a set of familiar double doors.

"Now what?" I mumbled.

I wasn't sure if I should knock or just open the door and enter. It swung inward, and a familiar face stared back at me.

"Why must you always be late?" Risa groaned, and pulled me into the room after her. "The wards are about to be activated."

I sucked in a breath between my teeth. That was the secret. The wards were timed to work at night. In the day, they weren't armed because elves and fae came and went as they worked, but at night, the wards would kill anyone heading toward the princesses rooms . . . or anyone leaving them.

I did my best to keep my gaze down as I stepped into the interior wing of the palace. Its ceiling was painted to resemble a sky. We gathered in a sitting area large enough to have multiple chaise lounges, a piano, and a long dining room table. Risa was pacing in front of a large clock, watching the hands move slowly toward midnight.

"Stop it," Lisbelle ordered Risa, and then hovered over

the tea set that was sitting out on a silver tray. Her hands trembled as she adjusted the tea set, checking the pot with her hands to make sure it was still warm. Her eyes flickered to me before narrowing with hatred. I could tell there was no love lost between the sisters.

I stopped to take in a lifelike landscape and tried to place where in the seven kingdoms it was depicting. The painting on the wall depicted the forest, but unlike the Northern Woods, the trees were darker in color, their trunks more twisted.

As I was pondering the origins of the painting, and watching Lisbelle out of the corner of my eye, the door opened behind me, and King Leonel came in with Lord Dyer. I stayed in my spot by the painting while listening to the king give instructions.

"Now, tonight my daughters will retire to their room, then all of you will be locked in. You are not allowed inside any of their rooms, and they are not allowed to leave this wing under any circumstances."

"That seems easy enough," Lord Dyer said. He was a younger lord with sandy hair and a small, thin mustache. He rubbed his hands together as if it was a challenge.

"One would think, yes. If something happens to them, I cannot guarantee your safety. You will have to face the repercussions of your failure."

Lord Dyer chuckled nervously. "I make sure they are protected, then come morning I will be rewarded?"

"Up to half my kingdom and one of my daughters to wed, as we agreed." King Leonel gestured to the table in the middle of the room. Lord Dyer sat down, grabbed a set of cards, and shuffled them.

The king headed out, and I watched as he pulled out a

gold key and locked us inside. I felt another tug on my skirt, and was about to reprimand Nimm, when Lisbelle appeared at my side.

"Look at the trouble you caused," Lisbelle hissed at me. She pointed toward Lord Dyer who pulled the tea set closer to him and turned over a teacup. "I hate you," she seethed. "You never should have been born."

Before I could react, Lisbelle spun on her heel and headed down the hall toward what I assumed was their bedrooms.

"Which one's mine?" I whispered to Nimm, who I had hoped was still guiding me. A tug on my skirt pulled me to a door that was halfway down the hall on the right.

I slowed and reached for the handle, but another hand grabbed it first. I could tell by the skirt it was probably Lisbelle.

"Next one down, Grace," Lisbelle snarled irritably. "Really, I think you're going a little mad. Oh wait . . . too late."

"Mm," I mumbled and followed the furiously tugging Nimm.

I waited at the next door and didn't grab the handle until I felt his push from behind.

"All right. I get it," I mumbled. I pulled open the gold handle and stepped into a luxurious room with sage green wallpaper and a satin four-poster bed with silk bedding. There was a fireplace that had already been stoked and was crackling softly. It wasn't until I walked the whole room did I notice that there wasn't a single window. Not even the outer sitting room had windows. I realized I was in an inner cell of a jail.

I sat on the bed looking around my room and felt the mattress dip as Nimm hopped onto the bed next to me.

"What now?" I whispered.

Nimm slipped out of the room. My guess was to spy on the other sisters. A few moments later, he returned and pointed to the wardrobe. I slipped off the bed and opened up the oak doors to see a deep green dress with scoop sleeves. There were matching slippers as well.

"I'm supposed to change into another dress?"

Nimm nodded. Thankfully, this one stretched, and I didn't need someone to lace me in. There were two ties, so I could to cinch the dress closed. I made my way over to the dressing table and mirror, and tried my best to fix my hair.

Nimm hopped on the table and pulled open a drawer, handing me a comb and some unique pins that helped hold a curl in place. After a few laborious minutes, I noticed it looked half decent. I applied the face powders and a bit of tint to my cheeks and lips.

Gone was the girl who wanted to run through the woods, climb trees, and shoot arrows. In the mirror, a confident woman stared back at me. She was beautiful, even. Her dark eyes twinkled with secrets, and her hair pinned in so brown waves tumbled down her back. The dress exposed my neck and the thin red scab. I touched it, and it was still tender, so I tried to hide the brightness of the mark with powder, turning the red mark into pale pink.

It would have to do for now.

I kept running my fingers along the dressing table and was apprehensive about my hands. I curled my hands under and worried again unnecessarily as Nimm handed me a white face mask and long gloves that matched my dress.

"Where did you get this?" I asked.

Nimm pointed to a secret drawer in the dressing table. The mask covered most of my face, leaving only my lips and eyes uncovered. No wonder Grace wasn't worried about anyone recognizing me. As long as I didn't say anything, I would be fine.

I moved to a chair by the fire and stared into the flames. I neither had the enchanted knife that Rhea had given me, nor Rumple. As I sat in silence, I began to miss his voice and his constant chatter, even his foul language.

The fire flickered and went from a bright orange to a white for a split second. I heard the crack of a log breaking in the grate, and a piece of ember shot into the air.

Except it wasn't an ember, but a slim strip of paper that floated in the air with its edges were still burning slightly.

I took the strip and blew the edges, recognizing familiar handwriting. I held it close to my chest, afraid to look at the words written across it.

Taking a deep breath, I pulled the slip away and focused on the flowery letters on yellowed paper.

"Don't drink."

Frowning, I turned it over again and looked at the backside of the paper. Blank.

When I turned it over again, the paper disintegrated in my fingertips. Nimm sat on the other chair next to me, his little legs kicking back and forth happily. He gestured to the paper with a raised eyebrow.

"It says *don't drink*," I said in a clipped tone, trying to mask my disappointment. The first message to me from my adoptive mother was one about not getting intoxicated?

"How long am I supposed to wait here?" I asked Nimm. He pointed to the lack of winding clocks and windows and shrugged.

"Just great." I fiddled with the silk gloves and kept readjusting them on my hands, before fidgeting with the mask. It was uncomfortable and itchy, for the secrets it held seemed to make it weigh more upon my face.

I had given up all hope of any kind of adventure tonight and was about to take a nap on the bed when my bedroom door swung open silently and silence followed. I stared into the hall and could see the other princesses grabbing their cloaks and heading toward the sitting room. I grabbed mine from the wardrobe, flung it around my shoulders, pulled up the hood, and stepped into the hall behind eleven other princesses.

Lisbelle peered into the sitting room and the man had fallen asleep at the table. Lord Dyer had fallen forward, his hand of cards had scattered across the table, and he was snoring soundly.

"Idiot," Risa chuffed as she placed a duplicate teapot on the table.

She took the previous one and dumped the contents into the nearest potted plant. From her pocket, she pulled out another teacup; this one was smaller and without a handle. Each of the sisters lined up in front of Risa as she poured a green liquid from a glass vial into the small cup and handed it to the first sister.

Princess Willa drank the contents and handed the empty cup back to Lisbelle. One by one, each sister took the offered drink and handed it back.

My mother's warning came back.

Don't drink.

My hands were shaking. How was I going to get out of this?

As I was fretting over it, something was tucked between my fingers. I opened them to see a bit of sponge. I stepped out of line and turned around and coughed loudly as if having a fit, and then tucked the sponge under my tongue. When I came around, I was next in line.

Risa handed me the cup, and I quickly titled it back and let the drink slowly pour into my mouth, hoping the sponge would soak it up. I kept my mouth closed and handed the empty cup back to Risa.

Being careful to not bite down or drink any of the liquid that was soaked up in the sponge in my mouth, I turned, grabbed the edge of my cloak and coughed again, spitting out the sponge. I squeezed it so it would soak into the black cloak, and then I could discard the sponge. Despite my attempt to not drink any of the liquid, some slid down my throat.

Risa went over to Lord Dyer and carefully added a few drops from her vial into his open mouth, making sure to close his lips until he had drunk the same amount as we did.

She stepped back and snapped her fingers, and Lord Dyer opened his eyes and sat up, completely under a spell of compulsion. She looked over at each of us, her eyes filled with sadness—but she ignored me.

"I'm sorry, but this means protection for only one of us. Do your best to survive another night."

Risa tilted her head back and drank the last of the vial, letting it fall to the ground with a thud on the rug.

Despite my resolve to not drink, I could still feel the effects. The room spun. The floor moved like waves, and I was pretty sure the trees in the painting were moving in the wind.

Not only that, but I could also feel the wind in a windowless room.

My feet moved of their own accord, and the hardwood disappeared. I was walking on soft earth through the woods.

CHAPTER TWENTY

W e were no longer in the palace. In fact, I wasn't even sure if we were in Sion. The surrounding trees were sordid; their colors just a bit off as if they faded in the sun before deepening. We had walked through the painting in the sitting room and transported somewhere else.

The painted trees became clearer. The bark lost its brush strokes and turned into actual bark. As we walked, I brushed my hand against the tree and felt the scrape of the wood. It was real.

The forest shifted as we came to the edge of the painting. A black stairwell led down, and Lisbelle lifted a lantern high, headed into the darkness.

Nimm was invisible and was struggling to keep up with all the stairs. He tripped and fell down a few steps and brushed against Willa's leg.

"What was that? Something touched me," Willa called out fearfully.

"No one touched you. Keep up," Risa said irritably.

I focused on Nimm cowering against the wall while trying to avoid getting bumped again. As I descended to his step, I kneeled and scooped him up. Quickly, he climbed up onto my shoulder and clutched my hood.

"Have you ever seen this place before?" I whispered.

I felt Nimm's head shake.

We walked until the stairs evened out, and we stepped into a grove of trees. The moon shone against the silver bark and leaves, and it seemed to glow a reflective white. Never had I seen such an oddity, and I found myself slowing to brush my fingers against the leaf. The leaf was cold to the touch, just like silver. I thought nothing could top the beauty of the silver grove until we entered a grove of golden thorn trees.

Immediately, I recognized the tree and the correlation to the golden thorn comb Ardax had given me.

This was Thornhaven. I did it. We passed into the sacred realm through a painting in the palace. A painting enchanted and connected to a ley line.

The other princesses weren't as enthralled with the trees as I was. In fact, they seemed to have picked up their pace as if in a hurry. I grabbed the hem of my dress and followed suit, racing after them and trying not to stare like a poor man in a market as we ran through a diamond forest.

As we ran, I could feel my slippers sink into the earth, and then the earth turned to sand as we were on a sandy bank. In front of us were twelve colorful boats bobbing on the water. Sitting in each boat was a man, dressed in black clothes wearing a white mask, waiting patiently.

One by one, the girls stepped into the boat, the masked men standing to help them settle before reaching for the oars.

I hung back and waited as the others had already selected their boat and were casting off across the moonlit water. I approached the last boat hesitantly. The man in my boat didn't press me, but waited patiently.

He cocked his head and gestured to the bench seat. I wasn't a fan of water, and I was terrified that I'd fall in and drown. Silly for a trained fighter such as I, but it wasn't so much that I couldn't swim. I had an unnatural fear of water if I couldn't see the bottom. And during this dark night, the bottom of the lake could have been endless.

But tonight, I wasn't Honor. Tonight, I was Princess Grace, who had probably taken this same ferry ride across the lake before with this same man many times. I had to gather my courage.

I took a deep breath, lifted the hem of my dress, and stepped into the small boat, and it rocked. I let out a yip and quickly plopped down on the wooden bench, grasping the edges of the boat for dear life.

I heard the man chuckle, and he reached out and grabbed the handles of the oars and pulled, shooting us across the water. He too, wore a cloak that covered his shoulders and head. The black mask was so obscure, with deep-hooded sockets and a wide nose that it made it cast his eyes in shadows, but it left his mouth and chin exposed. The whole outfit made him look menacing.

Even more so when he seemed to focus on my neck.

I tensed, and absently touched the quickly healing wound.

Was one of these men the son of Allemar? Were they in league with the southern elves? This was very powerful magic, indeed. I wasn't even sure my mother could conjure this spell, but an apprentice of Allemar could. I needed to be wary and keep my guard up.

"You can relax your grip." His voice was husky. "I'm

not going to capsize us. The boat is too wide bottomed for that."

Feeling a bit better, I lifted my hands to place them in my lap.

"See." To make a show, he shifted his weight side to side, causing the boat to sway and water to splash up, but there was little movement. I slammed my hands back on the edges again.

I heard a chuckle, and I glared at the big-nosed mask, letting him be the recipient of all of my hate. Of all the escorts, I got the idiot.

He seemed to quiet down after my cold stare. I only hoped it was haughty and princess-like, and not Honor's *I'm going to kill you in cold blood* look.

The lead boat with Risa had already pulled up to the other side of the lake, and they were mooring the boat to an ash tree. Because of my hesitation in getting in the boat, we were still pretty far away from the others. Risa and her guide headed into the woods, and I felt myself tense.

"Don't worry, I'll get you there on time." The apprentice leaned back with each stroke, and our little boat picked up speed, skimming across the water and overtaking the last two boats.

"Slow down," I hissed. "You're making a scene."

The boat was still coasting so fast we practically crashed into the embankment, and I flew forward into the chest of the apprentice. He caught me and helped steady my balance.

"Careful, now. You're not supposed to fall for me." I could hear the teasing in his voice, and it didn't sound at all like I thought it would for a deadly apprentice.

I pushed against his chest, causing him to fall backwards and land on his bottom in the boat. I lifted my skirt and stepped into the water in my rush to get far away from him.

I adjusted my mask and found myself standing next to Willa. She frowned and looked behind me at the man who was fumbling in the boat.

"You sure got the cream of the crop tonight," she said worriedly. "I hope he doesn't have two left feet."

I had sworn to not speak, but I couldn't help myself. "I think it's not his feet I have to worry about. It's his mouth that won't shut up."

Willa winced and reached up to grasp the hand of her escort, who led her through the woods, but this time, as soon as she stepped off the path, she was swallowed up by an inky, black mist.

I stared at the miasma and reached out to touch it, and it felt cold, but there was something familiar about it. I tried to step into it, but was met with a solid wall. I tried to push, but again, it fought my entry.

My heart raced as I watched all the princesses disappear through the mist, and I was left standing alone.

"No," I gasped, reaching my hands out and feeling along the black wall, unable to penetrate the magic. I was left behind.

A fumbling came from behind, and I turned to see my escort wringing out his cloak from the water.

"Thanks for waiting for me. Oh, that's right. You don't have a choice." My escort held out his arm, and I stared at it, not wanting to touch him, but I knew I needed his help to get through.

I laid my hand across the top of his hand, and he walked forward without giving me any sign of his intention. The blackness swallowed me, and I felt a cold trickle cover my whole body. I tilted my head back and let the magic course through me. I knew this feeling. It was a protective magic, like the veil in the northern realm. It was used to conceal and protect an area.

But the north's magic was warm and full of sunshine. This magic was cold, like ice in my veins, and I almost liked the pain of it more than the northern's gentle touch.

Then we were through, and I felt the coldness leave my body, and I longed to step back into its icy grasp.

Ruins surrounded us. Pillars broken and destroyed, overgrown with moss and clover. Stone steps, cracked and broken, as if the earth rebelled and tried to push them upward. Even the trees that had overrun the ruins were twisted and grew at odd angles.

Was this the sacred hollow of Thornhaven? The farther through the ruins we traveled, the more I believed it was. But where were the guards? Why were we walking right to the hollow?

My escort looked at my arms hanging by my side, and then up the row of princesses, and their arms were still interlocked with their escorts.

He reached for my arm and tucked it into the crook of his. I tried to pull it away, but he pressed his arm against his ribcage, trapping my arm in a pressure lock.

"Don't be difficult, Princess. I'm trying my hardest to make a good impression."

"Well, try harder," I hissed. "You're hurting me." I stopped walking and yanked my arm so hard that I almost punched myself in the face. His lips pinched together, and I knew he was holding back a laugh.

"Laugh, and I will gut you," I seethed, and immediately covered my mouth with my hands. That was not princess-like at all, and I worried I had blown my cover.

But instead, my threat seemed to have been what my escort needed. The smile dropped from his face, and he stood tall, leaving his arm out and parallel, waiting for me to take it. I refused, and held my skirts and followed the other princesses, inwardly fuming. I couldn't care less who he was trying to impress. I didn't want to touch that man, or have him touch me, ever again. I wanted nothing more than to find a way to sever his arm. A man didn't need two arms, did he?

My thoughts turned dark as I found myself dreaming of ways to punish the sorcerer by my side. I didn't care how charming he was trying to act. He and his kind were causing problems all over the seven kingdoms. And I hoped that tonight I would get the answers I needed. Maybe I could torture a few of them and get the truth?

I couldn't hide my malicious grin as the princesses and their escorts headed into the open courtyard, and every ten feet or so was another enormous, detailed painting that hung between two pillars. I slowed and stared at the paintings, and the lifelike detail that was put into each one. None of them contained people. They were all landscapes.

One was a beach with aquamarine waters and a waterfall. Behind the waterfall was the barest hint of a sandstone palace, and I recognized it from my mother's mirror when she would scry on the other kingdoms. It was the southern beach in the kingdom of Isla. Another painting depicted a snowy range at the base of a very familiar mountain that led into the mines of Ter Dell in Kiln. The third painting was just outside the capital city of Thressia in Candor. One painting caused my heart to flutter as I saw the inner court of the Northern Woods. The stone dais, the natural raised grassy platforms, and the circle of willow trees, but the painting had a giant rip, as if it was torn and then repaired sloppily.

My stomach roiled, and hard knots hit my gut as I turned around and looked at the painting directly across from the elven inner court. It was a painting of a familiar grassy field.

It was the exact spot where I'd woken up after the attack, but this painting included the remains of the hellhounds.

When I jumped through the veil of magic in the Northern Woods, did I enter this room and somehow knock the sorcerer and his demon hounds backwards and into another picture? Is that how I ended up in a field in the middle of nowhere?

I counted the paintings. There were at least twenty-seven in all that linked to key points in the seven kingdoms.

Some paintings were smaller than the others, and they were locations just outside of small villages. I recognized the town as where the first rumors of the son of Allemar appeared. As I walked the room, I could match up each of the paintings with an attack linked to Saphira's map.

My mouth went dry. The expanse of their reach, and the amount of magic needed to funnel into each painting to create a portal was intimidating.

"Greetings, my apprentices." A voice echoed off the marble walls. "You have been faithful in your attendance, and you shall all be greatly rewarded, but our work is not yet done."

Everyone in the hall turned their focus on the upper balcony that overlooked the twenty-four of us. There wasn't anyone standing on the balcony, but I could see a plush velvet red curtain and it moved, signaling that the speaker was behind it. This was it. The person I had been hunting for. I stepped away from my escort, but a hand reached out and grabbed mine, keeping me close by. I tried to pull my hand away, but I was getting strange looks from the other escorts.

"In three days' time, we will be ready for the final battle. We won't let what happened in the Northern Woods deter us. That was a fluke. Our armies have grown in numbers, and we are ready. So tonight, my disciples, I bid you to once again give yourselves for our cause so we can grow in strength and defeat our enemies."

A faint clattering of applause followed, and a long-gloved hand slipped between the curtain and pointed toward an archway on my left. I could see steps that led to a beautiful black circular dais, which gleamed like it was made of onyx.

In pairs, the apprentices and the daughters of Sion descended the steps and spread out to stand over a symbol on the circular dance floor. Carved into the dark stone were golden astrology symbols. It wasn't just the twelve symbols of birth months, but they were arranged like a clock in a circle. Soft music flowed as if by a spell, and a bell toned somewhere in the temple ruins.

Willa began to move with her partner, as did Risa and hers, and I froze, not understanding what was happening. But my partner grasped my hand and pulled me after him into a dance. I tensed, knowing that I would immediately give myself away if I didn't get ahold of my nerves. Why didn't Grace tell me there would be dancing? I wouldn't have agreed to the charade if I'd have known.

I stumbled over a misstep, and my escort caught me easily. His hand wrapped around my waist as he lifted me off the floor and swung me around for the intricate dance move without missing a beat.

"Thanks," I whispered.

His eyes flickered to me briefly before focusing over my shoulder. I had hoped the song would end soon, but just as the music faded out, it picked up again with another rhythm and verse. We must have danced over a candle mark and we weren't given a break.

My heart started to race and my breathing picked up as the exertion caught up with me. I tried to slip away and stop dancing, but my escort gripped my back.

"No, don't. You can't stop."

"I need a break," I whispered.

"You stop, you die."

Adrenaline kicked in, and I looked right into my escort's face. That's when I noticed the tenseness in his jaw, the muscle that kept clenching and unclenching from stress. I looked toward my fake sisters and saw that all of them were just as exhausted and showing signs of weariness, but they had a determined look in their eye.

I shouldn't have spoken up. I should have already known the consequences. Grace had warned me. *Whatever you do, don't stop.* I focused on the other dancers and the markings on the floor. After only a few numbers, we shouldn't have been this exhausted. I had trained to run miles without stopping, and I'd never gotten this tired this fast.

Something else was at work here.

That's when I saw it. The golden glow on the floor. As each princess passed over the symbol as they danced, there was a flicker of magic trailing from them, sinking deep into the floor. I frowned. We were dancing over the sacred hollow, but there was a spell circle in place.

It was a magic circle, and the pattern we were dancing in was a magic sigil. With each turn or spin on the symbols, we were activating and powering up the spell using our own life energy.

Just as I made the connection, we passed over another symbol. My escort spun me and I felt it, a pull on my heart, and my body grew slightly weaker. Even my escort showed signs of the spell affecting him.

"How much longer?" I whispered.

"We dance until dawn."

"Are you sure it's not dawn yet?" I muttered weakly and smiled up at him, trying to charm him, but knowing my lessons on wooing were woefully lacking.

"You're different from before," he whispered.

"How so?" I turned my face away and watched the other escorts and their partners.

"You won't stop talking." I immediately my lips pressed together. I'd given myself away. "I'm sure you noticed that very few of the others are talking. They don't have the energy for it, and you have never spoken a single word before. It's like you're a different person."

I needed to run, to get away, but I wasn't sure how without revealing myself. I had no idea how to get back to the portrait and into the sitting room.

My escort tightened his grip around my waist, pulling me close. His other hand that held mine released and slowly reached for my chin and lifted my gaze to meet his. I could feel my body tremble in fear at having failed.

I cast my eyes downward, unwilling to look at him and admit I wasn't who I was pretending to be.

"But you were always different from the others, Honor," he whispered so softly I could barely hear. My eyes shot up to meet his, and my lips parted in shock. "I told you, no matter what disguise you wear, I will always know you."

I tried to stop in the middle of the dance and pull away, but he wouldn't let me.

"I warned you before, you can't stop," he growled.

How had I not seen it? I felt a fool, that he recognized me, but I hadn't recognized him.

"Percy?" I whispered.

"We don't use names here," he hushed. He was watching the other escorts carefully to see if anyone had overheard me. None had. In fact, most of the dancers had started to slow. Many of the princesses had collapsed into the arms of their escorts, who were doing their best to keep them up and moving.

"What are you doing here?"

He was silent.

As we passed another symbol, I felt the familiar tug again, and the draining feeling overwhelmed me. The fear of harming others overtook my need for information.

"I have to get out of here," I whispered frantically. "I really can't take much more of this."

"We're almost done," he said, trying to soothe me. "Then we'll be released from the spell."

"I don't think I have that much time." I gasped as I felt the familiar pangs as I unconsciously started to reach outward for magic. "I'm scared someone will die," I whispered.

"I'll protect you."

"But who will protect you?" I gasped as a shock of pain ripped through my stomach, and I seized up as I fought the urge. My body froze as I could feel my body temperature drop, and goosebumps ran up my arms. This was going to be bad. Very bad. What would happen if I started to siphon from a room full of sorcerers?

"Honor, what's wrong?" he whispered as I buckled and he caught me, holding me upright.

I shivered, and he pulled me close. I rested my cheek on his shoulder, tucking into the crook of his neck. There was no hiding that Percy had picked me up and my feet no longer even touched the floor as we danced.

I could barely keep my eyes open as I struggled to lock away the desire within me. I would never harm Percy. I would die before I harmed him. As we danced, his sleeve slipped down, revealing a dark triangle tattoo mark upon his wrist. The one he had always hidden from me.

My blood ran cold.

It was the symbol of Allemar's apprentice.

"You're one of them?" I pushed at his chest, but he wouldn't release me. He'd said if I stopped dancing, I'd be killed. But if I didn't stop dancing, I would kill Percy—by accident or on purpose, I didn't know which.

"If you don't release me, I *will* kill you," I warned, my anger seething.

"You've already threatened to kill me."

"I mean it." I grimaced as my stomach dropped, and the stabbing pain began. Soon a desirous hunger would be released, and I could accidentally kill any of those with me. As I closed my eyes, I saw the golden light of his soul. It was so bright, his magic, and I wanted it. Tears of remorse and anger flowed as I struggled to get my curse under control.

I could feel myself reaching for the light, wanting to possess it—then snuff it out for its betrayal.

"Honor . . ." Percy gasped in pain as I touched the light within him.

I didn't care what happened. I had to stop this. Right now.

I reached up and used a pressure lock on his arm, but before I did, someone else stopped dancing and a heavy hush fell from the room, and the music stopped playing. The spell was broken, and I felt a snap of energy release back into me.

The escort who had danced with Lisbelle fell to the ground. The girl stood over him. A cruel smile crossed her face as she looked at me and raised her chin in victory. She cast her eyes toward the balcony and gave a little wave before turning on her heels and heading out of the hall, stepping over the prone body of her escort. I hoped he had passed out and wasn't actually dead.

The other escorts released the princesses, who stumbled away, their heads dropping in weariness as they shuffled out after Lisbelle. Many were limping, and a few of their slippers were coated in blood.

Now that the dance was over, I pushed away from Percy and tried to put as much distance between us. I threaded myself through the sisters and noticed that we were short not one, but two escorts. As Lisbelle had held onto the other arm of Risa's escort as they passed through the dark veil, I did the same with Willa's escort, grabbing the edge of his sleeve and even climbing into his boat with Willa.

Some of the princesses were asleep by the time they got to the boats and their escorts had to carry them. It seemed that most of the escorts were struggling just as much as we were, and now they had to row the boats.

From my boat in the middle of the lake, I saw Percy arrive at the shoreline and look for me. I turned away, not wanting to see him.

As I listened to the sounds of the oars hitting the water, I found myself unable to stay awake, and despite all my training—I fell asleep.

CHAPTER TWENTY-ONE

I woke to tugging on the front of my dress. I opened my eyes to see nothing, and then my dress was released. My head fell back and knocked against the headboard.

"Ouch!" I grunted.

A small invisible hand pressed against my mouth, silencing me. Instantly, I was aware of my surroundings. I was back in Grace's room, with no recollection of how I got here.

Nimm's glamour dissipated, and he waved for me to come to the door. Quickly, I slipped out of bed and opened a crack to see soldiers coming down the hall. They were knocking on each door and entering, searching the room.

King Leonel himself ranted loudly. "Another suitor is dead."

"W-what is going on?" I stammered in front of the king, terrified that he would instantly see that I was not his daughter. I dropped into a curtsy, my head hanging so low my hair fell forward and brushed along the floor. My slippers and the edge of my dress were both destroyed by the hours of dancing and traipsing through mystical woods.

He turned his hands, covering his eyes in shame. "He's

dead. Lord Dyer is dead. First it was Lord Rasmen, and now Lord Dyer is dead."

The news shook me, and I stumbled, forgetting my coy tactics. I looked right at the king; my face filled with shock. "Dead, but how? I don't understand. He was alive when we went to sleep."

King Leonel studied me closely. I couldn't fake my confusion, and it was news to me.

"You really don't know what happened?" He seemed taken aback. Captain Lathe came to the king's side, and he addressed him. "It seems that another of the suitors tasked with guarding the princesses against the daughters of Eville, have ended up poisoned. It must be her. Lorelai Eville is murdering my daughters' suitors. We must add more guards to our gates. She must be stopped."

"Right away, Your Majesty." Captain Lathe stormed out, signaling to more of his guards.

A cough came from the door next to mine, and King Leonel looked up to see Lisbelle standing there, her eyes narrowed in suspicion.

"Father," she said coldly.

"Lisbelle, are you well this morning?" he said stiffly.

"I'm well every morning, despite another murder in our suits. Thank you for your concern," she said with a smiling face, but her voice didn't match her expression. It was dead and filled with disdain. "I see that another candidate for the throne has passed away, so . . . conveniently."

"Lisbelle," King Leonel growled out in warning. "That is not the way to speak of Lord Dyer.

Lisbelle's eyes flickered to me. "No, I know nothing as to the unfortunate passing of Lord Dyer, or the tea left out for him. But you should stop offering to give away half your kingdom on a whim when you have no plan to do so. Perhaps it is the *nobles* poisoning their competition? Do you really believe a sorceress from another kingdom murdered them? Maybe you could just name an heir, and all this would stop?" She shrugged.

King Leonel's lip curled. "Soon it will all be over."

It seemed the king himself held no love for his daughter, and when he passed into the hall, I heard him raise his voice to order the body to be removed and the palace to be put on lockdown.

Lisbelle turned her vicious snake eyes in my direction. She stalked toward me, and I could feel her anger rolling off of her in waves.

"You've gone too far in this charade, pretending innocence. You are just as at fault for his death as we are. Don't pretend you don't have blood on your hands." Lisbelle raised her hand to strike me but I caught it midair, my grip squeezing her wrist.

"Don't you *dare* raise your hand against me," I said between clenched teeth. My warning was soft and deadly. "Or I'll have more than blood on my hands."

Lisbelle's face paled, and her lips sputtered open in protest before she spun on her feet and flounced away as if nothing had transpired between us, but I knew those flounces were deceiving. For that girl was as deadly as a viper dressed in lace.

Risa's eyes were red from crying, and there were dark circles of exhaustion evident. "You shouldn't rile her," Risa said.

"I can't seem to help it."

"You can stop it at any time," Risa added. "I know she's

238

difficult to handle sometimes, but she is trying." Risa moved closer. "He's not going to ever give in. I'm starting to agree we have to finish what was started," she said, as if to herself.

I nodded in agreement.

I wanted to question her further, but a commotion drew her attention to the door, and she headed into the hall. I quickly closed the door after her and ran to the closet in search of clean clothes. I needed to find Grace as soon as possible.

Even though I was mentally exhausted and drained, I fought through it, knowing I could restore myself if I slept in the warded tent.

I pulled a green silk scarf over my hair and dressed in the least extravagant dress in Grace's wardrobe. With Nimm's help, he led me out of the maze of palace halls and outside. Quickly, I skirted the guards and headed down a side path until I was in the gardens. With it being so early in the morning, there were hardly any visitors or palace staff out and about, other than a gardener.

Picking up my pace, I was almost running through the gravel path until I came to the farthest side of the gardens and slowed when I came to my tent. I took a deep breath and stepped inside to find it empty. My blankets were still folded from the night before. I turned full circle and looked at my sack of belongings.

"She's gone," Rumple said grumpily from within the pouch, leaning against the small three-legged stool.

"What do you mean, she's gone? I told her to stay here until I could get back safely."

"She ran away with all the money left in your coin purse."

"What?" I collapsed on my knees in front of Rumple. "You'd better explain right now."

"It seems that she took your pity on her as a way to escape the palace."

"I was duped."

"Duped, conned, tricked, bamboozled, deceived. She saw her opportunity to escape."

"Why didn't you stop her?"

"How?" Rumple cried out. "I don't have hands."

I saw the folded paper next to the stool, and I reached down to pick it up. When I unfolded it, I was surprised that I could read the script and that it wasn't spelled.

I'm sorry.

I can't survive another night in the palace or that . . . place. This was the only way I could think of to save myself. If you are reading this, then you survived the night. I pray that you are strong enough to keep on surviving despite the circumstances. Please forgive me.

~ G

I crumpled the note, tossed it onto the floor, and ran my hands down my face. What had I done, and moreover, what could I do?

"Where'd she go?" a voice called loudly, right outside the tent.

"I saw the princess go in that tent," another voice answered.

I backed up to the far side of the small tent and pulled the scarf down off my hair.

"Princess Grace, you are not allowed out without an escort," the voice called from outside.

"I'm coming." I stepped out of the tent and was greeted by none other than Captain Lathe.

"Because of unfortunate circumstances that have arisen, the king has asked all the princesses to remain inside the palace for their protection." The captain snapped his fingers, and a guard came forth, gesturing for me to walk with him.

"Rumple," I whispered. "Please get word to Bravado."

Silence followed as I was taken out of the tent and dragged back to the palace.

The palace was worse than a prison, except it had better food. Breakfast consisted of eggs, meats, breads, and cheeses. Our meals weren't in the dining hall, but in our wing of the palace, served buffet style.

Once again, I felt like I didn't know where to sit as I picked up a plate and stared at the long line of food. Risa was filling hers with pastries, Willa took only eggs, and Lisbelle ignored the food altogether. The plate shook in my hand as I tried to contemplate what Grace would have chosen. Then I saw familiar foods and found myself picking up slices of bread, pears, and honey butter. Just like in the Northern Woods, I moved away from the crowd and took the bench seat in front of a bricked-up window, feeling like it was as close to freedom as I could get. As I prepared my breakfast, I couldn't help but wonder how Percy had ended up in the sacred hollow. When had he become bound to Allemar? Did I ever really know him?

As I chewed my food, one of my fake sisters, Therisa, who had honey-brown hair, came and stood over me with her arms crossed across her chest.

"You eat the same thing. I wish you would change. In fact, I wish you would change . . ." She shook her head, changing her mind, and silencing her outburst.

The bread froze halfway to my mouth. What were the chances that Grace and I would eat the same unique breakfast? It didn't seem possible.

No longer hungry, I dropped the pear and bread. I looked into Therisa's green eyes filled with frustration. And maybe something else. I took a chance.

"You can speak freely with me."

Those beautiful green eyes filled up with tears and she wiped them away angrily. "It's fine. Never mind . . . I'm fine." But she watched me out of the corner of her eyes warily.

"About tonight. What do you think—?"

The door opened, and King Leonel stood in the doorway. His eyes passed over all of us, slowly scrutinizing. "These last few days have been an enormous strain on my kingdom, and many of the suitors have already withdrawn their offers after this morning's dreadful news. Daughters, I demand more of you."

Therisa started to speak, "Father, we are for—" Her hand slapped her mouth, and more tears came out of her eyes.

She turned away, quickly coughing into a handkerchief and hid it among her skirt, but not before I saw the blood.

Anger riled through me at the injustice. I balled up my fists and my jaw clenched. Therisa looked up at me in horror, her body trembling.

"What did you say, Therisa?" King Leonel turned to her.

She shook her head in fear and ran to her room, her hands covering her mouth.

"Why are the southern elves here?" Risa stood up from the chaise she had been reclining on. She pushed her long braid over her shoulder and faced the king, her face stoic and confident. "Send them away."

"They are here at my request. Allrick and I have an understanding." His eyes flicked to me.

"We are your heirs. It's only luck that none of us were boys, or there could be another daughter of Eville sneaking in our midst, plotting to steal this kingdom right out from under us. But no. That won't happen because our father is giving the kingdom away to a man!" Risa's voice continued to rise until she was screaming with rage. "Then I hear of your plotting with the southern elves? What have you promised them, Father?"

Analisa joined in Risa's argument. "Just choose one of us to be your heir. We are worthy or ruling, Father. We don't need a husband from this gathering of kings. We could take our time and marry for love."

King Leonel's face flushed red with embarrassment, then anger. "One does not marry for love. You can't afford to. It must be for the good of the kingdom. A marriage brings wealth, honor, and strength to the kingdom. If it can't bring those things, then your worth . . . is nothing." His voice trailed off, and King Leonel stared off into the distance.

I turned to see what caught his eye and noticed the mirror over Risa's shoulder. It was a gilded frame, and the reflective surface had gone white like snow, and shadows moved on the other side.

The king's mouth dropped open as the shadows blurred together into an outline of a woman.

"I gave you warning, Leonel. Your sins have come back to haunt you. You must stop this plan of yours. It will not work."

"Witch!" the king breathed out. He picked up a cup from the breakfast table and threw it into the mirror. Risa screamed and ducked as glass went flying everywhere.

King Leonel stood in the middle of the room, his eyes glazed over, his mouth turned down, and he was shaking with rage. "You will not force my hand!" he shouted at the mirror.

Twelve women stared at the king, unsure of how to move or respond. After a few tense moments, King Leonel seemed to come to his senses. He turned, pointing his finger at each of us. "I refuse to let her win. I will take the kingdoms back," he yelled.

"Well, that seems to be difficult when all the men who court us . . . end up dead," Lisbelle said sweetly. She came and put her hand on her father's arm, and he recoiled as if her touch burned him.

"No more," he whispered. "I will bring you more suitors."

"Oh Father, we are way past being mad . . .We are *furious.*" Lisbelle dragged out the words, which only seemed to make the king more uncomfortable.

He backed into a chair, causing the legs to scrape across the floor. I winced at the noise, and he stared at his daughters as if they were ghosts. The king fled the room.

Risa flicked her hands across her gown and her hair.

Little shards of glass fell to the floor. She stared out after her father's retreating form. "I've received word that the King of Baist, Candor, and Florin arrived this morning for the council. Be wary, my sisters."

Therisa returned, and a collective sigh came from the room. She turned to her sisters. "I heard one is a werewolf, and the other is a former apprentice of Allemar. Now is the time to be vigilant."

Ten heads nodded in agreement, and I stood there trying to put together the mystery that was slowly unraveling piece by piece.

"And be wary of the girl in the magical menagerie," Lisbelle warned.

"Which one?" Risa asked.

"The silk dancer with the painted face," Lisbelle answered. "I have a weird feeling about her. She seems familiar."

"But you always can read people. It's your gift," Risa answered.

"I know," Lisbelle said through clenched teeth. "There's just something odd about that one."

My mouth dropped open in surprise, and I covered it quickly with my hand, pretending to yawn.

One by one, the girls looked to Lisbelle, and a worried smile passed between them. Except for me, I raised my lips and tried to paste on a fake smile, even though I had no idea what was going on.

CHAPTER TWENTY-TWO

I s this what it was like to be a princess? I sat in the sunroom with the eleven sisters, and I finally took note of their names and figured out who was related to whom.

The king had married three times. With his first wife Helen, there was Analisa, followed by triplets; Karisa, Louisa, Marisa, and then Risa and Therisa. All of them were beautiful with honeyed locks and green or brown eyes. After Queen Helen passed from a mysterious illness, the king married Thena, who disappeared shortly after Princess Grace was born. The rumors were she ran away with a lover.

Not even six months later, in an attempt to secure his throne with a male heir, King Leonel married a beautiful noblewoman named Brielle, who died a few years ago. She birthed five beautiful girls; Annabelle, Clarabelle, Lisbelle —the blondes—while Maribelle and Willabelle were redheaded twins. All daughters went by the shortened version of their name—Anna, Clara, Mari, and Willa— except for Lisbelle. So there was a group I internally called the "Isa girls," the "Belles," and Grace. Seemed easy enough, especially when Grace was the outcast sister, as the only daughter of the king's second wife, who I learned was actually his favorite and possibly his one true love. It only created a greater divide and jealousy among the daughters, often leaving Grace segregated. For the time being, that helped me . . . thankfully.

Lunch was set out on the second-floor palace terrace, and the guests strolled through the glass doors to meet with the princesses, and I was one of them. I clung to the stone railing and looked out over into the gardens at the colorful tents beyond. My mind and heart were at complete odds with each other. When I had been in the tents, my goal was to get into the palace and find out what was going on so I could track down the son of Allemar. Now that I was in the palace and trapped impersonating a princess, I wanted nothing more than to shed the disguise and go back to freedom. Especially after everything I had seen from the night before.

There was no way for me to escape. I was being tailed by Ardax. Each time I tried to slip away, he was there, not even using glamour to try to disguise himself. I didn't know if the king commanded him to stay with us, or if he'd figured out who I was. The other princesses seemed just as uncomfortable by the addition of added elven security.

This wasn't a job for me. I had no magical abilities. This needed Rosalie and Meri, or even Aura. She could figure out who was behind this by listening to their thoughts and feelings. How was a blade going to fight magic?

It couldn't.

I suddenly felt unworthy of the task set before me, and I was utterly alone.

I couldn't trust Ardax, and I wasn't sure if I could even trust Percy, though I hadn't seen him since last night. I couldn't get a message to Bravado, and even Nimm had vanished early this morning. I had hoped he could get a message to Saphira.

I had spent the better part of the morning running from one end of the terrace to the other, avoiding the many suitors and their talks of money, land, and how many servants they had attending to their every whim.

The first suitor could not stop talking about his latest endeavor of removing all the hated gnomes and hobs from his province because their looks were an affront to nobilities.

"Surely, by removing the fae from your lands, you are almost guaranteeing drought and disease, for it is the fae's good fortune that brings healthy crops," I said.

"You must be joking," Lord Packer replied.

"I am not. The fae are magically tied to the land. Their health and happiness directly correspond to your wealth. If you choose to ban their entire species because they do not conform or look the way humans do, then be prepared to pay the price. Even trolls and goblins are a part of the very cycle of our kingdoms, and to disregard any species in favor of another is only declaring famine and possibly war."

Lord Packer quickly retreated, leaving me in peace until the next man filled in beside me with equally inane comments and questions. How could I possibly sneak away when I was under constant surveillance by every eligible male?

I had to draw the line in the sand and make it obvious that I wasn't available.

It became a game to see how fast I could subtly insult their intelligence and remove my name from the marriage market. By evening, the word must have spread because no man dared approach me.

But even more disconcerting was that from the second-floor balcony, I could see the slow disappearance of the Magical Menageries tents. One by one, the colorful canopies disappeared among the greenery, and soon they were gone, and with it—my magical charmed tent.

My hand clutched the front of my dress as I tried to settle my panicked breathing. This wasn't good. I couldn't be around this many people for long without negatively affecting them.

When I asked a passing servant, the man shrugged his shoulders. "It seems the owner of the menagerie has accused the palace of kidnapping and imprisoning one of their performers. So the king has asked their presence to be removed."

"No." I turned to stare at the last wagon as it headed through the front gate, driven by Ogress. As if sensing my gaze, she turned and pressed her green lips to her fingers, and held them up to me in a wave, wishing me luck.

Did she know? It sure seemed like she knew something was going on.

As her wagon passed through the gates, I watched as the guards pushed the two-story metal doors until they slammed close. I winced as the sound carried across the courtyard below, and more guards than I had seen the first day moved to stand in front of the gates.

Why were there so many guards?

What was happening?

And why did it feel like I was a prisoner?

∿

As the sun set and the moon rose into the night sky, so did the whispers among the servants and staff. A heaviness hung in the air like an invisible mist. Uncertainty could be felt among the guests all through dinner. Would the king make another announcement?

The king stood at the head of his table, and on his left were his twelve daughters arranged in birth order, from Analisa to young Willa. I was placed right between Therisa and Anna, and thankfully, three seats away from Lisbelle, who kept periodically leaning forward and giving me a strange look. Her eyes would narrow, and her brow would furrow as if she was sensing the difference in Grace.

Tired of being a victim of Lisbelle's bullying, I glared back at her.

Lisbelle smirked in response. She leaned back in her chair and reached for her glass, confident that she still had me under control in fear, and that I was Grace.

A sigh of relief escaped my lips, and I stood next to my chair, waiting for the men to file down the rows and take a seat in front of each of us. There were fewer men than yesterday, and even fewer than at this morning's tea.

With my gaze still downcast, I saw movement as each chair was pulled out, and a figure stood at the high table. Then two more guests joined the king. On his right was King Xander of Baist, with dark copper hair and an amber gaze that left a chill down the table of onlookers. Next to him was King Dorian of Candor, a half-elf; tall and domineering, with dark hair that hung over his ears, and gray-blue eyes as cold as ice. The third was King Aspen, a dark blond man with a cruel demeanor—and a former apprentice of Allemar.

When the king sat, everyone followed, and a servant

behind me scooted my chair in toward the table. I reached for the cloth napkin and laid it across the light green gown that I had taken from Grace's closet. All of her outfits were a shade of the soft green, as if it was her assigned color.

I looked down the row and noticed that we indeed were assigned a color based on the rainbow, with Analisa and Karisa's in deep red and pink. Louisa in orange, while Therisa was in a pale yellow. I was in the soft green, while Anna next to me was a deep blue-green. Lisbelle in her pale indigo dress only made her seem younger than she really was. I tried to think back over the last several days to see if any of the twelve princesses had changed out of their color order. No, they hadn't. Was this how I was fitting in so easily?

No one really dared to get to know the princesses, and we were just a color. As long as there was someone that looked like Grace in green, I was accounted for, and as the princess that was the most ostracized, it also worked in my favor.

I grasped the cloth napkin in my lap, wringing it over and over as if it was a noose tightening around my neck, letting my thoughts focus on the actions and surrounding conversations. I still wasn't sure if I could carry a full conversation face to face, or convince either Analisa or Therisa that I was their sister.

All through the meal, my eyes kept straying toward Dorian, Aspen, and Xander. None of them had ever met me, thankfully, but I knew enough to recognize them.

How was I to get to them and warn them about the coming war? And if I did tell them about the sacred hollow access and the magic paintings, how did I prove what I saw was the truth? Every time I attempted to touch the painting and pass through, nothing happened.

It was still canvas, with a wall behind it.

Would they believe me?

It was better to say nothing, to keep my head down, wait for nightfall . . . and what? Go back *into* the painting? Get trapped, forced to dance, and almost kill those around me?

The roasted duck tasted like ash in my mouth. I could no longer eat as my stomach knotted with worry. There had to be something that I could do, but I suddenly felt so alone. I was without Bravado and his troupe. Percy turned out to be in league with the son of Allemar.

I didn't know who to believe, or who to turn to for help. Especially since there were twelve elven soldiers standing directly across from us. I glanced up at Ardax, who stared at a spot on the wall behind Risa. His face was stone, his hand resting on his hip and near his weapon. Farther down the line was Percy, standing just as still, his muscles tense.

His eyes flicked toward me, and I was caught in a sea of green, drowning in his gaze.

My mouth went dry. The fork slipped out of my fingers and clattered loudly on the plate. I looked up toward the king to see King Dorian staring at me, his own fork held aloft—frozen midair. When he met my gaze, he quickly took a bite and leaned in toward Xander and Aspen and whispered. I heard a choke, and then both of the kings were staring at me among the table of princesses. I felt their intense gaze as if someone was boring a hole in the side of my head. Keeping my head down, I tried to ignore them, but I felt like I was snared in a hawk's talons. Their attention was so painfully directed my way.

Lisbelle seemed to have noticed the young kings' attention toward me, and her face scrunched up with frustration. Dinner dragged on, and it wasn't lost on me the dreary conversation I had as Lord Packer was sitting across from me again.

My hands trembled, and this time I knew it wasn't from trepidation, but fatigue. I pressed my fingers to my temple to try to focus on holding back the hunger. My worst fear was assaulting me again, and I had nowhere to run to.

Not here. Not now.

I bit the inside of my cheek until I tasted blood.

I needed to get away. Now.

The chair screeched across the floor as I quickly stood up and exited the room without a word. As soon as I stepped out of the dining room, I ran as fast as my slippered feet would take me, blindly rushing away from people even though I could hear footsteps as the elven guards and palace guards pursued me.

My chest burned, and I slowed, running out of energy, but I heard the rattle of armor and swords swinging against hips as the guards neared me.

Percy reached me first, and slammed into me, covering me with his body. My back pressed against the cold stone wall, and he pressed his chest against mine. His hands reached over me to touch the wall. He closed his eyes, and I felt a tingle run through my whole body. The air around us wavered as he used glamour to make us fade into the stonework.

Through a haze of glamour, three soldiers ran down the hall and split off, running right past us.

I'd seen the elves do this hundreds of times, knowing

they were touching a tree, a stone, and using magic to reflect the air around them, hiding their presence. Lorn had explained the mechanics of their secrets, and also why I could never truly join the scouts.

I would hamper their magic.

I gasped as the closeness was too much, and I could feel myself nullifying Percy's magic.

Percy's brow furrowed, and I could see his frustration as his magic wavered.

"You can't use your magic around me," I whispered, and pressed against his chest.

"It's okay," he said.

"I'm not okay. I'm what's wrong," I said, going weak.

"What do you need?" he asked.

"I need . . . I need to be alone." I braced myself against the wall, and a moment later, I heard the soft click of an invisible cupboard. One that the house-elves used. Percy pulled me inside after him and closed the door behind us.

There was barely room to stand, and the darkness only made the room seem smaller. We stood face to face, and I was increasingly aware of how close we were.

"What is this?" I asked.

"Looks like a broom cupboard."

"Why a broom cupboard?" I asked, struggling to stay upright.

He leaned in to whisper in my ear. "You said you needed to be alone."

I reached out with my hands to find out how big of a space we were confined within. There was barely enough room to sit or turn around, and I couldn't imagine hiding in here long, not when I was going cold.

Percy leaned close, his hands grasping my upper arms. "Why are you so cold? What's happening?"

"Leave me." I pushed at him again, stepped back and knocked into a broom. It started to slide against the wall, but Percy caught it before it clattered to the ground.

"Never. I'm not letting you out of my sight again. You always get in trouble when I do, and then I get in trouble just so I can be with you." Percy grasped my hand and settled onto the ground, situating me on the floor between his long longs. He pulled me back into his chest, wrapping his arms around me. "Honor, why do you keep lying to me?"

"Not lying . . . scared of the truth," I muttered.

"What do you need?" he asked, breathing against my temple. "Just ask, Honor."

"I can't. Please leave me. I don't want to hurt you."

"Honor, I know." He brushed the hair out of my eyes. "I know what you are."

Tears of shame threatened to spill down my face. "No, you can't possibly know."

In the darkness, the silence between us became heavy as he spoke the words of truth. "I figured it out last night. You're an antimage, and you're about to drain all the magic in the palace if you can't get yourself under control, and I can't let that happen. There's too much at stake."

"No!" I turned, putting my hands on his chest and tried to push away from him, but he grasped my chin. His fingers were hot across my icy skin. His other hand moved behind my neck and pulled me close.

"Take what you need from me," he whispered. "I can handle it."

"No . . ."

"Say it," he demanded, his voice husky.

"Say what?"

"Say you need me," he breathed out.

"I don't—"

Percy silenced my denial with a kiss.

Shock filtered through me at the initial contact. I inhaled in surprise as his lips pressed against mine to stop me from speaking. I expected him to pull back, but he didn't. His lips moved against my own. The gentlest question was a kiss, and he was waiting for me to answer. Years of wanting him, but knowing we could never be together, had built up so much tension between us that we had both been fighting for so long. I wanted to surrender to the moment and be taken captive as I melted into his embrace.

I answered his question with my own desire and the kiss deepened, crossing the line of friendship, knowing we could never go back without hurting the other. The kiss grew from gentle to demanding as Percy pulled me onto his lap, locking me to him with his strong grip. His hand pressed into my back, bringing me closer, and I wrapped my arms around his neck. I broke the kiss, gasping as my body pulled on Percy's magic, and it tasted so sweet . . . so beautiful. It was better than passing through the veil of the Northern Woods.

Tears filled my eyes, and I opened them. Even in the darkness, I could see the golden glow of magic from his heart flow into mine. He inhaled sharply, and I realized I was hurting him.

"No . . . stop," I whispered, talking more to myself than I was to him. Wishing I could give it back; return what I had stolen from him. "I'll hurt you."

Percy pulled me close, cupping my neck, his breath

warm on my lips. "This pain is nothing compared to the pain of being without you. You may not need me, Honor, but I will always need you." Then I felt his tears on my cheeks as he kissed my forehead, the tip of my nose, and then brought his lips to mine in a passionate kiss. I couldn't fight him away, as my desire for him only grew. The small cupboard glowed with the light that was shared between us.

He moaned and broke away. My lips were swollen, and I leaned in to kiss him again. "That's enough, or you'll surely kill me."

I gasped and moved away, but he brought me back into his lap. "Not me," he said through ragged breaths. "I mean, kill my control."

"Oh . . ." Heat rose to my cheeks, and I felt awkward . . . and very warm and content. He brushed his thumb across my wet lips.

"I've wanted to do that for so long. How do you feel?" he asked.

"Amazing," I rushed out, and then covered my face with my hands. "Embarrassed, ashamed."

He moved my hands down and looked into my eyes. "Never be ashamed of who you are." He kissed me on my nose and pulled me against his body. In a cramped hidden cupboard, I closed my eyes and focused on my breathing. I relaxed against Percy as he draped a hand over my waist, and I felt him lean his chin onto my head in a comforting embrace. I fell into a contented sleep.

CHAPTER TWENTY-THREE

A flutter of movement brushed against my hip, and I jumped up, my arm shooting out punching the air, my elbow connecting with something warm. I heard a grunt of pain as I sat up and stared at the surrounding darkness. Moments later, my eyes adjusted to the semi-darkness as the light from under the door seeped through. I was still curled up on the floor of a cupboard with Percy, who was rubbing his side where I'd accidentally elbowed him in the gut.

"Sorry, there's not much room," I said, trying to fold myself into an even smaller ball so as not to touch him.

"I wasn't complaining."

"How long have we been here?" I asked.

"Long enough for my legs to fall asleep, and long enough to worry the king."

"We should get going," I said, pulling away.

"Not yet. I'm comfy," he mumbled, pulling me back into his arms. He nuzzled my head. "This reminds me of a time I was hunting down rogue drakefowls. I had holed up in a cramped cave for hours with Ardax, waiting for them to come out. It was so cold, and I couldn't wait to get warm again. Only this time, the company is far more enjoyable." Percy nudged my arm with his knee.

"Why did you leave the scouts?" I asked, staring off into the darkness. "Why did you give it all up?"

"Do you really not know?" he asked.

"I don't."

"I gave it up for you."

My heart ached at his admission. "Why would you do that?"

"I never wanted to become a scout. That was your dream, which became mine to please you."

"Then why did you come to train in the first place?"

"Because I had to. At first, I resented that Allrick sent me and Ardax to the Northern Woods. Lorn knew right away who I was. He saw through my facade and confronted me. He blackmailed me; forced me to train with a human girl, or he would reveal Allrick's true motives."

"Which were?"

"To bring the two realms together, either by marriage or by force. No one has married outside the Thornhaven Court for hundreds of years. Our lineage and magic is weakening, and because our whole purpose is to guard the Thornhaven sacred hollow, our magic has become even more fractured because of our nearness to it." Percy picked at a loose thread on the seam of his knee.

I took a deep breath, trying to process all that he was confessing. "Did Ardax have a similar agreement with Lorn?" I asked.

Percy shook his head. "No. Ardax could never understand my motives for training with you. He thought I had gone soft and was betraying my clan. He was merciless to you, because he thought he was helping me." He shrugged. "I took the bribe, and Lorn kept my secret. Except Rulah fell for the wrong elf because I'd already fallen for the wrong girl."

"When I passed the final test, I returned to find you had left with Lorn . . . again. Every time you were away from me, I was unsettled, unable to sleep, and I couldn't figure out why. Honor, I don't know if you understand what I'm saying. It's like you were my compass. When you were by my side, things made sense, and when you weren't there, I was lost."

"You shouldn't say things like that," I whispered back.

The silence grew heavy. "It's true. There was a fire within you. I watched that spark grow to an ember, then ignite into the fiery, passionate woman you are. You cried when you were upset, got angry when you failed, and even got revenge on me, on Ardax—the more emotions you had, the stronger you became. Until that day when you turned your emotions off, when we were fighting. I saw that flame doused, and I didn't like that you hid behind a stony exterior. Your emotions don't make you weak. They make you strong. And I vowed that day to learn more about you, to share my emotions with you. I don't want to hide what I'm feeling. Not anymore."

The more Percy talked, the more my walls were crumbling. He was tearing down my defenses that I'd so carefully constructed, but no matter he'd just shared, I had to ask the question I was dreading. In the half-lit cupboard, I leaned away from him and turned to look him in the eye. Pulling up his sleeve, I revealed the dark triangle tattoo on his wrist.

"Are you—" I swallowed thickly, the moisture in my mouth drying up. "Are you the son of Allemar?"

"There's something you have to understand. A far greater power is at work—" he began, but didn't deny his involvement.

I cut him off as my heart started to break. "Explain this." I held up his wrist, exposing the blood tattoo. One that could only be gained by sacrifices. "You've sold your soul for power, Percy."

His head fell back against the wall of the cupboard, and he closed his eyes.

"Tell me what the southern elves are planning," I demanded. "Tell me how to stop them? How do I free the princesses from that midnight enchantment?"

"Honor." He opened his eyes and pleaded with me. "I can't."

"Can't tell me . . . or won't."

He fell silent again and wouldn't look at me. My anger rose to new heights. I couldn't tell if he was being stubborn, or if he was bloodbound to not speak about the son of Allemar.

"Did you know about the attacks?" I asked.

Percy shook his head. "No. You have to believe me. I didn't want this. I never wanted to hurt anyone." His head dropped, and his voice quivered with emotion. "But I have a sworn duty to . . ." he trailed off.

"Why are you lying to me?" I stood up, grateful to have my strength back, and I used it to push away from him and fumble with the cupboard handle until it opened.

Percy reached into his jacket and pulled out a slim dagger with a black-handled blade. "For protection from Ardax . . . or if it comes to it . . . me."

My gut twisted, and I couldn't believe what I was hearing. Lorn's warning from years ago echoed in my mind.

Do you really know who he is?

He's Percy.

Again, you seemed to have missed the purpose of your training completely. You still don't know your enemy.

"Please, Honor. Don't go looking for trouble. This is not the time nor the place for your adventures. Let things happen the way they are supposed to happen."

"Like what happened in the Northern Woods? You'd let that massacre happen again?"

His shoulders stiffened. "Sometimes death is the only way to bring about a new beginning; a new chapter."

"Well, your story needs a different ending," I snapped. "If you think I won't do everything in my power to rewrite the future, then you don't know me at all."

"I *do* know you, Honor. That's why I'm giving you this courtesy. I don't want to fight you because I may be forced to kill you."

I felt my blood run cold, like a bucket of water had been dumped on my head.

"Same. What are you planning, and why drag the princesses into this?"

He shook his head, and I saw the barest flicker of remorse and regret. "You know I'm unable to say anything just as they are? Anyone that has tried to question the king's motives has ended up dead. The real question you need to be asking is not why am *I* involved, but why are *you?*"

"What do you mean, me?" I dropped the blade to my side and hid it among the folds of my dress as footsteps came toward us.

"Don't you think it's odd that you arrive here in Sion, and there is a princess who looks *exactly* like you?"

"It's a coincidence."

"You don't believe in coincidences. You've always trusted your gut. What does your gut tell you, Honor? Why are you here? How did you get here? And where is Princess Grace?"

The footsteps grew louder, and King Leonel came around the corner with his guards.

"There you are, Grace! I've been worried sick about you. You weren't with your sisters. It's almost time." King Leonel came up to my side, looked up at Percy, and his face darkened. "Why didn't you escort her back to her room?" he yelled.

"Excuse me, Your Majesty, I'm on my way to do just that." Percy slipped past the king and grabbed my elbow, trying to usher me along.

I turned and yelled over my shoulder toward the king. "King Leonel, I will tell you where your daughters go each night, and how their slippers are destroyed."

Percy stilled, his hand gripping my arm painfully. "Don't," he hissed through clenched teeth.

"Your daughters sneak through a magical painting in the princesses' sitting room and go to the sacred hollow in Thornhaven where they are forced to dance all night to power a spell."

"Now you did it," Percy grumbled and stood back, his hands open at his side to show he was unarmed. We were surrounded on all sides; eight guards with swords pointed in our direction.

King Leonel turned, his hands going to his hips, his eyes wide in disbelief at my outburst. Then he leaned forward, his lips turned up into a cruel smile, and whispered so only I could hear. "You are . . . not my daughter."

"What?" I backed up and turned to Percy. "He knows . . . ?"

Percy gave me a small nod. "I told you not to say anything."

My heart hammered against my chest, and my hand went to my mouth as my breath froze in my lungs. I looked up at the king, whose eyes had narrowed in anger.

He grabbed my exposed wrist, looking at the jagged tree-shaped drakefowl scar. "What magic is this? Who are you?" he demanded.

"I'm Honor Eville." I gave a small curtsy.

This information sent the king into a blazing fury. "How is this possible? I've set up wards against this very thing." The king spun on Percy. "You were supposed to protect my daughters."

Percy's jaw clenched. "We are commanded to protect your daughters from death. Every . . . single . . . night. The day . . . well, that's another matter."

"Remove this glamour!" the king shouted, grabbing my arm and squeezing painfully.

"This isn't a glamour. This is what I look like."

King Leonel released my arm and froze. He took three steps back as if he had seen a ghost. "Tell me I'm dreaming. It can't be *her*. What is she doing here?" He waved his hands between us like I was smoke he was trying to dissipate. "Guards!" he yelled, and the two on either side of the king stepped toward us, followed by more from down the hall.

The king was still stuttering, murmuring to Captain Lathe as soon as he appeared with the last set of guards. "It can't be. I don't understand how she's here when there are antimagic wards." He spun on me, his eyes flaring to life with hatred.

It was as though a light had been snuffed out. Quickly the king switched between calm and collected, to paranoid and enraged.

"Arrest her . . . Now!" he screamed.

"You won't get away with this. My sisters will come, and they'll stop you."

King Leonel laughed. "By morning, my daughters will have given their lives, and my armies will invade all of the kingdoms at once. Without their kings to lead them, those kingdoms will fall. And the kings' heads will fall soon after. I will be the high king of all seven kingdoms."

"My sisters will stop you!" I yelled.

"They will be too late."

My cries fell on deaf ears as Captain Lathe's men pushed me to the ground, burying my face into the rough stone floor as cold manacles clasped around my hands.

My knees scraped against the stone, the thin dress doing very little to protect my skin. I gritted my teeth as they hauled me to my feet, and I noticed that I was alone again. Percy had abandoned me.

"What would you like me to do with the witch, Your Majesty?"

King Leonel waved his hands. "Put her in prison. We'll execute her at dawn."

My heart hammered against my chest as they dragged me away.

What had I done?

CHAPTER TWENTY-FOUR

The scratching of rats' claws echoed loudly as they scurried along the edge of my cold and dank cell. In the darkness, a rat brushed against my foot, and I recoiled in surprise. Pulling my knees up to my chest, I wrapped my arms around my legs and rocked myself, trying my hardest to keep my wits about me.

I replayed the confrontation in my mind. The king had reacted like he had seen a ghost. He wasn't at all surprised that there was another who looked like his daughter. In fact, he seemed to have known all along. Did that mean we were related? Could Grace really be my blood sister?

The squeaking of rats grew louder as they became braver, scurrying closer to my leg.

"Shoo!" I lashed out with my foot, sending the large gray creature scampering away.

Alone with my thoughts was a dangerous place to be. In the prison, there were no windows, and I couldn't tell the passage of time. A lone guard stood at the end of the hall, and every once in a while, he would walk down the row of cells.

From the dry hacking cough I heard farther down, I gathered I wasn't the only guest residing in the king's prison. The cell bars were solid, with well-oiled hinges on the doors. Rhea would have been impressed by the blacksmith's workmanship.

I stayed curled in my position, counting the steps the guard took on his rounds, listening to each step and the echo. I tried to judge how long the corridor was before the echo stopped as he turned a corner, and how many seconds before I could hear him return on his round.

I would have one chance.

Stretching out on the cold floor, I faced the door and feigned sleep, peeking an eye open slightly to watch him.

The prison guard, his hair dirty and eyes red-rimmed from heavy ale consumption, took a torch off the wall near his post. Pausing to check at my cell, he raised the torch, and I closed my eyes, focusing on keeping my breathing even and deep. When my cell darkened, I knew he had moved on. I sat up and slipped the dagger out of my skirt. Thankfully, the guards hadn't thought to check me for weapons, and I worked on sliding the blade tip into the lock on the u-shaped hinged shackles. In the silent dungeon, each time the thin blade slipped, it scraped against the metal and sounded like a loud, echoing screech. I was sure the guard could hear everything I was doing.

Halfway.

I knew my time was running short. Sweat dripped down my brow as I released the first cuff and worked on the second. I wasn't sure if I'd get another chance to escape. I didn't know what time it was, but I knew that all the kings would arrive by morning, and that my execution was scheduled shortly after. I didn't think there would be another change of the guard before then.

Click.

The second manacle released, and it dropped from my hand. I kneeled in front of the lock on the door. My hands slipped through the bars. Turning the knife around, I dug into the keyhole searching for the pin, hoping to twist the blade and release the lock.

My hands trembled in the cold, and the blade slipped from my fingers to clatter loudly on the stone floor outside the cell.

I froze.

The footsteps sped up.

Laying prone on the ground, I reached through the bars, my cheek pressing into the cold metal as I grasped at the edge of the dagger, but it was just out of reach.

The hall grew lighter as the guard returned with the torch lighting his way.

My fingers dug into the earth, and I scraped and stretched, trying to claw for the weapon. I brushed the handle, and it spun further out of reach.

My face dropped onto the ground, straw stabbing my cheek and I could feel my heart aching. I laid there helpless, watching my last chance of freedom slip from my grasp.

Then the blade lifted up into the air, suspended as if by magic, and shot through the bars toward me. A shimmer in the air made me smile. Nimm had found me.

I grabbed the dagger, tucked it under my body with the shackles and lay back down facing the wall, tucking my hands into my stomach just as the guard returned and stared into my cell. His torch rose high into the air while I froze with fear. *Did I cover the shackles? From his higher angle, could he see I was free?*

My heartbeat pounded loudly in my ears, surely even

the guard could hear it. The light on the wall flickered, and the guard moved back to his post, the light growing dimmer until I was left in darkness again.

A few moments later, Nimm slipped through the opening in the bars and materialized in front of me.

"Nimm, I'm so glad to see you."

Nimm lifted his hat, and his beady eyes gleamed at me. He handed me his scarf, and I unwrapped it to see the gnome had pilfered the guard's keys and wrapped them in the fabric to silence the rattling.

"Oh, thank you so much," I whispered to him.

He gave me a wave and disappeared again. I was surprised he left me alone. Then I saw the guard's torch suddenly flicker out.

A high-pitched scream pierced the air. "What is that? What touched me?"

I grinned. Nimm was providing the perfect distraction. Within moments, I used the key to unlock my cell. I turned to make my escape, but then paused.

Turning full circle, I stared down the dark prison hall at the other occupied cell.

I should leave, but instinct told me not to. I had to save the other person.

I ran, my slippers making hardly any noise as I checked every cell. Most of them were surprisingly empty. Where were all the prisoners? Usually, jails were full.

When I came to the only other occupied cell, I saw a prisoner curled up in a ball under layers of rags.

I inserted the key, and the door swung open. The pile of dirty rags shuffled and then moved, and a great mound of unruly hair sat up. Dark, hollow eyes surrounding a pale, deathlike skull stared back at me.

It was a woman, and she blinked at me in surprise. Her eyesight was more accustomed to the dark than my eyes were.

"You're free. We haven't much time to escape," I said.

The women tried to stand up, but collapsed back to her knees.

"I can't leave. The door is warded."

I looked at the frame and saw the sigils etched into the metal. These I could read. It was warded against magic, and it was trapping her inside.

I pressed my hand onto the symbols, and like I had done on the others, I absorbed the magic, nullifying the wards. The wards glowed and slowly fizzled out, dissipating like golden sand and falling to the ground.

"The wards are gone." I came to her and kneeled down, giving her my hand.

The woman trembled; her arms were bone thin, and her eyes filled with tears when she saw me up close.

I wondered if maybe she didn't want freedom.

"Grace? Is that you?" her voice cracked from disuse.

"No," I answered coldly.

I pulled the woman to her feet and was surprised to see her tower over me. Tall and ethereal, despite her hollowed shell of a self. I could tell she was once a woman of means and power by her demeanor.

"Follow me," I commanded. Now it was up to her if she wanted to escape. I couldn't afford to carry her.

"Honor?" The voice whispered, this time with hope. "Is that you?"

I froze, my hand gripping the bars, and I turned around again.

"How do you know my name?" I asked. Fear raced through my body, and goosebumps rose on my arms.

"Because I'm Thena, your mother," the woman said. Her eyes filled with tears and her thin hands covered her quivering mouth. "And I would know my own child."

Even with all of my years of training, nothing could prepare me for confronting my past, and I did the only thing I could think of doing.

Deny it.

I shook my head. "You must have confused me with someone else."

Her brow furrowed. "No. I can prove it to you. I come from a long line of magic-touched women, and we have a special gift. It passes down in sets of twos. Always twins. My sister and I shared the gifts, as do you and your twin."

"Grace?" As I said her name, my chest constricted. It was hard to breathe. The air was getting thin, and my vision blurred. "I-I'm not—" I started.

"You are. My gift—the gift of my ancestors—is very powerful, and it has two sides." Thena held out her hand, and now that the ward was gone, she could use magic. Thena conjured an image of a golden two-headed coin, and it spun in the air. One side was gold, the other dark. "One daughter would possess great power, the other daughter, the antithesis of that power. A dark and a light. Grace is the natural-born mage, which means you, Honor, are an—"

"Antimage," I answered.

"But like this spinning coin, one magic will cancel the other out to survive." As she narrated, the coin stopped spinning, and it fell down, rattling until it stilled, leaving the dark-faced side up, the golden light from the other side of the coin went dim.

Thena reached for my hands, her face streaming with tears that left white tracks down her dirty face. "Yes. Grace's power is the strongest in ten generations, which means your gift when it manifested would be just as potent. And it was too dangerous to keep you two together. You had to be separated at birth, just as my sister and I were separated. As soon as you were born, you were powerful. Your power was so strong, you almost killed the king. To protect you, we sent a nursemaid to take you to the nearest ley line in hopes of keeping your curse at bay. The king didn't want you to come back, and he ordered for you to be killed."

I tensed as I realized I was finally going to learn the truth.

"They didn't make it to the ley line in time. The nursemaid died, and the guard was terrified of you. So he made it look like the elves had killed the nursemaid. He told the king you had died with her."

"How did she die?" A lump formed in my throat, and I dreaded the answer.

"You already know." She looked at my hands, and she felt the callouses along them.

I hung my head, unable to fathom what she was telling me.

"I killed her?" My breath burned in my lungs.

"You were a baby. Innocent. This was not the life I would have chosen for you."

I pulled my hand out of hers. "It's the only life I know."

"It is one of loneliness, but it was necessary for survival."

I nodded my head, my heart breaking even though I understood her reasoning. I was too dangerous. It was the safest choice. One I'm not sure I would have been able to make as a new mother. Was it not the same choice Lady Eville had made? Separating me from my adopted sisters to protect them?

Learning more about who I was didn't make it any easier to swallow.

"So, King Leonel. He is . . . I mean. He's my father?" I struggled to say the words. If it was true, it meant that I really was a princess, and not just any princess. A princess of Sion.

"No," Thena breathed out. Her face turned red. "And that is my shame I must forever bear, and why I was imprisoned here."

My head snapped up. The mental daydream I had created dissipated, and I was once again left feeling numb.

"It is as it should be. My life could have been forfeit," Thena said. "I'm grateful that I can at least see my other child one more time."

It was as if she was saying goodbye. I had just met her, and already she was being distant, separating herself from my darkness, from my curse.

I bit down the bitter disappointment and put my focus on escaping.

Lorelai Eville was my mother. Not this woman before me.

When I returned to the entrance, the guard was gone.

"Nimm?" I called out.

A shadow slipped out of the dark corner and lit a torch holding it knee-high. The flames reflected upon Nimm's smiling face.

"I'm glad you're okay. Where's the guard?" I asked.

Nimm pointed with the torch to a dark corner where the guard was passed out. There was a huge knot on his forehead. I looked at the low hanging beam and realized he must have run right into it. Once he was knocked unconscious, Nimm tore his scarf up and bound his hands and shoved a wad in his mouth.

"Very well done. Saphira would be proud,"

"Saphira," Thena murmured. "I remember a Saphira."

Nimm's bushy eyebrows rose as he leaned to look at the strange woman following me.

"This is my birth mother," I said, angling my head toward her.

Thena put her thin hand on my shoulder for support.

"Something's wrong." She clutched her chest as if it was in pain. Gasping. "We must hurry."

There was no hurrying, for Thena could hardly make it up the stairs. With each step she took, she had to brace herself against the wall, and wait moments before taking another one. I wrapped her arm around my shoulders and supported her weight as we made our escape.

"A gnome," Thena said softly. "It has been ages since I've seen one of your kind."

Nimm reached out his hand and tried to help Thena up the stairs. As we neared the top of the prison steps, there was another door with no handle. Running my fingers along the wood, I searched for a way to open it, but found nothing to grip. Pressing my cheek between the frame and the door, I saw we were locked in from the outside. At the top of the door was a small, barred window that let in fresh air and moonlight.

"Do you think you could fit through?" I asked Nimm.

He cocked his head, measured with his hands the width of the spacing between the bars, and then brought them to his pudgy waist. He shook his head and shrugged his shoulders. He was willing to try.

Gripping Nimm under his arms, I lifted him above my head. He grabbed the bars, put his foot on the bottom frame and worked on angling his body through. First his head, then his chubby belly—which got wedged between the bars. He kicked his legs, and he pulled with all of his might, but he couldn't get through. He was stuck, and I knew when he gave up as his feet dropped and he hung there like a fancy door knocker, feet above the lock.

"Do you think . . ." I turned to my mother and pointed to the door. "Do you think you could release us?" I asked.

Thena shook her head. "I can't . . . with you so close."

I pinched my lips together to hide my frustration. Once again, I was the problem, not the solution—and even my mother was afraid of me.

"What if I go back down into the prison, far enough away from you. I wouldn't hamper your magic? Then maybe you could open the door and save yourself?"

"Honor, you don't understand. Conjuring the illusion of a coin is one thing, but if I used anything other than small amounts of defensive magic near you, the whole kingdom could pay the price. I don't want to lose you when I just found you." Her brown eyes pleaded with me to understand.

With a scream of frustration, I pounded my fist into the door with a thud. Pain traveled up my arm, and it actually felt good. I did it again, and again. I pounded the meat of my fist into the wood, releasing all of my pent-up anger and frustration.

What good was I if I couldn't save anyone? If all I did was hinder?

Years of training, and I couldn't even get out of a prison cell. I had nothing going for me.

A squeak of fear came from Nimm. Something he saw coming near us scared him. His legs wobbled, and he tried to force himself back into our side of the door. When that didn't work, he went invisible.

A second later, a heavy thud hit the side of the wooden door, and dust came raining down from above us.

I backed away from the entrance in fear. Creaking followed, and the wood splintered, and a crack appeared on the inside of the door.

A high-pitched voice hollered, "I'm coming for you, Honor!" Another thud, and more of the wood cracked.

"Rumple?" I called out in surprise through the door. "Is that you?"

"Of course, I'm here to rescue you!"

"Shut it, you stupid axe! You're going to alert the guards," a muffled voice followed.

"Bravado?" I almost cried when I heard his voice. A third swing of the axe and Rumple had cut off the wood around the lock, and it fell to the ground. The door swung outward, and a wonderful sight greeted me.

Bravado, Amaryllis, Sorek, Saphira, and Humperstink.

"You came back for me?" I stepped through the door, helping Thena who seemed terrified by the outside world.

"Of course, we came back. You're part of the family, and we don't leave anyone behind." Bravado put Rumple on the ground and reached out to give me a hug, followed by Amaryllis.

Tears formed in my eyes, and I turned back to the frail woman who was clinging to the broken door.

"Everyone, I'd like you to meet my mother, Thena."

Amaryllis immediately went into protective mode. She pulled the cloak from around her shoulders and covered up Thena, rubbing the fabric up and down her arms, and speaking words of encouragement to her. She motioned to Sorek, who handed over his skin of water, and Amaryllis helped hold it up so Thena could drink.

When I had exited, I took in the surroundings, just as I had done when I was taken to the prison. We were in an outer courtyard by the guardhouse, and normally it was heavily patrolled, but now it was empty. Burners were scattered throughout the yard, and flames flickered, casting shadows upon the stone walls.

"Where are the guards?" I asked, turning to Bravado.

"Gone," he said simply.

"I don't understand. What do you mean gone? There were hundreds out here earlier this evening."

"Yes, we know, but something happened, and they deserted their post. There was a commotion on the other side of the palace. We would've come sooner but couldn't. That distraction is what allowed us to get you out."

A squawk came from the door, and Saphira laughed when Nimm revealed himself again. With the door opened, we only saw his bottom half, still hanging facing outward, and his front was pinned against the outer wall.

Sorek moved to the door, and with his massive hands, pulled on the bars enough to release the gnome.

"Really, Nimm," Saphira chastised. "You should have easily been able to squeeze through that. You might need to give up the sweets for a while."

Nimm made a disgruntled noise and stuck his tongue out.

"Hey, don't forget to thank me!" Rumple yelled from against the wall.

"I'd never forget you." I leaned down and picked him up.

"You forgot me a bunch of times. Whatever happened to running into danger? Seeing action and fighting? All I've seen is the back of the ogre's behind."

I crinkled up my nose and held back the laugh.

"Watch your words, Dwarf, or you'll rue the day you insulted Ogress De La Cour." From beyond the courtyard, Ogress towered over the wall. Gone were her colorful robes and her daintily painted makeup.

She was draped in a furred garment, a necklace with a deer skull, and streaks of paint ran vertically down her face. She held a club larger than one of her ox. Against the many fires that burned, she looked intimidating; a beast of enormous power, and many would have said ugly. But not to me. It was her real armor, meant to intimidate and put fear in her enemies.

"Ogress," I called up to her, and she bent down. "You look wonderful."

Her green lips curled up in a smile around her bottom tusks.

"Thank you, child, but it's time for you to prepare for war as well." She motioned with her hand to the other side of the palace where the night sky was lit almost like day, and orange flames flickered against the sky.

Now I understood where the guards had gone. The palace was under attack, but my only question was, by whom?

CHAPTER TWENTY-FIVE

With Rumple in his holster across my back, I raced across the courtyard to the other side of the palace to see the guards lined up at the front gates. Catapults were being armed, and archers were stationed across the wall, arrows at the ready.

King Leonel paced in front of the palace gates, hundreds of his guards behind him.

In the distance, I could see one person standing on the other side of the palace gate. One woman requested entrance. I only knew of one woman whose very presence could send the king into a frenzy like this and start a war.

Lorelai Eville.

My adopted mother, and the king's ex-betrothed.

"Leonel," Lorelai called calmly through the gates, "has it come to this?"

Mother stood tall, her raven hair fell freely past her shoulders to her hips, her dress was finer than any I had ever seen her own. It wasn't her usual high-neck black dress or her brown work dress or apron. This was a dress befitting of a noble daughter of Kiln.

It was a deep red dress that hugged her hips, with billowy long sleeves, and enough cleavage to make a man drool, but hide her assets. Around her neck was a ruby gemstone as large as a fist. It was the only piece of jewelry she wore, and its presence nestled between her breasts seemed to upset the king.

"I want you gone, Lorelai," the king seethed. "You have no place here."

Lady Eville stepped forward, each step taken with purpose, her hands brushing her hips. It was slow, intoxicating. She was making a show, using her womanly weapons. Ones that I had yet to learn to wield. As I watched her, I suddenly understood their purpose. She was distracting the king. Using her wiles to pull on strings to gain the king's focus, and it was working. She was ensnaring him, using nothing more than her body. She was the puppet master, and he was the puppet.

"Pity, for I had a place here once. It was at your side, do you remember, Leonel?"

She brushed her fingers across the necklace. "Do you remember giving me this as a token of your everlasting love? When you asked me to marry you?"

"You are the worst kind of woman," King Leonel spat out. "Because I no longer loved you, you cursed me."

She tossed her head back and laughed. "Oh Leonel, it wasn't love. Maybe at one time, yes. When we first met, and you fell in love with a young, foolish girl who only cared about pleasing you, and you boldly asked my father for my hand in marriage. I thought nothing could come between us. But I was wrong."

She took another step toward the gate, and the nearest guards raised their bows and pointed the arrows right at her heart. They would surely kill her.

I moved to rush to her, but Bravado pulled me back to

the side of the storage building before the guards noticed me.

"Let me go. They're going to kill her!" I said. "You don't understand how much the king hates her."

"No, Honor. We mustn't interfere. You do not step between scorned lovers. This is a battle, one that has been brewing for over thirty years."

Lady Eville placed her hands on the bars of the gate, wrapping her fingers around the metal. She looked at the king. "But I was wrong. For you were seduced by another."

"Lies," Leonel scoffed, waving his hands. "There was no one else."

"There was, but it wasn't a woman that seduced you away from me. It was something far more dangerous."

King Leonel raised his hands to signal the archers, but he held his hand and even from this distance, I could see him trembling. He was listening to Lorelai and what she had to say.

"Yes, my father's merchant ships were lost at sea, and we lost most of our money and influence, but ask yourself: Who was behind it all?"

"It was fate that the sea took your family's fortune."

"No, it was Sirena, the sea witch . . . on behalf of another. But surely our love was stronger than physical things. It was more than what wealth I brought to the table, or so I had naively thought."

"It wasn't until the council of kings when my father pleaded with you to honor your vows that I saw the darkness within your heart. I knew then that my place in your heart had been filled by another. A desire for power. I saw the first tip of the poisonous arrows that were aimed at my family. You were a pawn. A means by someone more powerful than you, whose sole purpose was to destroy my family."

"I know not what you mean." King Leonel stepped forth and was now only paces away from Lorelai.

"Do you not see it? Even now, my father's death wasn't an accident. He was poisoned, just as your heart was poisoned against me. Just as your daughters poison their suitors . . . for you. What a fine show you put on. The charade, the disbelief, all an act to wipe away your enemies."

King Leonel flinched as if he was slapped, and he stepped back, shaking his head.

"You were only a prince at the time, and still under the influence of one greater than yourself."

"Are you accusing my father of killing yours?" he said.

"No, not him. But think about it, my prince. Who swayed you to end our engagement? *Who* was the one who served my father the tea at the high council?"

"I don't remember." He waved his hands and turned his back on her.

"You do remember," she hissed.

"I do not." He walked away.

"You were not the first man to ask for my hand in marriage," Lorelai called through the gates to him. "You were the second."

This seemed to be news to the king, and he stilled.

"I had no love for the vile and wickedness I saw in his heart, but he never forgave me for turning him down. And when I had found happiness with you, he tried to destroy *our* future. He ruined my father's fortune, took his life, influenced your father to break our engagement, and then he turned your heart against me. I was telling the truth when I said you were seduced by another. It wasn't a woman. You were seduced by *power.*"

"No."

"The power that Allemar promised your father, and in turn, you," she said.

"I tire of your nagging. Begone before my men lose their hold. Even now I can see their arms trembling. One slip of their finger, and you'll be out of my hair forever."

"Leonel, your threats never scared me." She laughed. "It wasn't your fault that your father didn't love you. That he loved another more than you. Bestowed on the bastard son all of his love, and saved none for his crown prince."

Leonel went white as a sheet. "How could you possibly know this?"

"You mean, how could I know about your father's first born bastard son;, who should have taken the throne if he was legitimate? How do I know of the man who secretly despised you, and at the same time, wanted to be you?"

"No, he wouldn't."

"He did," Lorelai said. "It was your brother, Allemar, the long-forgotten bastard. But I saw his wickedness. I refused him, and when we became engaged, it ignited a hatred that could not be doused. Since then, he'd spent his life trying to destroy me and take not just one kingdom. He wanted to rule all seven."

King Leonel's face paled. "No, he didn't want to marry you. He told me how wicked you were. How selfish."

My heart thudded loudly in my ears as I finally understood the lifelong battle that Lorelai had secretly been fighting behind the scenes.

"No. It is *you* who are selfish. Stop. It's not worth it. You are sacrificing your daughters for a greater kingdom."

"Not just one kingdom. Seven. If I had sons, this wouldn't have been an issue, but because of you, I'm forced to take what I want."

"Daughters have value," Lorelai argued.

"I do value them, and their sacrifice will not go in vain. They are gaining me more land than any one marriage alone could bring. And all because of Allemar."

"It's not too late to stop it. Save your daughters. Save yourself. If you don't, hundreds will die tonight. You and your men; I've foreseen it."

"Guards!" King Leonel backed up, tripping over his boots and falling into the gravel.

"You leave me no choice." Lorelai's hands glowed with power, and the bars disintegrated into dust. She stepped through the destroyed gate, and the first arrow came flying straight for her heart.

Lorelai brushed her hand through the air, and it went above and behind her.

"Kill her! Kill! Attack!" King Leonel yelled, and then hundreds of arrows flashed through the night sky and were swallowed up by a ball of fire.

Lorelai was magnificent. Her hands waved as if conducting an orchestra of water and fire. She destroyed the oncoming attacks with defensive magic, not once raising her hand to strike.

The closest drum of fire flickered near me, and a paper shot up out of the flames. I caught it and read the words across the thin parchment.

"Don't be afraid. You must do what you were born to do."

Looking up at the woman who raised me, I saw Lorelai across the courtyard. With her hair flying behind her, she looked like a banshee from Rya. Our eyes met, and she nodded, and mouthed the words. "Go!"

"I can't leave her!" I rushed toward her, but Bravado held me back.

Amaryllis faltered. "It isn't our battle."

An explosion rocked the courtyard, the force of the blast knocked off our feet.

My head throbbed in pain, stars flitted across my vision, and I struggled to sit up. Sorek, Bravado, and Saphira were knocked unconscious. Amaryllis and Thena had been blasted ten feet backward, and were cushioned by a hay bale.

"What was that?" I muttered, feeling like I was going to throw up.

"I don't know, but I don't want to go through that again," Rumple groaned. Flames engulfed the gate and I realized Leonel had used a catapult filled with explosives.

"Mother!" I screamed at the pyre of white fire that had been there only moments ago, where Lorelai had stood. Angry tears poured out of my eyes, and I struggled to stand. I couldn't breathe. Unimaginable pain filled my chest as I saw my mother killed.

Rage raced through my body. I didn't know how it happened, but I ended up in the middle of the fray, fighting every person in a yellow uniform. Swinging Rumple and screaming like a banshee, I fought. Down they went. Every sword that rose against me swiftly fell as I cut a path toward King Leonel.

The king's jaw dropped open when he saw me. "Kill her! Kill the imposter!"

More soldiers filed in front of me, but all I saw was practice targets. Captain Lathe stepped in front to challenge me, but the earth opened up and Captain Lathe, sunk down to his knees. Humperstink grinned evilly, dancing around the yard, using his earth magic.

I could see King Leonel through the flames. His visage burned into my mind, and I felt a burning hatred that fueled my anger.

I screamed, racing toward the king, and gasped as a sharp pain stabbed me in my shoulder. I faltered, and Rumple slipped from my fingers as blood coated my hands.

The ground rushed upward, greeting my knees in a painful kiss, and I saw the arrow protruding from my shoulder. White flecks dotted my eyes, and I knew I could pass out if I didn't handle the pain. I broke the end of the arrow off and pulled out the shaft. Gritting my teeth against the pain, I made a few of the soldiers back away when they say my fearsome determination.

A cranking followed, and I saw the catapult turn my way. I didn't think I could outrun it.

A great roar shook the earth as Ogress stormed across the courtyard, smashing the catapult with her club, breaking it in two. She picked up the frame and swung it over the gate.

"Ogre!" Captain Lathe screamed as he struggled to pull himself from the ground. Arrows flew, piercing Ogress's arms and legs. She roared in pain, dropping to her knees, then pushing herself back up. Her eyes blazed red with fury, blood running down her sides, as she became the target of hundreds of arrows.

"Ogress!" I cried, pushing myself forward, dragging Rumple along the ground with my left hand. I couldn't make it in time.

The earth rumbled a second time as she fell, bringing everyone to their knees.

"Ogress," I whimpered as I made it to her side.

The barrage of arrows had stopped, satisfied that they'd taken down an ogre. I looked upon her form.

"Why did you do that?" I sobbed, pressing my hands to her face.

Ogress's eyes fluttered open as she struggled to breathe. "It was your mother's instructions to us, to protect you at all costs." She coughed, and blood bubbled up out of her lips.

I tried to soothe her by stroking her rough cheek, but I could feel her heartbeat slowing as the ground around me turned dark red.

"Do it for Honor." Ogress sighed, her eyes fluttering close, and she exhaled.

"No!" I screamed.

"Honor!" Pale hands pulled me away into an embrace. Thena was there holding me. I buried my face into her chest and cried great, heaving sobs; a mix of grief, anger, and sadness.

"It's okay. It's okay to cry." She stroked my hair and gave me a kiss on my forehead. I looked up and saw the bright circle of light she was casting around us. A protective shield against the arrows, and it was quickly getting smaller as her power waned.

Thena's grip on my shoulders tightened, and she gave me a sad look. "I'm sorry, Honor. That I wasn't there to protect you. I'm grateful that Lorelai was able to be the mother you needed when I couldn't be. But I will do my best to protect you now." She pressed her hand to my shoulder, and I felt heat like a branding iron burn into my muscles as she forcefully healed me.

Blinding white pain almost made me pass out, but I shivered as cold overtook me. I knew the signs. I needed magic.

"Not yet, sweetie," Thena said. She gave me one last hug and stood up, brushing her rag like dress. Her power was waning, flickering, and I could see how painful it was to keep the spell up.

"I'm sorry," I sobbed.

"Your mother, Lorelai, was right. You must go. Do what you were born to do."

"I don't know what that is?" I cried out.

"You will. But for this to work, for both of us, you must *run*. Run fast. Run far away from me, and don't look back." She gave me a push, and I ran to the edge of her protective shield.

I hesitated and cast a fearful look at her.

She nodded. "Go, darling."

I passed through the bright light, and as soon as I did, the shield of magic collapsed and exposed us.

Thena turned toward the king and stepped barefoot across the gravel. I knew it must hurt, but she never once winced or wavered.

"Thena?" King Leonel gasped in surprise when he noticed the dirty woman.

"Hello, dear," Thena chuckled, and gave a little twirl to show off her raggedy dress. "I'm sorry that I'm not properly dressed for our first meeting in almost twenty years."

"That's because you betrayed me. You bore me a monster."

"Love is never a betrayal. I can forgive you for imprisoning me, but not for trying to kill my daughter."

"She tried to kill me," King Leonel said. "I held her, and she tried to kill me."

"She was a babe, and didn't understand her power," Thena yelled back.

King Leonel shook his head. "That's why she was banished. She should never have been born, and I should have killed you as well. Guards! Kill her!" the king screamed, and the archers turned on her.

I slowed when I got to Amaryllis.

"Go, Honor." Amaryllis pushed me toward the palace. "You shouldn't be here."

"She can't do this alone. She's too weak. She'll need help," I rushed out, knowing that it was taking every ounce of strength left for my mother to walk upright.

"It's okay. I've got this." Amaryllis shooed me away, and raced out to Thena's side, taking her hand.

Thena looked at Amaryllis. "Are you sure?" she asked. "You know what it means? I will take everything you have."

Amaryllis swallowed, and looked back at her prone husband. "I'm sure. My future was foretold long ago. I knew this day would come. We do it for Honor."

Even from a distance, I could see Thena trembling, struggling to stand up and face her captor. Amaryllis wrapped her arms around her in a hug, holding her upright.

I was still too close. I could feel myself pulling on Thena's magic. I needed to save her, and the only way to do it was to run away.

I ran for the open doors of the palace as fast as I could,

trying to give her enough space where I wouldn't nullify her magic. Just as I passed the palace threshold, I looked back and saw Thena raise her hands, and a bright light flickered across the courtyard, emanating from her chest. Amaryllis screamed.

Another blast followed, and I flew backwards into the foyer, hitting a marble column, and darkness followed.

CHAPTER TWENTY-SIX

"Get up, you lazybones!" Rumple growled. "You're squishing me."

Groaning, I rolled over on my side and saw the court-yard was empty. Piles of dirt lay everywhere. Hundreds of people, decimated into dust.

I screamed, realizing what had just happened. "No . . ."

Thena had killed everyone. Fueled by Amaryllis, in a blast of magic, she had destroyed the entire courtyard, the king's army, and herself.

Ogress, Amaryllis, Thena, Lorelai . . . all gone.

I couldn't do this. I didn't even know what I was supposed to do, or where I was supposed to go. Nothing made sense.

I picked myself up, stumbling through the carpeted halls of the empty palace. As I passed a portrait, the frame swung open, and I saw the beady eyes of the house-elves watching me.

I wandered aimlessly and crossed a deactivated ward. My slipper passed over it, and I felt a twinge of guilt. Was this my fault? Had I started the avalanche of circumstances that led to everyone's death?

If I hadn't jumped through the veil and followed the trail to the city, I wouldn't have ended up at the palace. I never would've met Bravado, and his magical menagerie, or Saphira. They'd all be alive.

A small cough surprised me.

Turning, I saw Nimm, his clothes singed, and part of his face was badly burned.

"This is all my fault!" I cried out, dropping to my knees. "Everyone's dead because of me."

He shook his head and pointed down the hall toward the princesses' wing.

"I can't."

He grabbed my collar, slapped my face, and pointed again. "I don't understand."

He pointed down the hall and then to his ears.

"Listen?" I guessed. "I am listening to you. I'm trying."

He shook his head *no,* and signed again, his fingers flying as he tried to act out what was going on. Hopping around, dancing, pointing at his ears.

"Elves?" I said. "Percy ... the princesses ..."

Immediately, my focus shifted from grief to worry, and I was once again surprised by the lack of people roaming the halls. The house-elves were in hiding, but where were all the servants? Where were the elves? Where was the leader of the southern elves?

"The painting!"

Nimm jumped up and down in excitement. I knew what was going on. There would be another attack that would happen tonight, and I had to stop it.

As I ran, I passed the ballroom and saw the storage closet. I paused, and I stared at the trunk, then down at my tattered dress and knew it would hamper me. Quickly,

I changed into a performing outfit, dropping the bloody dress on the floor. Slipping into another pair of puffed pants and striped leotard, I tucked the dagger into my belt. There weren't any boots in the trunk, but I'd make do.

Every hall I turned into, I passed another deactivated ward, and each time I had an eerie feeling. I came to the golden double doors, and I went through.

Empty. Just as I'd suspected. I looked up at the painting and ran my fingers over the dried paint. How did one get through the painting? What did I need to do to activate it?

"That's a horrible imitation of Thornhaven Court," Rumple said.

"You recognize this place?" I asked, pointing to the painting of the silver trees.

"Of course. It's the birthplace of magic, where the very first ley line erupted out of the earth centuries ago. It's said that its magic was so wild and rampant, it turned the trees into diamonds, gold, and even silver. From this ley line, the fae were birthed, even the dwarves." Rumple seemed proud of his knowledge.

"How far away is it? I mean, how long would it take to reach this place by foot?" I asked.

"I don't know. No one does."

"Then how do I get there?" I growled in frustration.

"With our help." A deep voice came from behind me, and I turned to see Kings Xander and Dorian. Behind them, four more people stepped into the room. Liam of Rya, Brennan of Isla, Aspen of Florin, and Kash of Kiln. The rulers of the other six kingdoms.

Immediately, I bowed, dropping my head.

"Will you look at that?" Kash said. "I never thought I'd see the day when this would happen."

"Sissy hands!" Rumple roared in delight at seeing his favorite king.

"Don't tease her," Liam said, his handsome face scrunching up. "Can't you see how much turmoil she's in?"

"Can we stop this yet?" Aspen asked, scratching his arms. "This really itches."

"You're no fun." Brennan elbowed the shorter Aspen. "I want to see how long it takes her to notice."

I frowned, staring at the royals before me. Their demeanor was off, even though they were in much larger and more muscular bodies. Their hand actions and movements were wrong, and very feminine.

Liam was watching me, and a smile cracked his lips. "I think she's figured it out."

I couldn't believe it. I took each of them in and tried to figure out who was the one holding it.

Not Xander; he had crossed his arms and was grinning at me. Brennan looked uncomfortable and kept switching his feet back and forth.

Dorian. I zeroed in on the tall, dark-haired king and grinned. Stepping closer and closer to him, we waited for my gift to nullify theirs.

Dorian's face scrunched up. "I can't hold it over Meri anymore. She's making it harder."

"Then maybe you should've used one of Rhea's charms instead," Xander taunted. He shook his head and looked toward Dorian. "It's okay. You can let it go."

"Phew!" Dorian released the glamour, and a shimmer dropped from Brennan and Meri. Meri laughed, running her hands through her red hair.

One by one, either the glamour dropped, or one of my sisters pulled a charm out of their pocket and dropped them on the ground. It was Rosalie's glamour of Xander that lasted the longest against me.

"Don't test me, little sister," Rosalie teased, and bopped me on the nose. My eyes welled with tears.

"Oh no," Aura cried out, her blue eyes filling with tears. She wrapped her hands around Eden and gave her a hug. "I'm so sorry."

"What?" Eden asked, confused by Aura's immediate empathy.

Rosalie looked at me, and my tears spilled over.

"Eden's birth parents are . . ." I couldn't finish.

"What? No . . ." Eden gasped, and I nodded.

Eden's lip quivered, and she fell to her knees. Aura dropped to the floor beside her and wrapped her arms around our sister.

Meri joined in the hug, and she sang softly.

"I'm so sorry, Eden," I said. "It was an accident. The king and my mother, and there was an explosion, but not—"

"Mother . . ." Aura's face became distant as she read my mind.

"Not Lorelai," Maeve gasped.

It didn't take long for all six of my sisters to start bickering. I didn't know how to comfort them. I didn't know how to relate because I was always the one on the outside— looking in. I wasn't as close to them.

Even now, I stood there helpless as they mourned.

"You could have saved them," I spoke up. "All the magic contained in this room in the six of you, and none of you were there when she needed you . . . You were all playing at being kings, hiding behind these glamours." The anger and betrayal poured out, and I found myself blaming them. "It's all your fault. All of you. If you had gotten here earlier, you could've saved her. You could've . . ." I started to hiccup and gasp as I tried to process everything.

Rosalie came and put her hand on my shoulder. Her face was cold and hard as she turned her anger not toward me, but focused it on the issue at hand. "We did what she wanted us to do. You took down the wards, which allowed us to slip in, but the king suddenly denied entry to the glamoured Liam, Brennan, and Kash. I think he suspected something was up when they arrived without an honor guard or troops. Mother chose to distract the king and his army so Aura, Meri and Rhea could sneak in to help you."

I shook my head. "That's not true. She wouldn't have done that for me."

"*All* of this is for you, Honor. I know it's hard to believe, but everything we've done up till now had been carefully planned to aid us in getting to you. For this very night."

Aura's eyes were glassy, her cheeks flushed from crying. "There will be more casualties before the night is over. You must hurry."

"You're right." Rosalie moved before the painting and opened her palms. The image began to fade and glow, and her brow furrowed as she fought my nullifying magic. "Uh, Honor, do you mind standing over there? This may take a while. It's been years since I've accessed this kind of power, and you know you . . . tend to make things harder."

Chastised, I moved to the far end of the room. In awe, I watched Rosalie direct Maeve and Meri to either side.

Meri sang, and Rosalie wove a spell strong enough to turn the painting back into a portal.

Eden was still crying while Aura held her, whispering comforting words to her. I watched as Aura pressed her finger to Eden's temple, and soon my sister was asleep. Only Rhea moved to stand by me. Her hands buried in the pockets of her dress.

"How are all of you here?" I asked.

"Well, we weren't going to let our husbands walk into an obvious trap, and we couldn't get through the wards unless someone on the inside could disable them all. And there's only one sister that can do that." She gave me a knowing smile.

"Why didn't you tell me?" I asked.

"You know that's not how we work." Rhea leaned over and ran her hands across Rumple's handle. "How are you doing, old friend?"

"Where's sissy hands?" Rumple grumbled.

"Where all of our husbands are," Rhea answered. "They're with their armies in their kingdoms, preparing for whatever walks through the veil."

"How did you know about them?" I asked. "I just found out about them yesterday."

Rhea smiled sadly and pointed to Nimm. "He worked with the house-elves, and they were able to get word to their network, and we had enough time to prepare. We knew something like this was going to happen. Ever since you warned Rosalie, we've been preparing for war. It only made sense that we leave the armies to the men and the magical warfare to us."

The room wavered with power, and I felt a pull toward

the painting. I clenched my teeth and tried to hold back the desire to absorb all the magic in the room.

Rhea could see my pain and struggle.

The painting shimmered, and like before, the trees moved within.

"It's open," Rosalie called. "Honor, get moving!"

I stared at the painting, and anxiety and doubt washed over me. This wasn't right.

"I can't do this," I said, turning to Rhea. "Come with me," I begged.

"This is not our story," Rhea said. "You must write the conclusion."

"How do you know that . . .?" I started, but then released a sigh. "Mother."

Rosalie nodded. "She knows what it is you will face on the other side and has given us our orders. But know that we will be with you." She turned to face the painting, and Rosalie gestured with her head. "We have our own battles to fight. Now, go!"

My arms pumping, I ran right through the painting, and this time I ripped through the magic veil and rolled, tumbling down the stairs and landing hard. I grumbled, got to my feet, and ran down the rest until I burst out into the woods. Without a skirt to hamper me, I was easily racing through the silver trees.

The trees weren't any less beautiful as I ran blindly, following an almost non-existent trail. How did the princesses find their way before?

The silver branches reached for my hair, pulling strands out, but I swatted them away. When I got to the gold forest, I again didn't slow down. As lovely as the woods were, it seemed like they were reaching out with their glittering branches, trying to stop my progress.

I hissed as a branch scratched my cheek, and warm blood dripped down my face. Another scratch followed, and a sting on my arm told me it had connected. I dreaded the last trek of woods. The diamond forest.

It wasn't my imagination. As I approached the diamond trees, the woods cracked and moved, closing off the path, making it deadly and impassable.

I took a deep breath and pulled the golden double-headed axe from my back, testing the weight of Rumple in my hands.

"How do you feel about destroying a forest of possessed diamond trees?"

"Mmm," he murmured. "You know dwarves have an obsession with treasure. I've been waiting my whole life for this moment."

"That's what I wanted to hear."

As if the trees could hear me, they moved, reaching for me. I swung upward, connecting and breaking off the largest branch. Turning in a circle, I brought it back down and severed another.

Swish. Crack. Swish. Crack.

For every branch, there was a swing, and a glittering broken limb that lay in my wake. But I wasn't making much headway. Step-by-step, I fought against the enchanted forest.

"Why?" I wondered aloud. "Why are you fighting me, when all I want to do is save the princesses?" And why didn't it react to me the same way the last time I was here?

I continued to fight, but I was losing steam. I didn't have the energy, and I could feel myself start to wear out.

"Keep going! Ha ha!" Rumple crowed with excitement.

Rumple was growing heavy in my arms, and I struggled to keep swinging, and the forest seemed to go on forever with no end in sight.

When my body wanted nothing more than to give up, I saw a mirage, or maybe it was a ghost.

Beyond the forest was an ethereal figure standing there. Thena.

"Keep going, Honor. Don't lose your way."

Tears stung my eyes as the diamonds continued to shred my vest and pants. Tinkling followed as the branches seemed to gather in momentum as a final wave of sharp, glittering diamonds rushed toward me. I swung the axe, jumped and rolled through an impossible opening as the branches collided with the ground.

I lay on the sandy banks of the lake. I had made it through the deadly forest alive. My heart raced, and dirt clotted the fresh wounds. The brush of water soaked my slippers.

This realm—the birthplace of magic—once felt so beautiful, but now it was deadly, and I had a feeling I knew why. And the thought of it scared me.

Sitting up, I brushed off the sand. All the boats were gone. My guess was that the princesses and their escorts were already on the other side, dancing and spinning a spell strong enough to send an army through the veils. I stared at the black lake and shuddered. I was going to have to swim.

I tiptoed to the water until it went up to my ankles. The blackness swallowed my slippers, and I couldn't see anything below.

"Oh stars," I breathed out, and walked till it came up to my hips, the freezing water turning my blood cold. I shivered as I took another step, and the ground beneath my feet disappeared. I screamed once, and water filled my mouth as I slipped under the murky lake, the heavy weight of Rumple dragging me under.

Down. Down I slipped beneath the waters, and no matter how much I kicked and swam, I couldn't make headway with Rumple on my back. It was as if an unseen force had gripped the axe and was pulling both of us down into the lake's mysterious depths.

"It's okay," Rumple said, his voice muffled through the water. "Let me go."

I couldn't do it. This was his greatest fear. I fought harder, slicing my arms upward, my feet kicking hard, and I only sank farther down into the blackness.

My lungs burned, begging me to take a breath. Bubbles escaped my lips, and I knew I didn't have much time left.

Forgive me, Rumple.

Grasping at the strap, I pulled him off my shoulder, and as soon as I did, I shot right up, as if repelled by a burst of water.

I broke the murky surface with a gasp.

"No, Rumple," I choked out as more tears filled my eyes. "Rumple!" I screamed, my voice echoing across the lake. I didn't care who heard me anymore. I dove below the water again, searching, but it was dark and impossible.

When I came up for air again, a hand was there to grab me by the back of the jacket, and I was yanked upward and over the side of a boat.

I flopped onto the bottom, my cheek slamming against the bench seat, and I turned, coughing up water.

A rough hand hit my back over and over as I continued to spit up the black liquid. Water shouldn't be black.

When the racking heaves stopped, I flopped over onto my side to see who my rescuer was.

The moonlight illuminated the dark figure as he leaned forward, his hand reaching for my throat.

I screamed on instinct, until my mind caught up with who I was seeing.

"Lorn!" I threw myself into his arms and babbled incoherently. "I'm so glad you're here. Wait, how are you here? I don't understand what is going on?"

Lorn pulled away and stared at me. His face was once again unreadable and void of emotion, which meant he was struggling to hide his pain.

"I'm here because Lorelai asked me to be here. I've been waiting." His voice cracked, revealing the agony he was experiencing. "Because she said you would need my help for this part of the journey."

I sat on the bottom of the boat like a wet rag doll as he reached over to grab the oars. With swift, sure strokes, he pulled us across the lake.

"How did she know?" I asked. "There's no way she could have foreseen everything that's happened. My real mother, the attacks on the kingdoms, her death . . ."

"She knew," Lorn said, leaning forward to pull on the oars.

"Not true," I cried out. "If she had foreseen her own death, then she would've known how to avoid it. She could've prevented all of this." I slashed my hand through the air in angry motions.

Lorn didn't flinch. "She did what she could."

"Well, it wasn't enough," I said, my voice breaking.

"She was one of the most powerful sorceresses in the seven kingdoms. She should have saved herself, and all the others. Eden's parents, my mother, Ogress. All of them. She could have saved them all, and she didn't."

"It's okay to be angry," Lorn said softly. "It's a form of grieving."

"I hate her," I said numbly, dropping my elbows onto my knees and burying my face into my hands. "She could have told me."

"It wasn't her place to tell you, and if she had, then you'd have only hated yourself."

"She could've found a different way," I argued weakly.

"It was the choice she had to make, to give you the opening to save even more lives. Don't forget, she saw every outcome. This one had the least amount of impact on the world. She sacrificed herself to save those she loved; her daughters."

Tears flowed down my face, mingling with the water dripping off my clothes.

"If I remember right, you did the same thing in the Northern Woods, and if you hadn't, more people would have died," he said.

I didn't like the analogy. I didn't like the comparison. "She was selfish," I breathed out, just as the bottom of the boat touched the embankment.

"We are all selfish," Lorn said. "It's in our very nature to be selfish, and we fight it every day. But you, Honor, you've always fought for others, even when it hurt you."

Lorn stepped out of the boat and into the water, pulling it the rest of the way to shore. I gripped the sides of the boat, unwilling to leave the illusion of its safety, because once I did, I knew I would have to step through the miasma and face whatever was waiting on the other side.

He stretched out his hand to me, and I took it as he helped me out of the boat. We walked up to the edge of the swirling mist, and I stared into it.

"Lorn, what will I face on the other side?"

"You already know the answer to that."

"But I can't stop them alone."

"You have everything you need." He tapped my chest. "Right here. Are you ready?" he asked.

I wasn't, not really.

"What is it?" I asked, touching the darkness. "It feels like the veil that protects the Northern Woods."

"It is much older. When the old elven king tried to tap into the sacred hollow, it fractured. They knew what they had done was wrong. They saw the deviated magic, and the effect it had on the woods and creatures around us. They made the decision to protect it with a veil, and since then, all of the southern elves have been sworn to guard it for generations. That is their purpose."

"You mean Percy and Ardax."

"Yes, it is their clan's punishment for tainting the ley line. They are duty bound to be Denizens—guardians of their sacred hollow. But they would not be needed for many years to come except . . ."

"They're dying, giving their life to protect the princesses and the sacred hollow."

Lorn nodded. "Ardax and Percy were called back decades earlier than they should have been to fulfill their roles. And at the same time, aiding the son of Allemar because they are generationally bound by a bloodcurse," he added. "It was that very first sorcerer who tricked the king of the elves into corrupting that ley line, and in doing so, he bound them to him—as servants. Allemar is a direct descendant of that first sorcerer."

"I saw Percy's wrist," I said. "He bore the mark of Allemar's apprentice, which means that he is—"

"Bound to Allemar, but not just Allemar; his son as well."

"But how, when?" I asked. "It wasn't there before. I would have seen the mark years ago . . ." I sighed. "The leather bracers . . ."

"It was always there, but he hid it well."

"How could I have not known? You even warned me. He was my enemy, and now I have to fight him. How do you fight someone you love?" I asked.

Lorn grasped my shoulders, and turned me to face him, his silver eyes filling with unshed tears.

"I didn't train you and Percy together because you would one day have to fight him. I did it so that you could one day save him."

With that sorrowful warning, Lorn pulled me into the mist after him.

CHAPTER TWENTY-SEVEN

As soon as we passed through the protective veil, I heard it. The music, eerie and somber. Not beautiful like I had once thought, but heartbreaking. I could imagine the princesses, their faces masked with pain, and their escorts doing everything they could to keep dancing and stay moving.

Walking through the ruins, I could feel the hum of magic, and I knew the spell was in full swing. As I stepped through the hall filled with arches, I looked down onto the black dance floor. If I concentrated, I could see the sigils filling with power, sucking the energy from the elves and the dancers, and flowing into the paintings.

What I was most surprised to see was that before six of the paintings, were hundreds of servants lined up, their expressions blank and unmoving, like the masks the escorts wore.

"What's going on?" I asked Lorn.

"They're preparing for war. As soon as the spell is complete, the paintings will open, and they'll spill over into the realms."

"But they're not fighters. These are nobles, lords and servants. I recognize Lord Packer and the palace guards.

Look, there's Wentworth, and even Randolph the guildmaster."

We passed through the rows of immobile, passive people. Saphira had said that people were disappearing from the city, and now I understood where they had been going. They were being taken into the sacred hollow.

"Once the spell is complete, they'll pass through." Lorn sidestepped a man whose glazed-over eyes followed him without moving.

"Rhea said there are armies on the other side waiting for them. They can help them get to safety."

"No, Honor. After you went through and Ardax closed the veil, the demons that attacked the Northern Woods shifted and turned back to their former shape. They weren't hellhounds. They were human. Rethulian recognized the twisted magic. Once they step through those portals, the twisted magic of this ley line will shift them into something else. Something inhuman. It didn't work on you because you're an antimage, and you countered it. There will be no hope for them unless we stop this spell."

I grabbed the closest woman to me and snapped my fingers in front of her face.

"Hello, wake up," I said loudly. I shook her, and then moved to the next person, shaking them. No one moved, for they were all under a powerful enchantment. I focused on each person and tried to see if there was a hint of residual magic about them.

There was none.

"Drink the tea, dance till dawn. The tea," I muttered, remembering the tea the daughters gave the men who guarded them. "They're drugged. It's not magic that I can counter or nullify."

"It's the tea that binds them to the spell and allows them to be controlled."

The closest painting humed with energy, and the colors within began to melt and merge together.

"You're running out of time," Lorn warned.

He was right. I ran, no longer worrying about bumping or knocking into them. If I couldn't stop the spell, then they were all going to die, either from the transformation, or at the hands of the six armies waiting on the other side. Then war would break out for sure.

I ran down the steps toward the dais and burst into the circle full of dancers. Eleven princesses and their eleven escorts.

I immediately picked out Percy, dancing with Lisbelle. The young princess had a gruesome smirk on her face, as if she was enjoying torturing my friend. Percy's eyes were closed, his mouth pressed into a thin line. I knew he was doing everything he could to keep going.

"Lisbelle, stop now."

A bitter scoff escaped her lips. "I'll never quit." She turned to address me, her face contorted into an ugly snarl, and her eyes filled with rage. "But you know that. I will *never* lose to you, no matter how much you torture me."

I blinked, confused by her reaction.

"Release them from the spell," I demanded.

Lisbelle barked out a laugh. "As if I could."

Nothing I was saying was getting through to her. Percy gazed up at me through his white mask, and I could see his hesitation. The slowing of his movements, his feet dragging, not keeping up with the tempo of the music.

"No, you can't," Lisbelle hissed, her fingers digging into his arm. "You stop, you die!"

With a renewed energy, he picked up his pace and continued to dance, and I felt hopeless at stopping them from weaving their spell. The magic was gathering. I could feel its energy and power trickle across my skin, causing the hairs on my arms to raise, then I sensed a malicious presence.

I turned to see a man in a red robe; his gold mask was unlike the other escorts. Along his arms were blood tattoos, and physically the energy pulsed outward in waves.

"Ardax," I addressed the man in the mask.

"No, that one's Ardax." The man pointed toward the dancers, aiming at a tall man in a white, hawk-nosed mask.

"Who are you?" I asked.

"I'm insulted that you don't recognize me, although I tried to make a lasting impression." The man lifted the gold mask from his face, revealing familiar amber eyes.

"Nathin?" I said, in surprise. "You're the son of Allemar?"

"Hardly." He pointed to the scratch on my neck. "I'm glad to see that you're healing well. But that goes to show you come from good stock." He pulled out the kerchief from his pocket, the one he'd used to dab my wound. He lifted the cloth to his nose and inhaled like it was a fine perfume.

"Please stop this," I begged.

A sigh escaped Analisa's lips, and she fainted into her escort's arms before they both tumbled to the ground.

"Analisa!" Lisbelle screamed and tried to stop dancing to race to her sister. But Percy grasped her arms, pulling her against his chest, smothering her cries.

Analisa wasn't the only one to succumb. An exhausted escort slipped and fell, pulling Therisa with him. Then

Risa collapsed, her escort unable to keep her moving. One by one, the ley line was taking everything the dancers had to fuel the magic spell.

The others continued to dance, the remaining sisters stifling their cries while stepping over the prone and fallen bodies.

"Enough!" Lisbelle screamed up at me, tears falling down her face. "Grace, please stop. No more. You're killing us!"

Air rushed from my lungs, and I faltered, grasping a pillar for support.

"Grace?" I whispered. She thought I was Grace. It wasn't Lisbelle who was behind these attacks.

Thena's words came back to me. *One daughter would possess great power, the other daughter, the antithesis of that power.*

In slow motion, all the clues replayed in my mind. The distance the sisters kept from Grace; the aloofness. The contempt they displayed toward her. The wards were placed around the palace, not just to keep daughters of Eville out, but to dampen and contain Grace's power.

It was Grace.

"Well, it looks like you finally figured out mother dearest's dirty little secret," a haughty voice said from behind me.

Spinning, I faced . . . myself. No longer dressed in green, but draped in the blood-red robes of an apprentice of Allemar, was Grace. She smiled, a cold and cruel display that made me shiver.

I now understood the attempt on Grace's life the day of the parade. The princesses were desperate to save themselves.

"You're Allemar's apprentice?" I asked.

Grace rolled her eyes and ran her hand through her hair, then glared at Nathin. "She can't possibly be related to me?"

My eyes widened as I saw the expression I so frequently used. The one look that always confused Percy.

Nathin nodded, breathing in the bloody kerchief. "I checked her blood like you asked. She's your twin."

Grace cocked an eyebrow at me and pursed her lips. "I'm not just his apprentice." She raised her hands and laughed. "The world's most powerful sorcerer tried to seduce Lorelai Eville, but she saw through his facade. Years later, Allemar tried to strengthen his lineage, and did his best to seduce the second strongest natural-born witch, our dear mother, Thena. He succeeded in making her love him." Grace clapped her hands together and cackled. "But Lorelai had already cursed the royal lineage of Sion to bear only daughters, and guess what? That bloodline included his bastard half-brother, Allemar. He had twin daughters!" Grace was laughing so hard, tears were forming. She was wiping at the corners of her eyes, and then settled down.

The air was sucked out of my lungs, and I struggled to breathe. She had to be lying. I wasn't the daughter of Allemar. He couldn't be my father. "You lie."

"If only. But just like King Leonel, he only valued sons. So Allemar turned all of his energy into training apprentices. But they were nothing more than weak replicas. Then he went and died without accomplishing *anything*." Her eyes flashed with anger, and a fizzle of energy gathered around her, causing her hair to rise. "I will not fail, nor will I make the same mistakes he did. I'll carry on his legacy as the true *heir* of Allemar."

The music on the dance floor rose in volume and pitch. The dancers were forced to keep an insane pace, and it was clear that Grace's aim was to kill them. She'd been draining them slowly, fueling the magic over time, and she wouldn't stop until every person on that floor was dead. It was all she needed to complete the final spell.

A willing blood sacrifice.

That is where all the guardians of the sacred hollow had been going. They'd been bloodbound and ordered to protect the princesses, and in doing so, it was their sacrifices and lives that were powering the spells to open the portals.

"Why?" I asked, stepping closer to Grace, hoping she wouldn't notice my attempt at nullifying her magic.

"Because I can." She grinned. "I had hoped that by sending you in my place that you would succumb to the spell and die, or at the very least, kill one or two of my miserable sisters for me."

I pulled at her, touching the light within her chest very slowly, and she caught me.

"Stay back, Honor!" she hissed. "Or I'll kill him." She pointed at toward Percy, who was barely dancing. His feet were dragging along the floor, and it wasn't just Lisbelle he danced with; he'd grabbed Willa and was holding both of the princesses—and he wasn't the only one. Ardax had done the same. He danced with Mira, and had Clara over his shoulder as he tried to make his way to a dancing elven escort that hadn't fallen, but who no longer had a princess.

"Both of them are new to my cause. They've lasted longer than any of the other southern elves. It has been so sweet to taste their sacrifice, fueling my power." She clenched her hand and Percy grimaced, almost dropping to one knee.

It surprised me to see Lisbelle lean down quickly as they tried to keep moving, placing his arm over her shoulder. With a great cry, she lifted Percy and Willa. She was fighting for their lives.

"Stop this, Grace, or I'll be forced to stop you," I threatened.

Grace laughed. "You? You can't do anything. You have no power, but I do. Join me, and I'll put an end to his pain." Grace held out her hands to me, beckoning me like a lover into an eternal kiss of death. "It's our destiny, dear sister."

"Drink the tea, dance till dawn," I repeated under my breath the words she had spoken to me. Her grand plan. "If you lack the strength, you become a pawn." I glanced down toward Percy and Ardax, and those that had collapsed on the floor. "Sacrificed for the old king's sake." They were forfeited because of the old elven king's greed—he was the *old king* in Grace's poem. I looked to Grace and spoke the final words. "To kill the queen, and a new world make."

"Stop that incessant chattering," Nathin muttered.

This time, it was my turn to smile, and it made her cringe. "You can't do it, can you? Not until you kill me."

Her beautiful smile fell from her face, and her eyes darkened.

"That's why you tried to kill me at the show. I know it was you."

Grace bit the bottom of her lip, closed her eyes, and rolled her shoulders. It seemed like her body was undulating with an intense pleasure. She was feeling their pain. I took a step forward, standing between her and the dancers. When the pleasure stopped, she opened her eyes and glared at me.

"Because I'm not complete," she said. "I'm not whole while you're alive."

"Two halves of a coin," I said quietly. "One magic will cancel the other out."

"Looks like you've been talking to our mother. How is dear Thena? Still in the dungeon, making friends with the rats? Did she tell you she killed her antimage twin to attain her full powers?"

My mouth dropped slightly.

"I see she didn't. And the guilt *ate* at her for years. She tried to lie to me, but I knew different, because I couldn't manifest to my full potential—which meant you were still alive."

Grace was drunk on power, and I was struggling to nullify it. When I tried to block the flow of magic, it moved around me. I was a pebble in a raging river of magic.

Once again, there was very little I could do to stop her, and I knew it. I might end up dead, like all the powerless antimages before me.

"Honor!" Ardax screamed, and I looked down at his face. Was he crying blood? No, blood was dripping out of his eyes and ears.

Percy and Ardax watched me, and I could see Percy pleading for forgiveness for keeping secrets, while Ardax's gaze was filled with hate. He gestured with his chin, and I knew the signal. Ardax was encouraging me to attack. To fight.

I tried to keep my face neutral as I faced off against my sister. Nathin had moved just over her right shoulder, still watching us, but paying more attention to the paintings.

I might only get one shot. Reaching my hand into my pocket, I fingered the dagger.

"Light and dark," I whispered, looking at Grace. "I always thought that I was the dark one, being the antimage."

Her brows furrowed in confusion.

"But I'm a bringer of light," I said.

Using his finger, Ardax drew a heart shape on his chest. He was telling me to go for the heart. I faltered. I didn't know if I was strong enough to do what needed to be done. My knees trembled, and I felt weak. I struggled to refrain from the magic around me, knowing it was tainted. That it was made from death. I narrowed my eyes, focusing on my target.

Grace laughed. "You can't bring light when you're trapped in the dark." She clapped her hands, and all the torches in the ruins went out . . . just as I let the dagger fly from my hand. I heard its whisper as it cut through the air. Its impact thudded as the blade hit flesh, and a body crumpled to the floor.

I followed after, my head touching the cold stone.

"What have you done?" Grace screeched. The torches blazed to life, and she raced to Nathin's side to find her lover dead, my knife buried in his heart.

I didn't dare attempt to kill her. I didn't trust myself to have that much power.

"Honor!" Ardax screamed in rage. "Command me!"

It was in that moment that I understood. The blood-curse. Not only were they bound to my sister as the heir of Allemar. They were bound to me . . .

"I release all the southern elves from this curse. Do what you must to protect the princesses!"

The symbols on the dais went dark. The ebb and flow of magic faded away to a trickle. Everyone collapsed. Mira and Clara embraced each other with heaving breaths, and great wailing followed as Lisbelle and Willa crawled toward their prone sisters. The remaining elves didn't give them time to mourn as they pulled them away, putting them over their shoulders, and rushing the survivors back to the boats.

Percy and Ardax raced up the stone steps and split, Ardax rushing to Grace while Percy raced to me, picking me up.

"I'm so sorry," he whispered into my hair. "I wanted to tell you so many times, but I couldn't."

Great sobs filled the ruins as Grace buried her face into Nathin's robe. Ardax approached her, but she turned on him.

He grimaced as his back cracked, and he was frozen, his arms pinned to his side. "I'm not done fighting yet," Grace said. Her brown hair had come unbound from its bun, and it flew about her shoulders.

Her lips moved, but no sound came forth, her hands forming a spell; weaving magic.

I pushed Percy behind me and ran toward her, knowing it was an attack spell.

"Honor, no!" he yelled.

Fire flared up around her palms, and I knew I should duck, run the other way—but I couldn't. I had to end this.

Grace's eyes narrowed. She smiled in triumph, and released a ball of fire toward me.

I flung out my arms, making myself an even bigger target as the spell hit me square in the chest.

I screamed as the fire engulfed me, but I didn't burn or

incinerate. I *absorbed* it. The fire ran up my arms, and I watched as it moved like water, then I closed my fists and the magic dissipated into me. My body was humming.

"That tickles," I laughed.

I had spent my whole life afraid of magic; afraid of harming people that used magic. I had built up a mental wall around myself to protect others by pushing their magic away. Thus nullifying it. But the more I pushed it away instead of accepting it, the more I tried to possess it. The harder I fought the monster, the hungrier it became.

Whenever I walked through the elven veil, it felt different. Beautiful, warm and serene. I wasn't scared of it. And then I realized . . . *all* magic was still magic. Dark magic, protective magic, offensive magic. I was a sieve. A conduit. All magic wanted to flow through me.

"No!" Grace cried out and sent another wave of attack. Shards of ice, blasts of water; all of them hit me, moved across my body, and then slowly absorbed within me until I felt full.

With each attack, I continued to advance, raising my hands.

"Stop it!" Grace backed up and tripped over a broken pillar.

I stood over her. "Give up Grace, it's done."

In her fall, she had bitten her lip, and now her cheek was smeared with blood.

"It's never over." Her eyes flicked behind me, and I turned. Ardax had a knife pressed to Percy's throat.

"Ardax!" I opened my mouth to command him.

"Say a word, *any* word, and he's dead," she hissed.

I bowed my head in submission, pressing my lips together.

"It's only fair," Grace said, moving to stand next to Ardax and Percy.

There was the barest shimmer over her shoulder, hidden in the archway.

She raised her hand to Percy's face, running a nail down his cheek. "You killed my love. I get to kill yours."

I shook my head.

"Ardax, Ki—"

"No wait!" I said, ignoring her order. "It's me you want. If you kill him, then I'll do everything in my power to destroy you. But if you let him live, I'll submit to you."

"This is a trick," she said, her eyes narrowing.

"It's not. I won't raise a hand against you." I turned to Percy. "I've lost so much tonight. I can't lose you." Facing her again, I said, "I promise that if you release Ardax and Percy, I will swear to never kill you."

Percy shook his head. Slowly, he showed me the mark on his wrist, reminding me what the bloodbond meant. Ardax and Percy couldn't attack her either. They were bound to her in life *and* death.

Percy's nostrils flared, and he raised his chin again in the barest of nods. He was giving me permission to kill her . . . and him by extension.

My eyes flickered to Ardax, and he gave me a slow blink. Another yes.

Grace smiled. "Okay. Ardax, Percy, hold her."

Ardax grimaced as he tried to fight the order, but he grabbed my left wrist, Percy grabbed my right, and I was forced down onto my knees. Grace walked back over to Nathin's body and pulled the dagger out of his chest.

She stared at the bloody blade in awe before bringing it close to me. "Drag her down there. Her life will be the last sacrifice needed to open the portals. We don't want her death to be in vain, do we?"

She looked toward the portrait hall. "Where have my armies gone?" she seethed. "What have you done?"

I raised my head as the shimmer grew closer. "I did what I was supposed to do, Grace. Distract you."

"I'm going to kill you," she said, spit covering her lip. She raised the dagger, and I flinched.

The air around Grace shimmered as Lorn appeared out of thin air, his short sword plunging deep into my sister's back.

The dagger fell from her hand and she gasped, slipping to her knees, and staring at me wide-eyed in disbelief at the blade that was coming out of her front. "Y-you, stabbed me?"

"No, I didn't raise a hand against you. My godfather did."

Grace coughed, and a gruesome smile crossed her face. "You weren't the one to kill me. You'll never be whole or all-powerful."

I reached for Percy's hand, and he threaded his fingers through mine, then I turned to Ardax and held out my other hand. He didn't hesitate to take it. "I am complete," I said.

Grace choked, and I could see her life fading. "I'm the more powerful sister." Her gaze settled on the paintings. "I almost did what he could not. My armies would've been strong enough. I did it. I could've taken the seven kingdoms. They would've been proud."

Allemar and King Leonel never valued her. They used her. I felt pity for a girl who had two fathers and couldn't gain their love without resorting to destroying herself and others. She was trying to fulfill two family legacies, and neither one would have loved her, no matter what she did.

"No, you wouldn't have gained the kingdoms. My sisters and I would have stopped you."

"Your. . . sisters?" she choked out, confused.

"We are the daughters of Eville."

Her eyes widened with understanding, and she let out a humorless huff. "I never stood a chance then."

I reached for her hands and clasped them in mine. "Grace, you had the chance to be the greatest sister, but you chose power over love. Be at peace."

Grace's eyes flickered, and I saw a tear in her eye. "My sister." She clutched my hands and then breathed out her last breath.

I turned and buried my face into Percy's chest while he held me close.

"How are we not dead?" Ardax asked Lorn.

"Because Honor is still alive," Lorn answered. "One twin survives. So half of the bond is still intact."

Ardax's lips pinched together, and he glared at me.

"Oh what? Did you want to die?"

"It would have been a glorious death." Ardax turned his back to me and placed his hands on his hips. "Now, I'm indebted to *you*."

"I can't believe you," I snapped. "Are you complaining about being alive? Instead of moping that you're not dead, why don't you celebrate? You can go kiss Rulah now."

"It's not worth it if she doesn't love me back." Ardax turned and pointed a finger at Percy.

"Oh, I think she does," Percy countered, and the two of them argued.

I walked away from them and stared down at the dais.

Underneath it was the ley line. The one tainted years ago by a sorcerer of my bloodline and an elven king that wanted power. This was what bound Percy and Ardax to be Denizens of the sacred hollow. This was what bound all southern elves into a reclusive life of guardianship.

"I wonder." I took the steps down and was surprised to see that all that remained of the dead was dust. It appeared the repercussions of Grace using the deviated magic from this ley line turned the fallen princesses and elves into nothing more than ash.

"Honor, what are you doing?" Percy called down to me as I kneeled onto the dais. "Stop! What are you doing?"

I turned to look up at him. "Righting a wrong."

"Don't!" he cried out.

I closed my eyes and reached for the tainted ley line and pulled it into me. A flashback from when I was young filled my mind. I had seen the gold lines of magic. It was so beautiful and warm, but the magic here was broken.

I knew what I had to do. Deep in my heart, I had the answer to fixing it. It had been there in my mind ever since I'd taken magic from Percy. His magic was of this hollow. It called to me.

The earth rumbled beneath me, and the last few remaining pillars fell.

Percy grabbed me to him, clasping my face in his hands. I opened my eyes to see his fear. "No, you can't, Honor. Hundreds have gone before you, and all of them have died trying. They turn to dust."

I smiled, my cheeks pressing into his palms. "That's because they were mages. I'm not."

"Don't risk it. It's too dangerous. You can't fix this alone."

"But that's the thing . . ." I smiled as more tears filled my eyes. "I'm not alone."

A clear and forceful melody echoed across the water, and I knew the magical voice of my sister, Meri. She added her power into me with her song, singing a thread of magic. It floated through the air and into my chest.

A raven flew down and landed on the dais next to me, then shifted into my dark-haired, spitfire sister, Maeve. "Did you leave any fighting for us?"

"How are you here?" I whispered.

"We're daughters of Eville. We find a way. Meri is singing and controlling the lake, bringing the others over. Lorn is already at the bank. I bet you they'll be here in three, two . . ." She counted down her fingers just as Rosalie raced down the stairs, followed by Eden, Aura, Rhea, and Rosalie, whose serious face softened when she met my gaze.

"We're here." Rosalie touched my back and added her magic, not to the ley line—she poured it into me. Her magic smelled of roses, and I felt my heart flutter. One by one, they touched me and fed me their magic. Maeve's magic was electric and sent a shock through me. Eden's tickled like a feather across my neck. Meri's was thunderous and angry, like the ocean, and I swore I tasted salt. Then came Aura's, and when she touched me, I felt peace.

Rhea hung back, unsure of how to help.

"Don't just stand there! We need to add our magic!"

My head snapped up as Rumple chastised Rhea.

"But I don't have that kind of magic?" Rhea said.

"I'm all the magic you need," Rumple growled at her.

"Rumple?" I cried out. "How?"

Aura showed me a picture in my mind of the lake

parting at Meri's command, and Rhea retrieving Rumple from the bottom. The actions played as though they were my memories, and I watched as she had taken over the minds of those hundreds of people standing in front of the portrait. She'd brought them to the lake, where Meri was helping them cross to safety.

Tears flowed freely down my face as love and magic surrounded me, but I could feel the pressure building. I was struggling to hold it all.

Then Rhea placed Rumple in my hand, and I could feel the power of the dwarf, and his earth magic that had been touched with Rhea's charms.

I nodded, and this time, I pictured all of the golden light inside of me, the magic my sisters had been feeding me. I pushed it out and through my hands, back into the ley line.

Like oil and water, the two kinds of magic fought against each other, light and dark. But it was my sisters' magic. I could see it chasing the dark strands deep into the earth, bringing it forth, upward like hounds chasing a rabbit.

"Oh, I can see it coming!" I cried out as another earthquake shook the ruins. The dais cracked as their magic burned through, rushing after the poison taint. It was racing for the surface to escape.

The dais cracked down the middle, and a great black liquid reached for the sky, but I didn't let it go. I caught it and pulled it to me. Like a fish on a line, it fought, but I wouldn't concede.

"You belong to me!" I yelled, and I could almost hear the magic laugh. "I'm the daughter of Allemar, the descendant of the one who cursed you."

The magic halted and stopped fighting, as if listening. "I remove the curse, by taking it into myself!"

Percy tensed. "Honor, you don't know what that will do."

"Trust me," I whispered.

The magic hung in the air, a moving cloud debating my offer, then like a hive of bees swarming, it dove straight for my heart.

I screamed as coldness ripped through my very being, and I absorbed the dark magic. Ice, fire, pain. I was drowning and overwhelmed. I fell backwards into Percy's arms, my body going cold, shivering.

"We can't stop," I gasped, and folded myself inward, grasping my chest. My body battled against me. "We're strong enough . . . Can't stop . . ."

Percy lifted my chin. "There's only one magic that is stronger," he whispered, looking deep into my eyes. "A magic so strong it burns for eternity. And that's love." He pressed his lips to mine and pushed his magic through me.

Pleasure replaced pain. I was no longer drowning, but flying. The fire of our love chased and burned out the darkness until we were surrounded by a blinding light.

A great burst of magic erupted like fireworks out of the ley line, and scattered across the ruins. We broke our kiss to see the surge hit the veil of magic protecting the realm, and it shattered. Gold, silver and diamonds rained down on us, creating a tinkling sound as it hit the marble dais.

Bright blue skies shone down on us and I tried to stand, but the world spun. Crumpling against the cold stone, my vision swam, and sleep claimed me.

CHAPTER TWENTY-EIGHT

Three weeks later.

"**D**o you think Lorelai foresaw this?" I asked, standing in the throne room. I watched my sisters and their husbands talk, flirt, and even tease each other mercilessly, instead of conducting council business.

A round table sat in the center of the throne room at the palace, and it didn't seem like any actual work was getting accomplished. There were supposed to be land deeds signed, and new titles to be bestowed upon the nobles and lords. There were new border lines being drawn up between the various fae races.

Eden glamoured herself into Dorian and tried to sign papers on his behalf, while Dorian chased around their toddler, a little blonde-haired girl named Elsie. She was running after Violet, Rosalie's daughter, and Violet had shifted into her wolf pup form. Maeve and Aspen tried to sneak out of the room, but Rosalie pulled Aspen back by the back of his cloak and pointed to a chair. "Sit." Then she waved her hands at the raven sitting in the window. "Maeve, get down here!"

Aspen groaned and shuffled back to his seat, while Maeve, in a flash of feathers and magic, shifted back into her grumpy self, and plopped next to her husband. Then Rosalie deposited her youngest child into Maeve's arms.

Maeve held the swaddled baby and looked up in absolute terror. "I don't do babies."

Kash was busy arguing with Rumple—who continued to call him names, like Nancy, sissy hands, and longface—and Rhea was busy reading a book and taking notes, obsessed with how we'd fixed the ley line. Apparently, when I'd healed the sacred hollow, it redirected the ley lines.

"I swear I saw a glimpse of another realm," Rhea muttered, her fingers covered in ink as she made more notes.

Liam stood next to Aura, his hand touching her shoulder; a magical shield that protected the empath from the barrage of thoughts in the room. Devin, the acting king of Rya, seemed overwhelmed. Aura was the queen of the fae. Since Liam didn't want to accept the throne, it fell to Devin, but the two were still brothers-in-arms, and in heart.

Brennan reclined in his chair, plopping his boots on the maps.

Meri swatted him in the back of the head. "Off!" And Brennan reluctantly pulled his feet down.

"Do I think Lorelai foresaw this?" Lorn repeated, then thought for a moment before he answered my question. "I'm sure she did." He looked out the window while he continued to speak. "I hope they get some work accomplished."

"Yeah, but I don't see that happening today. It has been years since everyone has been together. Lorelai would have wanted them to have this," I said.

"On the other hand, she would be chastising them for wasting time."

"True." I smiled at the thought. "But there's no hurry in choosing a new ruler of Sion."

"I think there are four very nervous daughters waiting outside to see if any of them are worthy." A sadness washed over me. Of the eleven sisters, only the youngest four survived: Lisbelle, Willa, Mira, and Clara.

Lorn turned to me, studying me with his silver eyes. "Are you going to put your name in? You are technically the oldest daughter."

"I'm also the illegitimate child of Allemar, the bastard firstborn," I said. "And no. I'm not made for a throne room. I've spent my life traveling the ley lines. I feel like I'm more at home on the road under the stars than stuck between four walls."

Lorn was staring down at the dais, his face forlorn. I reached out and placed my hand on his arm and leaned my head against his shoulder.

"I still can't believe she's gone," he said, his voice breaking.

"I know," I whispered.

"She knew. She foresaw all of this. Planned it out, down to the last detail. That's why she never said she loved me back, because she knew our love would be eternal."

The door opened, and Lisbelle came in dressed in pale

white, no longer wearing her assigned indigo color. Her blonde hair was brushed out and kept in a simple knot by the nape of her neck. I didn't realize how young she'd looked in those frilly dresses. She was older than I thought, and she looked so sophisticated.

When Lisbelle saw me, she tensed up in anger and fear —then a small smile formed, and she gave me a curtsy. I waved back, and she went to present her reports to King Xander.

"She's become quite the little leader," Lorn said.

"Yes, she'd be my choice to lead the kingdom," I agreed. "She was the only one who stood up to Grace even in the face of death. I've already spoken with Rosalie and Xander, and they see it too, but they won't make a decision hastily."

When Devin saw the beautiful Lisbelle, he almost fell over in his chair. She paused, gave him a side glance, and then she dismissed him coyly, using the tools that Saphira had tried to teach me.

But it wasn't so easy for Devin. He looked like he was put under a love spell. He couldn't drag his eyes away from her.

"Oh, *that* will be interesting," Lorn said quietly.

Lisbelle curtsied before the kings and queens while she greeted them, but her eyes did stay a little longer on Devin.

"This could be what they need," I said.

Rulah and Ardax came in next, hand in hand. Ardax grinned as he handed a scroll to King Brennon. It seemed after the Northern Woods attack, Rulah's true feelings were revealed when she had seen Ardax in danger. They had plans to unite the courts of Lightwood and Thornhaven and remove the centuries of stigma over the southern elves.

I grinned as Rulah leaned into Ardax, giving his hand a squeeze. When they turned to leave, Ardax gave me a slow wink. I nodded my head in return.

"This was an interesting turn of events." Lorn elbowed me as a shimmer in the corner of the room moved from the wall, and I saw Nimm, shuffling over to us, but now there was a tinkling sound. When Nimm appeared next to me, I laughed at his colorful ensemble of green-striped socks, a blue and red vest, and his stocking hat adorned with silver bells.

He made a face and pointed at the open door. I left the throne room and headed out of the palace doors to the colorful line of wagons. At the head of the first wagon was a tall elf, dressed even more ridiculously than Nimm.

His blonde hair was covered by a similar hat to Nimm's, with even larger silver bells. His green eyes sparkled mischievously as Percy jumped down from the wagon in a mismatched outfit that was raided from the lost and found bin.

"Percy, what are you wearing?" I covered my eyes and laughed, thoroughly embarrassed for him.

"I've joined the Magical Menagerie." He grinned, waving his hat and giving a bow. "Bravado and Sorek insisted I'm a natural. And I'm hoping a beautiful silk aerialist will fall into my lap." He raised an eyebrow at me. "Do you know of any?"

I couldn't hold back the laughter as I realized Percy had fallen in love with performing. He had always been fascinated with humans, and this seemed right up his alley.

In the driver's seat of the wagon behind Percy was

Bravado, his arms and leg still bandaged and healing from the fire. His glorious mustache was missing, but his eyes twinkled when he saw my look of shock over Percy's new wardrobe.

"I may not be as good with a needle and thread as my Amaryllis was, but I did my best," he laughed.

"It's perfect!"

I ached and grieved for everyone we'd lost, but tiny pieces of my broken heart were healed when I learned that Saphira, Bravado, and Sorek had survived, though not without some damage. Sorek had burns across most of his back and was being tended to by Saphira, who sold her inn and decided to rejoin the troupe. I think in part it was to stay close to Sorek. And with Nimm also came more gnomes, who all joined in to pick up Humperstink's work.

"What do you say, Honor?" Percy called out. "Shall we travel the kingdoms, maybe cause some havoc along the way?"

"Are you going to stay out of the taverns and stop cheating at cards?" I teased.

"What? You were the one who taught me how to cheat!" He pointed at me, laughing.

I blushed and raced down to him. Percy swept me up in an embrace and kissed me.

"Is that a yes?" he asked.

I narrowed my eyes at him. "You would really give up your duty to run away with me?"

"I told you, being a scout was your dream. My dream is being with you."

"What if I commanded you to—" I started.

Percy cut me off. "You can't command someone that

loves you. Those are the rules that I just made up. And I've loved you for years."

"Really?" I said in surprise. "That long?"

"I've shown it in every way I could. In all the hours I sat by you, cared for you, played pranks with you. It was to get closer to you. I was waiting for you to stop fighting your own feelings and admit that you loved me back. I knew you loved me. You're terrible at hiding your feelings. Everyone knew you loved me . . . except you."

He pressed his lips to mine, and I melted in his embrace. This was what I wanted. Him.

When we pulled apart, he was breathless. "Please, run away with me to join the Magical Menagerie."

"Well, the kings and queens will still need spies," I mused.

"And we could stay near the ley lines."

"It's perfect." I smiled at him.

Percy's eyes lit up with joy, and he kissed me. "I agree. My plans are always perfect."

"Hardly," I countered.

"Let's put itching powder in Ardax's uniform one more time before we leave," he whispered, and kissed me again on the lips.

I grinned. "He'll never know it was us."

"Yeah, he will," Rumple yelled out.

We turned to see a stunned Ardax holding Rumple in his hands.

Our faces flushed bright red with guilt.

Ardax's eyebrows shot straight up. "I *knew* that was you!"

"Somebody's in trouble," Rumple sing-songed.

"Why do you always have to be a pain in the axe?" Percy choked out.

Ardax hefted the axe in his hands and eyed Percy's head. "You better run!"

Percy took off, and Ardax chased him down playfully while Rumple screamed out in joy. "Run, ya little elf! I'm going to chop you down to house-elf size."

The two bantered, racing over and around the wagons, until Percy disappeared and hid his aura next to a grove of trees.

Ardax froze, unable to see where he went. He looked to me for help, as I could always find the elves and saw the shimmer. I pointed, and Ardax took off running again.

As soon as he caught Percy, he handed over the axe. "You take him. He won't shut up." Ardax laughed and bolted into the palace, turning his head slightly to yell, "And stay away from my uniform!"

I was laughing so hard my sides hurt. Even Bravado was wiping tears away as he said, "Come on, Percival, the invisible elf. Are you ready to hit the road?"

Percy jogged back to me, and Rumple now hung on his shoulder. "Are you ready, Honor? For our next adventure?"

"As long as you're by my side, I'll be ready for anything." I threaded my fingers through his, then hopped up onto the wagon.

"I'm coming too, right?" Rumple asked. "After all, the menagerie needs a dwarf to be complete."

"You're not a dwarf," Bravado called out. "You're going to be the star of the troupe." He turned and gave me a sly look. "How do you feel about chopping down targets while singing a cappella?"

"I'd love it," Rumple breathed out eagerly. "You know, dwarves have great singing voices . . . It's one of our many talents."

I placed my head on Percy's shoulder as he snapped the reins on Ogress's eight oxen. My heart filled with joy and excitement for our next chapter in life, because love truly is the greatest adventure.

CHAPTER TWENTY-NINE

Lorn rode up to the old guard tower. Smoke no longer rose from the chimney, the gardens had become overgrown, as the hob and brownie had moved on to find another dwelling.

As he crossed the bridge over the stream, he could hear a sad moan from Diesel, a fae water beast. Traygar the troll had gone back to the mountains.

It wasn't the same. There used to be lines of laundry blowing in the wind, butterflies and fae romping around the yard, and the girls' laughter filling the air. Now the home was silent.

Lorn unhitched his horse and let him wander over to Jasper, the workhorse, and Bug, the donkey, who were out grazing near the house. He was surprised that none of the miscreants from town had broken into Lady Eville's house yet.

He pushed open the door and crossed the threshold. The windows were shuttered, and light came in through small cracks. The long, mahogany table was coated with a layer of dust, and the fireplace hadn't been cleaned. But there wasn't anyone to tend to it. He crossed into the sitting room and paused to look at the high-back chair that Lorelai had brought from her old manor house.

His heart ached as he looked at all the empty chairs. It wasn't a home anymore, but a mausoleum. He took a deep breath. If he closed his eyes, he could almost smell her. The scent of lavender and honey, mixed with the herbs she dried for home remedies.

When Lorn opened his eyes, he was facing the mirror. The beautiful, framed mirror that Lorelai spent years in front of, scrying and searching for answers.

"Why couldn't you have seen me?" he whispered, pressing his hand against the frame. "You did so well; protected those you cared about, even the seven kingdoms. But you forgot about me."

Lorn let out a great sob of grief as he pulled the mirror down. Dust and cobwebs came with the frame, and giant holes were left in the wall where the mounts were pulled out.

Carefully, Lorn wrapped the mirror in linen and blankets and brought it outside. Then he saw Clove, the brownie, sitting on the donkey with Stankplant, the crankier of the two hobs. Sneezewort had left long ago to help Aura bring life back to the fae court.

"Go. You're free." He tried to shoo them away, but Stankplant just shook his knobby head. Clove grasped Bug's reins and raised her chin in defiance.

"Fine, you can come with me, but it's a long trip."

They nodded.

It took weeks; much longer than he would have expected traveling with the fae, and an extra horse and donkey. Clove ended up hiding in his saddlebag since she preferred to come out at night. And Stankplant was obsessed with protecting Lorelai's mirror. He polished it every night, staring into it, hoping she would come back.

The terrain changed as they headed up into the mountains, and he almost missed the turnoff for the manor gate that was still missing letters. Instead of Eville, it read *Evil*. He rode up to the stone manor, Lorelai's childhood home, and brought the mirror inside. As soon as he did, the hob moved to take Bug and Jasper to the stables, and Clove went right to the kitchen.

Lorn took the mirror into the sitting room and saw the empty spot where it once resided. The empty nail still hid on the crack in the wall, and he hung it.

"It is done," Lorn said. "Everything you asked of me. I have done it all—for you. I only—" His eyes filled with tears, and he brushed it off. "I only wish you were here to ask me for another favor."

There was a smudge on the glass, and Lorn reached out to polish it with his sleeve. The mirror grew warm to the touch, and when he stepped back, he could see an image reflected on the surface.

"Lorelai," Lorn breathed out, staring at the magical reflection.

"I have one more favor, Lorn," the image spoke to him.

"Anything," he whispered, tears falling down his face. "I would still do anything for you."

He wasn't sure, but it looked like Lorelai was crying too.

"Love me," she whispered.

"I do," Lorn said. "I always have."

"And I you." A hand touched his shoulder, and he turned to see Lorelai in the flesh.

Her hair was down, no longer pinned in a matronly

bun. Gone were her stark black or brown clothes, and high-neck dresses. She was in a soft purple gown, and she looked the same as the day she'd met him.

"You're alive? But why did you . . . how?"

"So I could be with you," Lorelai answered. "The last daughter is raised; the seventh kingdom is safe. There's no need for an old, evil sorceress to strike fear into the people. I have seven daughters for that."

"But shouldn't they know . . . that you're . . . alive?"

She shooed her hand. "Oh, Aura knows, and I'm sure she'll let the cat out of the bag one day or another. Stars knows, that girl can't keep a secret. But they're old enough to make their own decisions. And I've made mine. I choose you, Lorn. Now and forever. If you'll have me."

Lorn grasped her around the waist. "I'll choose forever." He was about to kiss her when a loud knock came on the door.

Lorelai furrowed her brows and cast a glance toward the foyer. "No one is supposed to know I'm here," she mumbled. She pulled away from his embrace and stomped over to the door, flinging it open and glaring out into an empty road.

"There's no one. . ." She paused and leaned down, lifting a basket into the air. From within came a soft and gentle cooing sound, and there was a yellowed piece of paper with a note written in a language long forgotten. She turned the card over, and her fingers trembled.

She looked up at Lorn with a small smile. "Here we go again."

ABOUT THE AUTHOR

Chanda Hahn is a NYT & USA Today Bestselling author of The Unfortunate Fairy Tale series. She uses her experience as a children's pastor, children's librarian and bookseller to write compelling and popular fiction for teens. She was born in Seattle, WA, grew up in Nebraska, and currently resides in Waukesha, WI, with her husband and their twin children; Aiden and Ashley.

Visit Chanda Hahn's website to learn more about her other forthcoming books.
www.chandahahn.com

Made in United States
Orlando, FL
29 June 2022

19223189R00209